A Celibate Season

•

A Celibate Season

•

Carol Shields

Blanche Howard

VINTAGE CANADA
A Division of Random House of Canada

Copyright © 1991 by Carol Shields and Blanche Howard.
Originally published by Coteau Books, Regina, Saskatchewan.

First Vintage Canada Edition 1998.

The article "Collaborating with Carol" first appeared in *Prairie Fire: A Canadian
Magazine of New Writing*. The review of *A Celibate Season* by Meg Stainsby originally
appeared in *Room of One's Own: A Canadian Feminist Quarterly of
Literature and Commentary*. Reprinted with permission.

Canadian Cataloguing in Publication Data

Shields, Carol, 1935–
A celibate season

ISBN 0-679-30888-1

I. Howard, Blanche, 1923– . II. Title.

PS8587.H46C4 1998 C813'.54 C97-932286-3
PR9199.3.S54C4 1998

Printed and bound in Canada

10 9 8 7 6 5 4 3 2 1

To Carol from Blanche and to Blanche from Carol,
and to the letters woven into the fabric of friendship

Foreword

Collaborating with Carol
Blanche Howard

Our family has a cautionary tale, part of the family folklore.
It seems that two sets of aunts and uncles on opposite sides of
the family became fast friends and decided to travel together
for three months in Europe. (European travel was considered
more exotic then than it is now.) After the travellers returned
and my mother phoned to hear all about it, she found that
neither couple was speaking to the other. Furthermore, they
were never known to speak again. Explanations were not
forthcoming. The aunt on my mother's side confined herself
to a disparaging sniff and made remarks about some people
not knowing the limits of civilized discourse nor the need to
accommodate anybody but themselves. Nothing, as far as I
know, ever emerged that was so beyond the pale as to
account for the disruption of what had seemed a solidly
entrenched friendship.

How much more dangerous, then, is it for two artists to
collaborate on a work! Gilbert and Sullivan, for instance,
were renowned nearly as much for the depth and ferocity of
their animosity as for their witty lyrics, and, indeed, at a
forum at the annual Sechelt Writers' Festival, one of the par-
ticipants asked Carol Shields if she and her collaborator in
A Celibate Season were still on speaking terms.

We were, and we are. Carol's reputation, when we started the novel, was burgeoning, whereas mine had languished after my three novels were published. I jumped at her suggestion that we do a novel together, recognizing her generosity in wishing to spend time on a work that might very well not further her career, and indeed might use up valuable time more beneficially spent elsewhere.

Carol is generous, and she is loyal. I emphasize this because generosity and loyalty have not been givens among the writerly talented, a goodly number of whom have abused their gifts in the disservice of others. In his final years Truman Capote alienated lifelong friends and benefactors not so much by his drunken and obnoxious behaviour as by the cruelty with which he lampooned them. The Bloomsbury crowd, too, thought nothing of accepting hospitality and favours from the likes of Lady Ottoline Morrell and then, with amusing (in retrospect) bitchiness, or downright malice, cutting her to ribbons. This is Virginia Woolf, in a letter to her sister: "it is said that Garsington presents a scene of unparalleled horror. Needless to say, I am going to stay there," even though Lady Ottoline is described as being "as garish as a strumpet."

Carol and I first met in Ottawa in the early 1970s, when a mutual friend took me along to the Shields' large brick house on the Driveway where Carol was hosting the University Women's Club book discussion group. My first novel, *The Manipulator*, had been accepted, and Carol's first small book of poems, *Others*, was being published. We soon recognized the other as a "book person" — by that I mean that the reference points we used for living our lives had come to a large extent from the voracious reading habits we had developed in childhood.

In 1973 the exigencies of politics booted my husband and me back to Vancouver, and I suppose Carol's and my tentative friendship would have stayed at that level had it not been for the contract she was offered in 1975 for her first novel, *Small Ceremonies*. At the time, she was in France where her husband, Don, was attached to a university during a sabbatical. My next two novels had been accepted, and so I must have seemed like an expert to whom Carol could write and ask for advice.

I don't remember what nuggets of wisdom I offered other than "Grab it," but I do remember well the astonishment I felt when I read *Small Ceremonies*. I had not read Carol's prose before, and I was, perhaps, unprepared for its magic: mature, elegant writing with the nicely turned and unexpected phrase. By the time I got to the very funny party scene where a woman is saying, "remember this, Barney, there's more to sex than cold semen running down your leg," I knew, with bolt-from-the-blue revelation, that I was dispensing advice to a quite extraordinary talent.

Somehow we fell into regular correspondence. Carol loves to get letters — once, visiting them in Paris, my husband and I were amused at the enthusiasm with which she watches for the daily mail, or twice-daily, as it is in France. She swoops down on the mailbox as if it might contain the meaning of life — and perhaps it does. Still, I suppose our regular letters back and forth over the years, even in the '70s before e-mail and faxes had begun whittling away at formal communication, was and is a somewhat Victorian diversion.

I stuck Carol's letters in a file, and eventually I began to put in copies of my answers as well. The file of letters is three inches thick now, and as I riffle through them trying to determine when it was that we decided to collaborate, I settle on April of 1983 when she came to Vancouver for Book Week.

By then the Shields were living in Winnipeg while we were still in Vancouver. They *had* spent two years in

Vancouver between 1978 and 1980, a time that gave Carol and me a chance to know that we enjoyed one another's company and not just one another's letters. And that our husbands liked one another. As everyone in a relationship of any sort knows, it frequently happens that the significant other is bored by or can't stand the sight of his/her counterpart. Carol's and mine is a lucky friendship; our husbands hit it off from the first. We had dinner parties; they sailed with us; we went dining and dancing with them.

Only two years and they were off to Winnipeg, where Don had accepted a job at the University of Manitoba. Now, besides writing letters about books, families, work, the state of the weather, and so on, we were beginning to read one another's manuscripts (a practice we still continue) and in 1981 I was commenting on *A Fairly Conventional Woman*, wondering if Brenda should have slept with Barry in her old flannel nightgown. (Carol was sensible enough to keep the scene.)

I suppose an epistolary novel was a natural for us, although at that time it was a form that was being shunned. Carol was the one who noticed that the feminist revolution had so liberated women that there were bound to be career conflicts, and so we decided to have our husband and wife faced with separation. Beyond that we didn't plan, which is the way I operate but is unusual for Carol. Usually she knows where she is going with her novels and is able to write three polished pages a day.

Separation has never happened to either of us in real life. Unlike our protagonists, Chas (for Charles) and Jock (for Jocelyn), Carol and I have settled quite happily wherever our husbands have taken us. This may be due in part to the social strictures of the times that shaped us; I was a young wife and mother in the '50s while Carol was still an adolescent, but in that decade when housework and husband-support was raised to what Galbraith dubbed a "convenient social virtue," it seemed a natural thing to do and be. Indeed, to yearn otherwise carried social disapprobation. When entering the hospital in labour, Erma Bombeck attempted to have "writer" entered under vocation, but a no-nonsense nurse scratched it out and put in "housewife." And, as Carol has pointed out, writing is a portable vocation that can be done satisfactorily whenever the children (five for Carol, three for me) are tucked into bed or off to school.

In *A Celibate Season* Chas says he's not prepared to abandon the middle class, since "the good old middle class has, after all, been good to us." The middle class is where most of us hang our hats, although following the century-defining '60s, many were bent on denying it. Jeans and headbands were in and skirts and pearls were out, and Carol and I joked at Writers' Union meetings in Vancouver about the need to shed our middle-class images, since writers above all were not supposed to be co-opted by the middle class.

In the end, it is Carol who has done the co-opting. With her Jane Austen-like asides that prod our foibles and pretensions, she has carved out her territory from the milieu in which she lives. In an introduction to *The Heidi Chronicles* Carol wrote, "Feminism sailed into the sixties like a dazzling ocean liner, powered by injustice and steaming with indignation." For a time the ocean liner came close to refitting itself as a warship, or even a destroyer, lobbing its ideological bullets at those with differing takes on the truth.

"Truth," Iris Murdoch says, "is always a proper touchstone in art . . . requiring that *courage* which the good artist must possess." Fiction is not the handmaiden of politics, any more than the bleaker side of sexual politics is the honest experience of every writer. We don't lack for novels that crawl into the many hearts of our darkness, and bookstores are lined with thought-provoking essays by articulate feminists like Gloria Steinem. What we have lacked, and what Carol has brought us, is an intelligent and articulate witness to the ordinary and often happy lives of women and families.

Carol and I met — or rather, didn't meet — Gloria Steinem once. At breakfast the day after *A Celibate Season* launched in Regina, we sputtered over an unpleasant review whose main preoccupation was with the names we had given our protagonists. By way of a restorative we hurled ourselves against an icy gale in minus twenty degree temperatures for several blocks to a bookstore. Almost nobody was there, except for a lone woman who was sitting in a chair waiting to sign books. "Who is it?" Carol whispered to me. "I think it's Gloria Steinem," I whispered back. It was. We didn't introduce ourselves. Carol thought it might be intrusive — and I agreed — since we hadn't read Steinem's new book. I regret it now.

But I'm getting ahead of myself. When we began *A Celibate Season*, Carol wanted to write the male part, and so I kicked off the process with Jock writing from Ottawa, where she has accepted a position as legal counsel for a Commission looking into "The Feminization of Poverty." I sent the chapter off to Carol on October 26, 1983: "Well here's chapter one, and I can't tell you how much more fun it is to write something for someone else's eyes than just to write for the faceless mass who may or may not read it."

It was enormous fun for us, lobbing curves at the other. "Killing off Gil was a stroke of genius." "Please feel free to revive Gil." I wrote that I laughed out loud at Chas' irritated postscript, "Fuck the purple boots."

When both Jock and Chas do something they can't risk telling the other, we had, somehow, to transcend the limitations of the epistolary novel. The only solution in a two-way correspondence is the unsent letter, although Carol was bothered, initially, by what she feared might be "the narrative dishonesty of it."

Since I was coming through Winnipeg in November of 1984, we vowed to complete the first draft by then. I stayed in the Shields' lovely Victorian-style home, the kind with oak panelling and big halls and a wide, sweeping staircase. On a bitterly cold and slippery night (me smug in the superiority of Vancouver rain), we went to the university to see Carol's delightful little play *Departures and Arrivals*, and the next day we worked diligently all day at the dining room table, each reading aloud our own letters and interrupting one another with corrections, cutting, adding, changing, arguing over commas. At five o'clock Carol announced that eight people were coming to dinner so we had to clear the table.

I remember that the evening was merry and that we involved the guests in a vigorous discussion of whether or not "A Celibate Season" was a good title. Some said yes, some said no, but nobody (including the authors) knew of a possible derivation that was pointed out later by an astute reviewer (Meg Stainsby, whose comments are included at the end of the novel): St. Paul, in a letter to the Corinthians, asserted that celibacy is desirable within a marriage, but only for a "season." As far as *we* knew the title was entirely original, but we may have been deceived; the brain has its hidden ways, it can explore forgotten recesses and toss used tidbits up like newly minted gems.

Carol sent along two reworked chapters in short order, and in December came the "big" chapter, the one where Chas admits to his somewhat bizarre episode of infidelity. She worried that I might think it "unacceptably kinky"; instead I found the letter "wonderful, pathetic and touching."

The end was in sight. Letters flew back and forth. We

started sending the manuscript to publishers in January of 1985.

I thought it would be fun to try adapting the novel to the stage, and by September, while publishers were (very slowly) considering the novel, I was sending drafts of the play to Carol in France. "Davina is better in the play than in our book, funnier and fuller, also more likeable," she wrote back. As for the novel, when Carol came to Vancouver in the spring of 1986 we still hadn't sold it, and again we went over the manuscript. The first third, Carol wrote to me after spending a July weekend on it, was perhaps too slow, the second third really crackles, and the final third was perhaps too amiable. Re-worked once again, and once again I started mailing it out until we had racked up nine rejections. In the meantime, the play was faring well; it was being workshopped by the New Play Centre in Vancouver and when I sent it to the Canadian National Theatre Playwriting competition, it was a finalist and came back with soul-restoring comments.

The Shields invited us to spend a week with them in Paris in the spring of 1987, and while there I read the galleys of *Swann* and was quite sure it would win the Governor General's Award. It didn't, although it *was* shortlisted.

By now the manuscript had been temporarily abandoned. Then at a conference in Edmonton I bumped into fellow writer and mutual friend Merna Summers. How did we expect to sell the novel, she asked, from a desk drawer? Get it out there, she urged, and she suggested Coteau Books. I sent it in September, and in May of 1990 Coteau agreed to publish it. In June we got word that the play would be produced by a small North Vancouver drama company in the fall.

That summer my husband and I rented a *gite* near the stone house the Shields had bought in France, and once more, in the sunny days of June, this time looking out over the lovely Jura mountains, serenaded by cows in the neighbouring fields, we went through the manuscript and began editing for publication.

Carol told me once that if she didn't write she would become neurotic. I think this is true of most writers; Freud may have merely put a new spin on an old truth. Certainly writing is a search that may, like psychoanalysis, lead us into secret labyrinths where thoughts we had never suspected are discovered, where ancient and forgotten fears thrust themselves, like stalagmites, into consciousness, where we catch glimpses of desires so evanescent that they scatter like cockroaches before the light. And always, the compulsion, the need, to know more.

The following summer we were returning on the ferry after Carol's appearance at the Sechelt Writers' Festival and Carol was gently probing me about my thoughts on aging. (I am older than she is.) "Carol, are you asking me for the meaning of life?" I asked, and we both laughed, and then I said, "I'll tell you what, if I find it I'll phone you," and, after a pause, I added, "and if you aren't in, I'll leave it on your answering machine."

Dearest Chas,

I bet you didn't expect me to pick up pen and Château L.
stationery ten minutes after your phone call. Surprise! Here I
am, huddled on one of their oversize beds, which makes me
feel as though I were drifting around the Strait of Georgia in
our leaky old dinghy. When I think of all the times *you've*
spent alone in hotel rooms — Regina, Victoria, Edmonton
— and how I used to envy your freedom, your *adventure*! It
never occurred to me that it might feel this empty.

What do I do now? A man, I suppose, would head for the
bar. (I can't — I'll drown.) I'll have to pour my own. Damn!
I just remembered. You know that little bottle of medicinal
Scotch you tucked into my briefcase? (Sweet you — oh God!)
Well, at the last minute I decided to bring yet another legal
tome and there wasn't room for the Scotch so I took it out.
All I have is a miniature bottle of gin supplied by Air Canada
— I suppose I could mix it with mouthwash. I deserve to
crawl drinkless across the Sahara — which, incidentally, the
dimensions of this room are beginning to remind me of.

Ingratitude! It was classy of the Commission to put me in
such a room, so royally maroon! Heavy maroon quilts,
maroon drapes tied back over white sheers that hide what
turns out to be two old-fashioned windows (with wooden
sills!) that actually open, reluctantly, from the bottom and
have to be propped up. But I'd have felt less bereft if the
room had been little, with, instead of two big double beds,
one modest, cell-like single covered with chaste white cotton
— why two doubles, anyway? Are there people so sexually
athletic that, having worn out the resilience of bed number

one, they roll — not coming unstuck — onto bed number two. . . . I'd better get off that line of thought.

I got off to a great country-bumpkin start — tripped getting out of the taxi. There's a step up to the revolving doors here at the Château, and I missed and would have fallen on my face (falling on my face — a hidden message from the psyche?) if the doorman hadn't had the reflexes of Rambo. I've got the jitters, no use pretending otherwise — about tomorrow, I mean. There I'll be, all got up in that great grey suit from Chapman's — Mother tried her damnedest to wheedle the price out of me, but I refused to blow my cover — in my suitable navy-blue blouse, navy-blue pumps (and matching soul) — clutching my leather Lady Executive Briefcase, stumbling in and introducing myself to Senator Pierce — oh Lord! How do you address a senator? I forgot to find out.

I keep remembering how sceptical Mr. Enright seemed when I told him I was taking a leave of absence. "Women's issues — " was all he said, and then sort of shook his head and grinned.

Tell me I won't blow it. This is high-powered stuff. I need you. To reassure me. In person, not over a disembodied electronic gadget. *And* I've got the guilts again about leaving you to cope.

Happy about Greg's two goals! I keep thinking of him skating out onto the ice and tossing his head back like Wayne Gretzky. That little head toss — I don't know why — keeps swamping me with tenderness. Imprinting the hero. Seeing oneself as a glorious hunter/warrior/pilot — maybe it's the male way of blocking any suspicion that ploughing around in muddy trenches or being impaled on a lance or tumbling in flames into the Atlantic isn't that much fun. I guess invading space must be next, that's what little boys dream of now. (Little girls? I notice no one ever cleans space up.)

I'm trying not to worry about Greg. Or Mia. Or about you, volunteering for this house-husband thing. No vestigial role-model anywhere, is there? Your father's ashes would ignite, and as for your mother, I did think she sounded a mite snappish when we told her, didn't you?

I'll write after tomorrow's meeting. It's only nine o'clock Vancouver time (midnight here), but maybe if I tunnel under the maroon covers my mind will shut down. Why didn't I steal *two* little gins?

Much, much love, and even to the rotten teenagers. Tell them I called them that — perversely, it'll make them feel loved.

Love,
Jock

P.S. My God, the lentils! I bought two jars; I was going to learn to make lentil soup. They're on the top shelf, seems a shame to waste them.

P.P.S. Sequins! Mia has to have them for her ballet costume. Don't worry, I'll think of something.

29 Sweet Cedar Drive
North Vancouver, B.C.
4 September

Dear Jock,

I'm sitting here by the kitchen window, which is where I moved my old drafting table and typewriter yesterday. Greg came out of his sulks for a whole ten minutes and gave me a hand carrying it up from the basement (my God it's heavy —

you can't beat good solid oak), while Mia stood by and exclaimed in that shrill piping way she has that it's a campy old thing and that it makes the kitchen look "unbalanced." Tell me, what do thirteen-year-old girls know about balance? "Never mind," I told her, "this is where it stays."

You wouldn't believe what this simple shift of furniture has done for my morale, which was draggier than usual after a weekend of heavy parenting — more about that later. Here I sit, king of the kitchen, in that wasted space between the fridge and the kitchen table. (We moved your bamboo plant stand into the dining room where your mother's old tea trolley used to be, and as for the tea trolley — more about that later too.)

At any rate, I feel this dreary morning like a man reborn. The sun is *not* pouring in — you wouldn't believe me if I said it was — but there is definitely something about the sight of tall, dark dripping trees that makes for a minor-chord melancholy that's one step up from basement-itis. God only knows why I put up with that basement room all this time. One more year of strip lighting and cinder-block walls and mildewed straw matting might have destroyed me totally. And so, despite the non-balancing kitchen and the sticky jam jar someone's left on my drafting table, I feel installed, ensconced, magisterial even.

Of course it's helped that your letter arrived this morning. I've read it through three times and feel a real pang, whatever the hell a pang is, reading about your snug maroon cocoon at the Château Laurier and that wasted width of empty bed. In retrospect it seems somewhat wacky to me that, when this Ottawa job came up, we didn't stop to discuss or even consider the problems that might accompany ten months of celibate life. Does this seem odd to you? A little suspect in fact? I suppose, like a pair of fools, we thought we could just shut down for a spell, the way we disconnect the pool in winter or turn off the furnace for the summer.

Speaking of the furnace, it appears we need a new thermal valve which is going to set us back — with labour — two hundred and fifty whopping bucks. When I flicked on the heat and got a series of little cheeping noises and then a crumpling sound and, finally, silence, I called our speedy twenty-four-hour emergency serviceman, who said he was awfully sorry but this was the busiest time of the year and he wouldn't be able to make it up here until Friday. "Well, that's just great," I said. "What are we supposed to do till then — freeze?" There was a pause, and then he said that maybe he could get over here on Wednesday if I could promise that the lady of the house would be in. "I *am* the lady of the house," I told him, "and I *will* be in." There followed another pause, longer this time, and then he said, finally, something that sounded like, "Yeah?" So it looks as if we only have to stay chilly for a couple more days. Which is another good thing about moving my table to the kitchen — I can open the oven door and bask in its fierce kilowatt-eating coil, never mind what the hydro bill's going to look like at the end of the month. (You didn't say, Jock, whether you are on the gov't payroll yet or not.)

Can't wait to hear how you made out with your senator. Put it in writing so I can savour it. Lord, I miss you!

Love,

Chas

P.S. Glad we agreed on the letter writing. I think it'll keep us sane. Greg says he could get us on e-mail if I'd just install a modem, but do we want the kids accessing our private disclosures? I think not. Besides, it costs money.

Château Laurier
Sept. 4

Dear Chas,

Well, *veni*, *vidi*, *vici* — except that I didn't conquer. In
fact I think I came a bit unstuck. I was half an hour early leaving the Château Laurier, and after a leisurely stroll to the East
Block I was still twenty minutes early. I was tempted to just
hang around, but the guards aren't great on hangers-around
so I walked over to the Centre Block and pretended intense
interest in the portraits of ex-prime ministers. One of the
guards told me to notice how Mr. Diefenbaker's eyes followed me around wherever I moved, a thought that did more
to unnerve than to uplift. But finally the clock in the Peace
Tower bonged eleven, so back I went. A guard phoned ahead
and gave me directions to Senator Pierce's office. He hadn't
arrived yet, but five minutes later he came bustling in and I
introduced myself. He looked quite uncomprehending.

"Jocelyn Selby," I repeated. "The legal counsel from
Vancouver. For the Commission?"

"*You're* the legal counsel?" he asked, with just the right
degree of astonishment. He managed — now this is subtle
— to imply that such a dish couldn't be such a heavy, but if
indeed he should be so fortunate then he would personally
get down on his knees and thank *le bon Dieu*. (In spite of the
anglo name his mother tongue is French. I'd never noticed
the slight and charming — what else? — accent on TV.) I
felt like a combination emancipated new-look career woman
and Playboy bunny.

"Well," he said, and flashed me a Robert Redford smile,
including dimple, "this Commission is going to be more
interesting than I'd thought." Injustice! The man must be fifty
if he's a day, yet I'll bet he looks, if anything, better than he

did at thirty. The blue eyes, the slightly silvering and perfectly styled (blow-dried) hair, the perfect suit, the trace of accent — and to top it off, he's not just another *beau visage*.

He went into a kind of crouch, and, with a sort of fascinated horror, I saw he was about to kiss my hand, when suddenly my eardrums were shattered by a raucous female voice behind me. "Still charming them, you old goat? Christ, you must be some kind of Dorian Gray. Where's the real you? Hidden in the bowels of the Peace Tower?"

I wheeled around to face the most unlikely looking woman — unlikely in that setting, I mean. She was — is — immensely broad in the beam and wearing brown cords that stretch tightly over her thighs and a faded blue plaid shirt, not tucked in. Long black greasy hair. Striped headband. Thick, eye-distorting glasses. Senator Pierce swept past me in my neat get-up and perfect hair, threw his arms around her, and said, "Jess, you old cuss, you still look like a leftover hippie."

That is Jessica Slattery. She's actually ON THE COMMISSION! Appointed at the last minute after the women's groups got so mad that there wasn't a woman commissioner on a commission to look into the feminization of poverty. (I suppose my sex got me my appointment too — a nice reversal on the usual theme.)

I've found out since that Jessica is the president of the Canadian Social Welfare Council (which I didn't know existed), that she's been riding the poverty horse for years, and that she believes in farting when she feels like it. Unfortunately she felt like it just as Senator Pierce was introducing us, and I didn't handle it with aplomb. I had managed my most gracious how do you do? when she let go, and the Senator guffawed and I would gladly have disappeared into a fourth-dimensional time-warp. (What I did was turn red and mutter, "Excuse me." And then I was mortified that the Senator might think I'd done it.)

Sept. 5

Sorry, got interrupted. I've been hunting for a place to stay, but so far no luck.

I haven't told you about the third commissioner, Dr. Grey. (Grey by name and grey by nature, my first impression.) He'll take some getting to know. He's a skinny grey man in a grey flannel suit with a grey voice. I was — am — astonished! Mother babbled on and on about Austin Grey — McGill University, economist, statistician, Rhodes Scholar, poet — and I don't know exactly what I expected, but I thought he'd be, well, not-grey. He's even greyer lined up against unbelievable Jessica and beautiful Vance. (Vance has asked me to call him Vance, but it isn't easy. Makes me think I'm talking to a movie star.) Jessica controlled her sphincter in Dr. Grey's presence — does natural dignity impose restraint on others, as Mother is always preaching? I'll watch, or rather listen, and let you know.

Love,
Jock

29 Sweet Cedar Drive
North Vancouver, B.C.
9 September

Dear Jock,

Your letter just arrived and it bucked me up no end, which makes two pluses this Monday morning.

I'm feeling more or less buoyant because I've had a lead on a possible job opening. You remember Sanderson and Sanderson Associates? Talbot Sanderson is the cretin who wore the black cape and eye patch at the Ticknows' New Year's Eve bash last year, and his wife is the one who trounced me in *Trivial Pursuit* the same night. If you'll remember, she couldn't get over the fact that I didn't know what Lassie's master's name was. The two of them run a fair-sized design company that puts out decent work, though nothing earth-shattering. They were big on urban development for a time, but like Robertson's they've had to lay off half their architects. Now they've landed that big harbour-development contract that was in the papers last summer — remember? — and will probably be taking on staff.

The unlikely person who put the bug in my ear was that old grump Gil Grogan, all *sotto voce* through the hedge Saturday morning when I was out hacking back the alder. There hasn't been anything public, he said, but the word was out that they'd be taking on two or possibly three temporary staff. Naturally I tried to find out how he'd heard the rumour, but he just stood there swaying and looking smug and mumbling about keeping the old ear to the old ground. (Now there's a man who seems to thrive on celibacy. Since Meg's died he's taken up jogging and other primordial sins such as grouchiness and neighbour-hood vigilance.) Still I was grateful and told him so.

I heard the same happy rumour about Sanderson, etc., from — guess who? — your mother. (By the way, her cold is better. She specifically asked me to tell you, since she's too busy to write, she says, until after the Fall Fair.) She stopped by on her way over to the church hall to bring us a coffee cake and an eggplant casserole. In some ways it was unfortu-nate we didn't hear her pulling into the driveway. She let her-self in the front door and caught us in the middle of carrying the drafting table up the basement stairs. Greg had the top end and I had the bottom and we were negotiating that narrow spot by the landing, Greg his usual grunting, unaccommodating self, Mia screaming at us from the top of the stairs to move to the right, move to the left, and me blustering away, I'm afraid, in my loudest sergeant-major voice and turning the air a smokey blue — in all, not exactly a Walton family picnic. Suddenly your mother appeared over Mia's shoulder, looking pale and puzzled and asking what in sweet heaven we were doing and were we sure that Jocelyn would approve. (I hope you do, my beauty, because I'd sooner dynamite the thing before moving it another inch.)

To smooth things over I asked her if she'd care for a sherry, and true to form and to no one's surprise she said, "Well, maybe just a teeny-weeny one." I also offered Greg a cold beer. (After all, that drafting table weighs a ton, and he *is* seventeen years old, and *I* was having a beer myself.) I wish you'd been here to hear the curtness with which your firstborn refused this kindly meant offer. "No thanks," he said (sneered), and walked over to the fridge and poured himself a large, wholesome glass of milk, which he drank eyeing me and my beer all the time with a look so pious it made me wonder if you and I maybe overdid the puritan principles. Your mother chimed in with, "I don't think a teeny-weeny bit of beer's all that harmful" — this while I topped up her glass.

The rain stopped for a whole ten minutes or so, and we were able to take our drinks out on the deck. (It's so green here right now. God, even the air is green. Do you suppose it's healthy breathing green air?) Your mother wiped off one of the deck chairs with a tea towel and settled down. She'd been talking to some friends, she said, and just happened to hear something about a firm called Sanderson and Something — had I heard of them? — that they were about to take on half a dozen new architects. Naturally I asked her precisely who had given her that information, but she just waved her glove in the air and murmured something or other about keeping an ear to the ground. (Do you think, now I've emerged from my cinder-block cellar, that I too will acquire an aptitude for crucial ear-to-ground skills? I can only hope.)

Sunday afternoon, after a lunch composed entirely of pecan coffee cake, Mia went roller blading with the Finsteads, those new people across the way, who have, they told me when they picked her up, a series of family outings planned — bowling next week, hiking the following Sunday, and perhaps an excursion to Squamish in November. Greg disappeared too, saying he had "plans." I pressed him. What plans? Well, he might go down to the rink. Was there a practice on? Not exactly. Who was going to be there? Coupla guys. When would he be back? Dunno. (I loved this kid once.)

I must revise and type my CV for Sanderson et al. and catch today's mail. We all miss you!

Love,
Chas

P.S. Quit worrying about how you'll do in the big time. My experience with bureaucracy is that anything above mediocre is considered brilliant. You'll do fine.

Château Laurier
Sept. 11

Dear Chas,

I've phoned down to the desk three times hoping for a letter from you (pretending an urgent message), so will give you an update on my adventures with the Commission while waiting.

After our initial meeting, the four of us had a get-acquainted luncheon at the Parliamentary Restaurant, which I found a tremendously glamorous thing to do. (Maybe, despite all our Vancouver years, I'm still just a Williams Lake gal.) It's a beautiful room with arched colonnades and windows looking out on the Ottawa River, and round tables, and all sorts of important people, and less-important people watching the important people and feeling important doing it. (I am among the latter category.)

I nearly yelped as we went in to find myself right behind the environmental minister (I never dreamed he was that tall!) and then noticed that his companion was the Minister of Justice (I never dreamed he was that short).

As soon as we sat down Jessica clawed around in a pocket of the awful pants and produced a rumpled pack of cigarettes (oh Lord! My sinuses!) and Senator Pierce — Vance — was rude to her about it.

"Where's your character, woman? I thought you were quitting."

"Yer not smokin' any more, Van?" she drawled. "Whatsa matter? Lose yer nerve?"

"No, found my senses."

Dr. Grey and I smiled weakly at one another and he said, "The buffet is rather good. I would recommend it."

In the end we all went to the buffet — which was superb! — and drank a couple of carafes of white wine. I noticed that Vance didn't look around or wave to anyone, and since everyone else seemed to spend a lot of time leaping up and trying to catch the eyes of others, I wondered who it was he was ashamed of. I mean, I'm still wearing my navy and grey uniform, but I blend in pretty well here, clothes-wise. (Matter of fact, I've become sufficiently de-dazzled to recognize that Ottawa is *not* the *haute couture* capital of the western world.)

Okay, I can sympathize with Vance for being a tad reluctant to draw attention to Jessica.

Not that Jessica was about to let him get away with it. "Hey, Van," she bawled, at one point. "Don't you know *anyone*? What's yer name — you, the legal counsel — "

"Jocelyn," I said weakly.

"Jocelyn — she'd probably like to meet some heavies."

"She's met you."

"Shit, Van, you'll have to do better than that — " and just then who should walk in with the Minister of Finance but Senator Kennedy — yes! U.S. Senator Kennedy. Up here to look (enviously, I presume) at Canadian medicare. You can imagine the stir that rippled through our hallowed eatery! And who do you think he recognized? Jessica.

"Well, well, surely not Jess Slattery. You turn up everywhere, just like a bad penny, don't you?" he said. "How come you're eating subsidized food?"

"I helped pay for it, didn't I?" Jessica shot back, and then she introduced him to Dr. Grey and to me (I stood up. Should I have?) and pretended to forget Vance, who was doing a knee-bend halfway between standing and sitting and said, *in French,* "Oh, et un *faux* senator, M. Pierce," and Kennedy smiled and murmured, "*Enchanté!*"

Everyone, even Jessica, speaks fluent French — how I wish mine were better! At that point I forgot how to say anything but *oui*, which is why I drank too much wine, I guess.

Sept. 12

Still no letter. The hotel clerk no longer answers with, "Yes, may I help you?" He just murmurs, "Nothing." Regretfully.

Must finish this. Not much more to tell. When we finished lunch Vance shot back the silver-clasped cuffs of his elegant French shirt and looked at his watch and said he had a three-o'clock appointment, but maybe we could get together a little earlier tomorrow before the hearings started.

"Where you rushing off to, Van? Got a new flame?"

In a voice that would have frozen Hawaiian rain, Vance said, "Catherine is the only flame I'll ever need." Catherine? Must be his wife.

Jessica was not frozen. "Lucky Catherine," she drawled, "and unlucky all the rest of them. Let's get the hell out of here. Slurping up the government booze isn't helping the godamn starving women of Canada."

"Surely no one is starving," I said, sounding about as assertive as talking Jello.

Jessica turned and glared — or no, she didn't exactly glare. I've been trying to analyse that look. I'd expected accusing or hostile or contemptuous, but that wasn't it. It was some sort of challenge, as though she were testing me to see if I was a fellow woman. I don't think I am. She scares the hell out of me.

She asked me where I was staying, and when I said I was still at the Château Laurier but was looking for a bedsitter she said, "I live in a group home — always room for one more." I told her I had a line on a place.

"Suit yerself," she said. "Holler if you change your mind."

When hell freezes over, I thought — but didn't say. (*I do* have a line on a bedsitter. Keep your fingers crossed.)

Know what? Writing letters is turning out to be therapeutic as well as economical. It helps me feel closer to home and also to sort out my own impressions. The phone just isn't a substitute. God, I'm lonesome! I wish we hadn't decided against Thanksgiving — is it too late to change? Although I haven't got the moola for a ticket at the moment. Have you?

Anyway, I'll look forward to talking to you this weekend — maybe you'll have my letter by then. They say the postal service is improving. They lie. At the moment I feel low. *Why did it have to be Jessica on the Commission?*

Much love,

Jock

P.S. Your letter just arrived. The hotel clerk phoned me! He sounded so excited I thought maybe he'd opened it. *Thrilled* about the Sanderson thing — what's happening? Phone if you get work.

29 Sweet Cedar Drive
North Vancouver, B.C.
15 September

Dear Jock,

Nothing yet on the Sanderson thing. A week since I sent the application — typed it on the drafting table, which I have in the down position to accommodate the computer. I spent two hours revising and typing the CV, shaping it along the lines you suggested, puffing up that bit about the airport job and playing down the university gold medal, which, all things considered, is now more of an embarrassment than anything else. I then wrote a long, obsequious, and painfully composed letter about how extraordinarily electrified I was by urban harbour projects — this will surprise you, Jock, as much as it did me — and how wonderful and competent and original an architect I am. All I needed was a young, aggressive, and modern-minded firm to hitch myself to and thereby channel my abilities. On and on, yards of it.

I think, to tell the truth, I got the right formula: about three-fifths self-congratulation and two-fifths professional grovel. At the age of forty-seven I don't suppose I should find it this easy to grovel, but it seems I have a knack for it, especially after nine months full time in the basement. I mentioned, of course, my fourteen years with Bettner's, disclaiming all connection with the Broadway-Peterkin lawsuit, and I also detailed my last eight years with Robertson's (note how cunningly I omitted mention of the free-lance year in the middle — what the hell) and pointed to "harsh economic realities" as the reason for my termination. I thought that sounded more forceful than "the recession" or "the present financial climate." What do you think? "Harsh economic realities" seems to me to have a slightly embittered tone but one that is moderated by the brand of pragmatism suitable for the New Unemployed Me I'm trying so hard to sell. God, I hope this works out. Even a temporary contract, six months or a year, could lead to something permanent, and even if it doesn't, we can get caught up on the household bills. I'll let you know as soon as I hear anything definite.

I made the mistake of leaving the computer on, and when Greg came whistling in at suppertime he read it. "Are you really going to send this?" he asked me. "Or is this just the rough draft?"

"What's wrong with it?" I asked. I was in the middle of serving up the eggplant casserole your mother brought.

"Oh, nothing." He said this in that maddening airy way that you surely remember. "It's okay, I guess."

I could tell he didn't think it was okay. He slunk out of the kitchen and into the family room with his plate. I asked myself, what does a seventeen-year-old kid know about business letters? Nevertheless, I pursued him. "What exactly is wrong with the letter?" I demanded.

"That jazz about 'harsh realities,'" he said. "It's sort of, you know, sort of — "

I had to prod him. "Sort of what?"

"Well," he said, "sort of like begging."

I told him as calmly as I could that I had considered the phrase carefully, weighed it, and decided it was the best possible choice. "Suit yourself," he said, and settled down to watch a re-run of Archie Bunker, whom I am sure, if he had a choice, he would prefer for an old man.

Anyway, the letter must be there by now, the die is cast, and now all I have to do is sit back and see what happens next. Waiting around is the worst — the walls seem to press closer and closer, and often I think of how you must have sat in this kitchen and waited for the kids to grow up and go to school and then waited around to hear if you'd been accepted for law school. What did you do with yourself all day?

By the way, we saw your Senator Pierce being interviewed on *The Fifth Estate* last night. I think your Robert Redford comparison is a mite flattering considering the good Senator's bobbling paunch and his stertorous huffing into the microphone. Mia said, all incredulity, "Is that Mom's new boss?" and Greg said, "If that turkey doesn't watch out he's going to injure someone with those cufflinks of his." He did make a certain amount of sense, though (Pierce, that is), especially that bit about the plight of widows.

We look forward to your further adventures. Yes, I agree that our letters seem to be working out better than the damn telephone. Doubtless it was our puritan mothers, bless the two of them, who plied us with guilt about the heaviness of long-distance phoning. Otherwise, why, when I pick up the phone, am I suddenly speechless or reduced to inanities about the rain and the roses?

I'm off to bed early tonight. Tomorrow I'm driving out to

Capilano College to sign up for the communications course
Gil Grogan recommended — might as well brush up on a few
skills while waiting to hear from Sanderson, etc. And in the
afternoon I'm interviewing a lady who answered my ad for
cleaning help. The woman your mother found didn't work out
at all; she wanted seventy bucks for six hours' work — rob-
bery — and said she was uncomfortable working in a house
unless the Mister and Missus (that's you, lovey) were out. I
explained that I would do my best to be inconspicuous and
quiet, but she said she had more jobs than she could handle
anyway. Maybe this new woman will fill the bill. She sounded
cheerful on the phone, and God knows a little cheer wouldn't
hurt. We do need someone to organize things a bit. Our shoes
are sticking to the kitchen floor, a most peculiar sensation.

Love,
Chas

P.S. What lentils? I can't find them — probably because I
don't know what the hell I'm looking for.

4 Old Town Lane
Ottawa, Ont.
Sept. 18

Dear Chas,
    I *love* getting letters from you — do you realize that
we've been married twenty years and have never written to
one another before? I feel as though I'm catching glimpses of a
whole new you that's been lurking there all along and that I
didn't even suspect. Do you feel that way? Actually it's even a
bit scary.

This is just a quick note to let you know I've found a place. Not grand (understatement), but not dreary either. It was advertised as a bachelor apartment, but it's a cut above that. It has a separate bedroom — the smallest in the Western World, but separate. In it is one double bed — which takes up a lot of room, but I cherish the hope you will visit at least once — and a night table that clears the door by exactly three centimetres. Tucked into the corner by the foot of the bed — with a whole twelve inches of clearance — is a shabby, brown, scarred dresser. Clothes cannot be hung in the bedroom but must go in a tiny closet at the top of the stairs — I know that sounds unlikely, but bear with me.

The combination living room-kitchen is small, but there is a little wooden balcony off it that looks out on a tiny park. Ottawa is full of parks — remember how we noticed that when we came with the kids? Dr. Grey pointed out in his gentle way that I should enjoy them to the fullest, since it's the taxpayers of Canada, not Ottawa, who pay for them.

In the distance, on the other side of the park, you can see City Hall, and if you were to lean way out over the balcony (only second floor, not too risky), you could see along Sussex Drive. When I mentioned to Austin — Dr. Grey — that the Prime Minister's house is almost within spitting distance, he said he didn't think he'd be able to resist the temptation if he were in my shoes.

He's actually quite nice. Yesterday I really boobed — changed Jessica's response to a brief on pay equity to conform to what I *thought* were the regulations. Turns out my source was two years out of date. Jessica slapped the hole in the knee of her jeans and yelled, "Christ, what kinda stuff are they passing off as law in Lotusland?" I really was mortified, felt so stupid I couldn't eat my dinner. This morning I found Austin's copy of the new regulations on my desk and a poem:

These rules are meant to ease the lot
Of women out for hire,
And if you say you know them all
You just might be a liar.

Anyway, just because my "pad" is close to the PM's doesn't mean the neighbourhood borders on posh. It doesn't. Do you remember that wonderful market in Ottawa that we took the kids to? Well, there is an area beyond it called Old Town that has a mixture of very modest frame and brick buildings, and some of them are being restored by the National Capital Commission. Mine is in one of the unrestored two-storey frame buildings, within walking distance of Parliament Hill (about twenty minutes) and very close to Rideau Street. So, location couldn't be better.

Back to the living room. Well, as I say, it's small. The furniture is terrible: a shabby chesterfield that pulls out to make into a bed (maybe one of the kids will visit?) covered in a cheap brown tweed material, a matching chair, an Arborite coffee table, and — unbelievably — a bay window. With cushions and a view! Nice. And, as I said, a glass door leading out to a little wooden balcony that makes me think of Charles de Gaulle. (Don't ask why.) The strangest thing of all is that the stairs from the front door are mine, all mine. They're part of the apartment! On the ground floor is a door, my door, Number 4, and when I unlock it I walk up this long flight of stairs and there, without benefit of further doors, is a small landing with the clothes closet directly in front, and on the right the living room. No arch, no curtain, it's just there. It gives me kind of a vulnerable feeling, their not being shut off like proper stairs, and I expect it will be drafty. (Also expect that I or someone else will tumble down.)

And that's about it, except for a very small bathroom,

which somebody in a psychedelic sixties freakout decorated in purple and pink. Purple tub, matching john, and every inch of counter space and walls brightly enamelled in "passion" pink.

Oh yes, kitchen is a sink, hot plate, microwave, tiny fridge, and small counter on the stairs side. I know it sounds awful (depends on your point of view; Jessica is loudly scornful — thinks it elitist), but actually it's nice. The living room has funny little angles, and the bay window and view of the park make it seem a bit homey. Or cosy, at least. I do need a desk — there seems to be some mix-up about my pay, but maybe when I get it I can find something cheap.

Just glancing over your letter and note with some surprise that you and the children think Vance looked paunchy on TV. Actually he's slimmed down, tells me he's gone back to jogging along the canal every morning.

About your cleaning-woman problems, did you ever stop to figure out what seventy dollars for six hours' work is per hour? About twelve bucks. Backs up what we keep hearing re the disparity in men's and women's incomes. I'll spare you the sermon that springs trippingly to the tongue and confine myself to pointing out that cleaning women charge *at least* fifteen bucks an hour these days. That's why we were getting along without one. (I'm not suggesting that *you* don't need one, love.)

Am dying to hear what happens re Sanderson et al. Phone when you hear, hang the expense. Wait — I don't have a phone. As soon as they connect it (promised for tomorrow) will call you.

Oh, I miss the kids! Do you think Greg is being especially difficult? If so, I wonder why. Would it have to do with my departure do you think? I would have thought Mia would be the one to react to that, but gather she loves being the little mother.

The mattress is lumpy on one side. Would gladly give you the good side if you were here.

Much love,

Jock

P.S. Would you ring Mother and give her my new address? She feels threatened if she can't locate me precisely on a map.

P.P.S. We start the hearings proper next week. We've been going through the written briefs, but now the Commissioners will get a chance to question the groups that submitted them. Vance says I shouldn't hesitate to ask questions, but I'm worried it might seem presumptuous. What do you think?

29 Sweet Cedar Drive
North Vancouver, B.C.
25 September

Dear Jock,

Well, kiddo mine, you've pulled off a real live *déjà vu*. Unbelievable! I'm sure it must have been unconscious on your part, but do you realize that your new Ottawa pad — except for the Charles de Gaulle gallery — is a dead ringer for the suite on Tenth and Cambie where you were living when I first met you? My God, I read your letter with dry mouth and dropped jaw. The same apartment — the bay window, the clothes closet on the landing, the missing door, and the sad little bashed-up dresser, and even (you must remember) a double bed with one lumpy side. What does all this replication mean? I ask myself this, being in a contemplative frame of mind this rainy Wednesday morning. What does it *signify*?

Yes, the rain continues and continues. We're setting some kind of record, apparently. Good for us. A government plot, no doubt, to keep our minds off "harsh economic realities." But despite cold winds and grey skies, the kitchen is one hundred per cent brighter since I took down those heavy old curtains of ours — you'll be amazed when you see the difference it makes. On the other hand, it leaves me more or less open to Gil Grogan's steady scrutiny. Every time I look up (contemplatively) from my drafting table I see the old bugger standing at his kitchen window, looking daft and lonely and waving a coffee cup at me. Your mother was sceptical about my letting Sue take down the curtains, but I told her you'd thank me for doing it. I gave them (the curtains) to her (your mother) to sell at her Fall Fair, though Sue says she can't imagine anyone going for that particular shade of purply-green.

Sue — Sue Landis, that is — is our new treasure and salvation. We no longer stick to the floor around here or kick up dust balls when we cross the living room rug. She even changes the sheets (first time since you left) and throws out the rotten oranges and cheese rinds and empty cereal boxes. The four-hour dynamo we call her, and worth every bit of seventy bucks — you were right, lovey, about the current pay scale for cleaning help.

She's been here twice now, and the place shines. Even Greg is looking somewhat shinier since she's started coming, but that's probably because she's taught him a new chord on his guitar — a bar chord I think it's called.

I have to admit that she wasn't quite what I had in mind when I put that ad up on the notice board at Cap College. Lord only knows what I expected, but when she turned up at the house last week I thought there'd been some kind of misunderstanding. She's young for one thing — well, thirty-two — and wears jeans and a sweater Mia would kill for, and has a head of crazy red hair. And she's intelligent! (Now, Jock, for crissake don't go and write me a Jessica-inspired sermon-ette about feminine stereotypes and male perceptions. Spare me this once, since I'm already chastened.)

Well, we sat down in the kitchen for a couple of Red Zingers (Sue carries her own teabags, feels caffeine is defi-nitely carcinogenic and has some impressive statistics to prove it), and she told me a little about her background. This clean-ing thing is just temporary, she says, just bread and butter until she gets her old job reinstated or finds something new. Until last August 15th she worked for the Department of Education as part of something called a Sexual Abuse Team that went into city schools and put on dramatizations of situations that kids apparently run into. At any rate, the gov't. decided it was nothing but an expensive social frill and cancelled the whole program. Sue maintains that the province will have to pay the real cost down the road. She gets fairly heated on these themes, and we've had a couple of lively discussions, downright arguments in fact, all of which is a hell of a lot more entertaining than analysing the stock market with Gil. (God, that man makes rotten coffee. Boils it I think.)

Sue was interested in hearing about what you are doing in Ottawa. She asked all kinds of questions, says it's about time someone took a good hard look at the economic burden on women and on single mothers in particular. But all the time she was talking I had a funny feeling that she was simultane-ously eyeing our laser printer, the Toni Onley in the dining room, the Chinese carpet in the hall, etc., etc., and wonder-ing what the hell a couple of bourgeois schmucks like you and me know about poverty.

Speaking of which, your good senator seems to be something of a stranger to the down-and-out set too, at least according to that cryptic profile in *Maclean's* last week (p. 52). Upper Canada College! Harvard, yet! A BMW! Good God, does he really "collect" rare burgundies and nineteenth-century sheet music? The kids were disappointed that the article didn't mention the people working for the Commission by name, but the bit about "Senator Pierce's unique ability to surround himself with dedicated hard-headed realists" was nice, and we all basked in the reflected glow of it.

Still no word from Sanderson's, just a letter saying they had received my letter and would be in touch soon. I hope they mean this week or next — I'd like to get that furnace bill taken care of, not that they're pressing me yet. The furnace repairs came to more than the original estimate — what else is new? Afraid that scratches a Thanksgiving reunion.

The communications course at Cap College didn't work out either. By the time I got there to register, after spending an entire morning standing in line and feeling like Old Man Time in my tweed jacket and necktie, I was told the class was filled. There was one other course open, they said — Creative Connections — so I decided I might as well give it a whirl. First session, so gotta run.

With love,
Chas

P.S. It's all right about the tea trolley. The white shoe polish did the trick.

P.P.S. If Vance says it's okay to ask questions, can't see why you shouldn't.

4 Old Town Lane
Ottawa, Ont.
Sept. 30

Dear Chas,

Yes, Vance does collect rare burgundies — I've actually been treated to a sip! He invited us back to his office after today's hearings, dusted off the bottle, opened it with a bit of joking ceremony, and handed around the wine in delicate long-stemmed crystal glasses that he just happens to have in his desk. It was so dry it took all my *sang-froid* not to make a face. But Dr. Grey — Austin — held up his glass to the light, squinted, and said admiringly, "*Formidable!*"

Vance preened a bit and allowed as how it was a nice little burgundy, and when Jessica and I said nothing (my lips puckered), Vance couldn't resist a dig. "No praise from either of the fairer sex? Not up to B.C. standards, Jock? Could I offer Baby Duck?"

He was trying to get a rise out of me, of course. I think I've been less than a barrel of fun lately, because, to tell the truth, I am feeling somewhat down, and besides we'd just heard a brief from a single mother whose home consists of two roach-infested rooms, and whose baby suffers from malnutrition!

"Ignore him, Jock," Dr. Grey — Austin (can't get used to it) — said. "Just because he's a senator doesn't mean he knows anything." He then remarked that it had certainly been a wrenching brief.

"Nobody ever said poverty would be fun," Vance said. "On the other hand, you have to remember that it is, to some extent, a state of mind."

I snapped at him. "Meaning those poor women should pull up their socks and snap out of it?"

Austin, who seems to be a bit of a peacemaker, said Vance was partly right, although poverty isn't a curable state of mind. "A state of mind that you, Jock, for instance, don't share."

"She isn't poor," Vance said. "How could she?"

"I've *been* poor," I said.

God, remember that first year I went to law school? When we just had the one car, and it took me an hour and a half on the bus to UBC? And how we'd count our pennies to come up with bus fare, and sometimes I'd have to skip lunch?

Vance sneered that I didn't know the meaning of the word, at which point Jessica, who had been remarkably silent, drawled, "Tell me, Jock, what would you do if What's-his-name — your husband — "

"Chas."

"Chas! What kind of a name is that?"

"A nickname," I said, a bit huffily. "For Charles."

"Oh. Where I come from he'd be called Chuck. So like I said, what would you do if Chuck — "

"Chas."

Jessica blew out cigarette smoke and looked sideways at me through the thick glasses and grinned very slightly. "Okay, Chas — if he walked out — or.... No. What if he had walked out when the kids were little? Before you got your law degree, say?"

Funny, I suddenly felt as though heavy cold air had wafted in from the Gatineau and was flowing over my body, the way they say you feel if a ghost enters the room. I hadn't known I harboured such phantoms.

I told her I probably would have taken my capital, and —

"Capital?" she said (sneered).

"Savings," I amended. "I would have taken my savings and done exactly what I did — go to law school."

"Poor people don't have savings." Still glaring.

"Chas and I weren't exactly in clover," I pointed out, feeling somewhat defensive by then. (She has that effect on me.) I explained about how we made do on a lot of beans and tuna casseroles and the occasional chuck roast and powdered skim milk, and how during the eighties recession when you were laid off we got along on as little as some people do on welfare.

"You weren't poor," Jessica said, maddeningly.

"We damn well were!"

I'm learning to stand up to Jessica. If you don't she bullies you; but if you do she treats you with grudging respect.

"We once figured out that we were ten per cent below the poverty line," I told her, and I went on about how we shivered through one winter with the thermostat set at sixty, and how I used to get my clothes at the Thrift Shop when I went to university.

"My dear," Vance said, "hand-woven jute would look good on you — or, even better, no hand-woven jute."

I groaned I was so frustrated, and Austin said there was a difference between being cash poor and poverty. "You knew you were smart enough to study law, and even though it used to be a man's prerogative you didn't sit still for that."

"And," Vance said, rather smugly, "no doubt you were able to make arrangements for your children."

I started to say that their grandmothers had helped, but Vance interrupted before I could get the words out.

"Ha! Now picture Granny — "

"She goes ape if you call her Granny."

"Whatever. But I want you to picture her in a welfare line-up."

My mother? In a welfare line-up? I had to laugh. "I can't get her mink jacket off," I said.

They all laughed and I cheered up a bit, and then Jessica bawled, "Here's to the poor!" and swilled down the rare burgundy in one gulp. She smacked her lips and pronounced, "Excellent appearance, not too faithful, maybe just a mite pretentious — no wonder you find it appealing, Vance. Well, thank God there's money in poverty so we can drink world-class."

With that she wheeled around, wound up like a big-league pitcher, and hurled the glass against the wall where it shattered and left splats of red dribbling down the white.

"You never could hold your booze, could you Jess?" Vance said in a steely voice.

The two of them squared off as though they were about to dive for their six-guns. Austin and I looked at the floor — a mistake; glass and dribbles of wine were scattered all over the pale-blue carpet — and in weird unison we shifted our gazes to the ceiling and started an inane conversation about the Third World that was interrupted by a loud belch from Jessica. She then swooped down on me and grabbed my arm — in a moment of madness I'd accepted an invitation to supper at her place — and as we left I turned and saw Vance and Austin looking thoughtfully at the second bottle of vintage burgundy. I'd have killed to join them.

"I get the feeling you didn't approve of my toast," Jessica yelled as she wheeled her rusted-out Volkswagen (beetle, formerly yellow) at breakneck speed down Rideau Street.

"I think you go out of your way to antagonize Vance," I answered, sounding hideously prim. (I have scary glimpses of myself turning into Mother.) "He's loaded, but that's not exactly a crime." Then I mumbled something about compassion not being a function of money, or a prerogative of the less-rich, either. I do believe all this, dearest Chas, but it sounds incredibly self-righteous written down, especially when, what with one thing and another, I haven't given an awful lot of thought to "women and poverty" in recent years.

Now, suddenly, it's all I'm thinking about. I think of it all day and half the night, and I'm grateful that something seems to be getting addressed. I told Jess that I'd been impressed by Vance's response to the Single Mothers' Association, that he seemed really concerned about poor women.

"Yeah, Van has some good points," Jessica said, sounding surprisingly conciliatory. "Just don't be dazzled by his fancy footwork, that's all."

Before I could ask her what the hell she meant by that she parked the car in front of the group home. As we got out she shot at me, "Well? Did you learn anything?"

Sometimes Jessica gets a bit tiresome, although I do enjoy a good discussion with her. I know I've painted you a pretty sordid picture, but Jessica's not just an uprooted bag-lady. She has a brain. And loves a good argument. On the other hand, I think she thinks it's good for me to see "real life" — this is twice now that she's dragged me to her place, an ancient brick house in Sandy Hill where we wallow in Group Home Modern. Pandemonium, what with eight mothers and kids of every age, a common living room dominated by TV, common eating areas, and common God knows what else — I could never live like that. (Why not? I ask myself.)

We parked ourselves on benches at the kitchen table and she ladled up nourishing stew and baking-powder biscuits — good, but I wasn't terribly hungry. She started in again about poverty being a state of mind. "During the Depression — "

I groaned.

"You got something against the Depression, Jock?"

"Sorry. It's just that everyone hauls it out when they want to make a point."

"That's called learning from history."

"Okay, okay."

Her point was well taken, even by me. Intelligent,

educated people then were poorer than plenty of welfare cases today, but according to Jessica they didn't *feel* poor. "They never thought of themselves as belonging to a social class defined by poverty, any more than you thought that when you went to law school." I have to admit that Jessica can be intellectually challenging, which was about the last thing I expected her to be when I first met (and heard) her. She went on about how I might be broke but would never be poor, "Because, one, you haven't got the negative social conditioning, two, you're educated, and three, even if your husband walked out tomorrow you'd manage very nicely."

No I wouldn't, Chas. I would *not* manage at all nicely.

"Your state of mind isn't poor," Jessica forged on, "*ergo* you aren't poor."

Ergo? I don't get Jessica. I mean, she affects this awful speech and those terrible clothes, but if she gets wound up she can't hide the fact that she's educated. I've tried to find out something about her background, but she isn't talking. I asked her if she'd ever been poor.

"Oh, I once went for a week without eating because I didn't have any money, and in the sixties I hitched through Europe and managed on a hundred bucks. Without selling my bod, in case that's what yer thinkin'."

It wasn't. In fact it was about the farthest thought from my mind.

"But I sure as hell wasn't eating at Maxim's," she went on. Ha! Would Maxim's have let Jessica in? Even with money? Not bloody likely. (Although I didn't say so.)

In some ways I suppose we've led sheltered lives, Chas. Contemplating my bedsitter, I've been feeling kind of — noble, I suppose, or self-sacrificing — being willing to live like this. *Temporarily*. But what if this was it, for the rest of my life? With no escape?

God, we are incredibly lucky to more or less own our nice cedar house. Glad you got a cleaning woman, but sorry she didn't like the kitchen curtains. I hope she doesn't start redecorating. Aren't you getting a bit chummy with the hired help? I thought you were the one who always made it a point to stay out of office politics and thought it strange that I knew all about my secretary's rather inspired love life. Anyway, I know the curtains were too heavy, but they were there precisely because of Gil. Unnerving, isn't it? I used to think the fixed regard was focused lustfully on that sexy grey jogging suit I wear around the house. But if you're getting it too, he must be just plain lonely.

I've finally found the perfect way to lose weight. When I couldn't eat today I thought I might be getting flu, and then realized it was just like the time thirty-five years ago when I went to camp and couldn't eat. Homesick — can you believe it? At my age? Let's look into cheap fares if you get the Sanderson thing.

Much love,

Jock

P.S. I guess Thanksgiving *is* a little soon.

P.P.S. Tell the kids to *write!* Those grunts on the phone aren't doing anything for me.

P.P.P.S. You *do* think we're doing the right thing, don't you? Today we heard a brief from a woman whose mother deserted her when she was thirteen, and she never got over it.

29 Sweet Cedar Drive
North Vancouver, B.C.
30 September

Dear Jock,

Couldn't wait to sharpen the old quill and tell you about
Creative Connections. (Remember, the substitute communications course?) I may say that after one session I'm having
second thoughts.

We sat around a seminar table, about eight of us, in a
little room with no windows (goddamn architects!), and I
can't remember when I've felt more ill at ease. The teacher
is a blowsy and frowsy woman who lost no time telling us
she was a published poet with a number of awards to her
credit. Davina Flowering's her name — do you know anything about her? She's one of those women — you know
the type — who manages to make an art form out of ebul-
lience. She stabs the air, shrieks, curses, clutches her hair,
yanks her sweatshirt — yes, Jock, her sweatshirt, and not
from Chapman's either — and pounds on the table. The
resonance soon had my teeth chattering. Two hours of this
and I was frazzled — and so were the others, I think.
Each of us sat there, dazed — and looking ashamed of
ourselves for having come, but Davina assured us that within
a mere week or two we would know the inside scrapings
of each other's souls. (If I decide to drop the course after
next week I can still get my money back; and maybe my
soul too.) She gave us an assignment for the next class —
to write a poem, Xerox it, and bring it for "workshopping,"
whatever that is. I thought I might dig out that parody I
wrote for the firm banquet when Bill Bettner retired.
You remember the one.

If you can keep a shaky firm together
Despite slow-paying clients all around,
If you can wangle contractors' agreements
Who for their fees are not ashamed to hound
Etc., etc.

Anyway it got a good laugh at the dinner, and Bill even asked me for a copy, if you recall.

In my spare time (laugh please) I've been doing some drawings, partly to pass the days while I wait for Sanderson's to come through and partly because I think I might have a work-able concept for the west side of the house. It occurred to me that maybe we're beyond the idea of a separate dining room, and if we knocked out that wall between the living and dining rooms and went out a couple of feet with glass panels — double, of course — we could get a kind of solarium effect, maybe even try some solar heating. I've got a good book from the library about it and it sounds feasible. What do you think?

October 8

Sorry if I sounded a bit glum, as well as fuzzy, when you phoned Thanksgiving night. The fact was that the festive family gathering I'd planned gradually disintegrated as the day wore on, and by evening there was no one in the house but me and an eighteen-pound turkey. First my mother phoned (at least she had the grace to call early in the morning) to say she was feeling a bit shaky and not up to driving over the bridge. I said I would come over and get her, but you know what she's like; said she didn't want to be a burden and a bother, she'd just make do with a Swanson's frozen dinner in front of the TV even though there was never anything to watch but foul-mouthed gangsters and young women with hair in their eyes, etc.

Around noon the phone rang again, this time *your* mother. She'd been decorating the hall at St. George's for the Fall Fair and was "all tuckered out." Would I mind if she passed up Thanksgiving dinner this year? She thought she'd make an early night of it, crawl into bed with a hot toddy and a good book. Not a word about the kids, *or* about the cauliflower casserole she'd promised to bring.

An hour later it was Mrs. Finstead on the phone — she's the mother of Laurie, that little friend of Mia's across the way (the one who looks as though she popped out of an ad for fresh milk). Mrs. Finstead — Marjorie — asked if it was all right if Mia came over for Thanksgiving dinner. They would just "love to have her aboard," she said. They were all "nutty about her." I didn't know what to say, but then Mrs. Finstead said — or whispered, rather — how sorry she was about, well...about...well, she didn't really know what to say, but she was just so very, very sorry.

I interrupted at this point and made it clear to her that Mia's mother was only away temporarily on a government contract, that we were not separated, that Mia was not a victim of a broken and uncaring family, and that I had just that minute been basting our own perfectly respectable turkey. At the same time, I could see that Mia was dying to go to the Finsteads, so what could I do without playing the part of the ogre?

That left Greg and me to tackle our golden beast. The phone rang, and Greg tore into the den to get it. Emerging a mere one-quarter of an hour before dinner, he announced that he had to go out. Naturally I asked why. Something had come up, he said, something he couldn't get out of. We stood in the kitchen facing each other for a good minute or two; I was reminded of a scene in *High Noon*. Neither of us said a word. Just how far can you press a seventeen-year-old kid on an issue like this? I could hardly say, given the circumstances, that he was disrupting a sacred family occasion. I shrugged and waved a weak hand in the direction of the oven, but I didn't want to get into my mother's brand of self-pity. Greg made a dash for the door. I yelled after him, "How about a turkey sandwich at least?" but I don't think he even heard me.

For about ten minutes I sat in the kitchen and listened to the countdown of the oven timer. Then the dinger went and everything was ready, turkey, stuffing, mashed potatoes, cran-berry sauce — my least-favourite dinner in the world, and there was a mountain of it. I happened at that moment to glance out the window and see Gil Grogan's smiling face. I waved him over, and between the two of us we made a small dent in the turkey and finished off the last two bottles of the Beaujolais your mother gave me for my birthday. It was a somewhat silent meal, just the two of us chewing and swill-ing, though once Gil mumbled something pious about how we had much to be thankful for. I wasn't up to the topic, I'm afraid.

Which all goes to say, my lovely and hard-headed real-ist, that we miss you from time to time around here. By the way, how do you make that turkey curry you used to do?

With love,
Chas

P.S. Found the lentils. Now what?

4 Old Town Lane
Ottawa, Ont.
Oct. 10

Dear Chas,

Rotten, rottener, rottenest — that's how I felt after reading about your Thanksgiving dinner. Quite simply, I felt the
rottenest I've felt since I left. What in sweet heaven was
wrong with The Mothers?

I've sat through countless harangues from mine, as you
know, on the subject of dinner guests who didn't have the
manners to let one know well in advance — "Don't they
know the amount of preparation...? No regard for a person's
feelings...Nothing but a servant..." Really, I don't know
when I've been so goddamned mad!

In fact, Chas, I couldn't turn off the mental harangue that
circled and swirled and harped away at me in a voice suspi-
ciously like my mother's. As I explained to Vance, the cauliflower casserole was the last straw, and when he snorted and
guffawed my first instinct was to punch him right on his aris-
tocratic nose. Fortunately, Mother's voice blipped off in mid-
sentence and I was restored to temporary sanity. No, I don't
discuss personal matters with Vance as a rule, but when I was
so obviously upset he was persistent, and Mother's voice
never needs a lot of encouragement.

He is a surprisingly warm man, considering, as you say,
the BMW et al. And he did cheer me up with a rather wry
account of his own Thanksgiving dinner, which was marred
irreparably by the poor burgundy that his wife had chosen.
What suffering!

My own Thanksgiving dinner was not lonely, although
loneliness might have been preferable. I know that sounds
ungrateful after Jessica was good enough to invite me to the

group home turkey spree, and other than a three-year-old who rubbed cranberry sauce in his eye, a dog who choked on a turkey bone and had to be clipped smartly in the dog equivalent of the solar plexus (dislodging the bone along with other stomach contents), a baby who threw her bottle at my wine glass and scored a direct hit (there was lots more wine — that kind comes in gallon jugs) — other than that, as I say, it was not bad and I wasn't hungry anyway.

I think my difficulty came from feeling out of place. Before dinner Jessica and I were having one of our interminable dogfights about background being a poverty determinant. She's bound she's going to radicalize me, but I'm not at all sure I'm ready to abandon the good old middle class, which has, after all, been good to us.

She had just launched into a tirade about power and how nobody — especially men — relinquishes it without a fight, when one of the women who lives in the house came over and asked if she could talk to Jessica for a minute, about a problem.

"Shoot," Jessica said.

"Well, like, I hadda quit my job and I'm gonna have trouble with the rent this month, so I was wondering if it would be a hassle if I didn't pay for a couple of weeks, just until I line something up."

"No sweat," Jessica said. "What happened to the job?"

The woman's eyes slid away. She's about twenty-five, I would guess, and quite pretty, and she was holding the baby that later spread my plonk over the tablecloth. (Plastic, fortunately.)

"Here, have a cigarette," Jessica said, getting up and pulling a pack out of the hip pocket of her jeans.

The woman helped herself, and Jessica took the baby while she lit up. The woman looked rather shyly at me, and all at once I was conscious of how I looked, in my good wool skirt and that nice silk blouse your mother gave me last Christmas. The young woman had on jeans and a polyester blouse and very high heels...no — it wasn't clothes that separated us. I mean, everyone wears jeans, it wasn't that, it was something else I'm having trouble defining. Here it is. If we met at a social event I would know instantly that she wasn't my kind and she'd know the same thing about me and in fact that was what was making her uneasy. What is it? The cut of our hair? the shade of lipstick? the jewellery or lack of it, the thousand little signals that say "different class" — God, I'm beginning to sound like Jessica.

"This here's Jock," Jessica said. "She won't harm you none, I mean, you can talk in front of her. Let's all take a load off our feet." And, still holding the baby, she plopped back onto the grimy chesterfield beside me and the woman — Jean — sat down across from us.

Jean blew out cigarette smoke rather self-consciously and said, "Well, like, I tried to stick it out but the manager — my boss — he doesn't own the restaurant but it's like, a chain, eh? Anyway, he kept coming on so strong, you know? I couldn't keep him off, so finally I just figured it wasn't worth it, he was making my life so miserable, eh?"

I was shocked, as you can imagine. I glanced at Jessica and waited for the explosion I thought was bound to come. But she just lowered her eyes and jammed her cigarette butt into an ashtray, then handed Tricia to me (I was nervous that she would spit on my blouse, silk is not a wonder fabric and I can't afford to get it cleaned) and said, "You don't need to take that kind of shit you know, Jean."

Jean looked terrified. "It's not worth it to start trouble, Jess. I've been through all that when I tried to get support from the kid's father. It just isn't worth it. I'll find something else, but for now I'll be a bit tight. I got some unemployment coming, I think, except I dread going in for the separation certificate."

"I'll go along if you like," Jessica said.

Jean's face lit up and she looked so pretty I could see why she might present a fetching target to that yahoo boss.

She reached over to take the baby (which *had* spit on me, do cleaners take Visa?), but for some reason I didn't want to give it up, and when she took it and hugged it I felt something like *envy*! Do you think, Chas, that absence makes the head grow softer?

"Listen, I made a real nice dip," Jean said. "Would you and Mrs. — Jock — like some?"

"Yer damn right. Pass it to Jock, she needs some meat on her bones." Thanks a lot, Jessica. But I ploughed my chip into the dip anyway and waxed enthusiastic over the stirred-up onion soup and sour cream.

All the same, Chas, I can see what Jessica means — about poverty being a state of mind, I mean. If I were sexually harassed on a job I wouldn't stand it for one minute. I'd state flatly that I was going to the Human Rights Commission if *he* didn't leave me alone and I'd point out to him that no doubt the restaurant chain wouldn't be too pleased to see *its* name dragged through the media. But Jean couldn't possibly do that, she hasn't got what it takes, the indignation, the sense of self-worth, the outrage.

I've surprised myself, since then, with sudden flashes of anger that attack without warning, like a minor mental blight. I can be listening attentively to a brief when a chance turn of phrase will trigger it, and I feel possessed, suddenly (as in possession, exorcist style), and I get a shaking in my limbs and a sort of blindness that blocks out my surroundings. Isn't it odd? I mean, rationally I've — *we've*, you and

I — long since come to terms with our masculine and feminine roles, and God knows you're the epitome of fairness, or
else why would you be back home coping with Greg and the
Mothers? I don't know — this rage must come from some
primordial identification I'm not even aware of. Do you agree
that this is odd?

Much love,
Jock

P.S. Greg's behaviour at Thanksgiving wasn't too great either.
What *is* eating him I wonder?

P.P.S. The hell with Mrs. Finstead.

29 Sweet Cedar Drive
North Vancouver, B.C.
15 October

Dear Jock,

Poverty as a state of mind, eh?

Hmmmm, yes. I can see what you mean. But have you
and your snorting pal, Jessica, considered, as a poverty deter-
minate, the effect of bodily health? One thing I've learned
this week: a three-day bout of wrenching cramps and diar-
rhoea goes a long way toward diminishing your belief in your
life choices or even in your viability as a human being.

Yes, dear Jock, we've all taken to our beds, Mia on Thursday, Greg on Friday, and I on Saturday morning. Now don't
panic, Jock, don't reach for that phone, don't grab a plane.
We are, it seems, on the mend — at least I can now hold up
a newspaper without being overcome by weakness.

The worst of it is, it seems to be my fault, and I'm being condemned on all sides as a careless parent, irresponsible citizen, etc. etc. Dr. Hopkins, who broke his physician's oath by paying us a house call — on his way to the golf course — came out loudly and rapped me on the knuckles with: "I thought it was common knowledge that..." Not easy to take from a man with a good suntan, but easier than listening to your mother's ringing remark that she was "taken aback" that I hadn't known better.

Actually, it was the turkey's fault. Foul Fowl. For several days following Thanksgiving we feasted on his glistening flesh, simply stripping away our protein needs as hunger prompted. For a brief while I thought I'd discovered a way to avoid the cooking and planning of meals — just keep a plump, roasted turkey in the fridge and grab a fistful of nourishment when necessary. Unfortunately, we also scraped away at the stuffing — delicious, if I do say so — which was rapidly building up vicious microbes and gathering strength for a full-scale salmonella attack.

But we are, as I say, recovering. Chastened and emptied out, we three shuffle around the house with our cups of steaming tea and vegetable broth. Greg has never been so civil, going so far as to inquire whether I slept well last night. Rest and liquids seem to be the standard treatment. We kept to our rooms at first, meeting only occasionally in the neighbourhood of the bathroom door, but now we're beginning to assemble in the family room for a little passive TV viewing.

And it's slightly surreal to be sitting snugly indoors, wrapped in dressing gowns and blankets and peering into the tube at the tumult of the universe. Well, not the universe exactly, but at what's happening here in B.C. No doubt you're keeping track of things from Ottawa, but I wonder if you can feel it as it really is. This strike seems to be inflaming passions from every side of the political spectrum, much more so than the myriads of strikes we've lived through in the past. It's all crazy out here. Management comes on the air battering away in the chilly relentless voice that seems to go with corporate success, and then, the next minute, we get a close-up of a union leader shouting or weeping or going through a set of agit-prop calisthenics that makes you want to cringe and cry at the same time. And then the inevitable pictures of riot police wrestling some overweight, beer-guzzling, inarticulate working joe to the ground. Dogs straining on leashes for a quick snack. What the hell is happening? I mean, is this really a police state? It's hard to believe when we sit here, insulated and safe and sipping our way back to health, that there's a bunch of bad guys out there putting the hammer-lock on us. Down among the workers there's a certain amount of tearful we-shall-overcome corniness, as you might guess, and some embarrassing rhetoric too, but the main "feel" of the crowd when the busloads of scabs go by seems to be numbed out-rage and a sense of disbelief that this could be happening in our own beautiful rainforest.

I have a problem with the whole thing, but not Sue Landis, our Ms. Clean. She's whole-heartedly on the side of the union. She phoned to say she wouldn't be able to come to clean on Monday because she and her "sex squad" were rigging up a little dramatic protest, but when she heard we were all sick here she promised to drop over in the evening. Well, she whirled in about six, made us poached eggs on toast, changed the sheets, swabbed the bathroom and kitchen, and generally got us glued back together. (Your reference to "getting chummy with the household help" struck me as a little raw, lovey. This girl — whom you would like tremendously, I know — is bringing order and healing into our ailing household.)

In some ways it hasn't been a bad few days. Relations among the three of us have grown almost weirdly congenial. Mia, the first to bounce back, mans the teapot and fluffs the pillows. Greg has thus far had the grace not to accuse me directly of poisoning him — in fact he is mainly a silent presence. I realize that this is the first time in a couple of years that I haven't been worried about where he was and what he was up to. A respite. All of us, despite the backdrop of Africa, international terrorism, union bashing, and the ozone layer, seem to have dropped into a sweet, peaceful pocket just outside of time. (Remember that snowfall back in '87, how we couldn't move for two days and how quiet it was, just us? How we had the fire going all day long and listened to those old Dixieland records by the hour?)

Everyone's been kind. The Finsteads sent a coffee cake, as yet untouched. My mother phones daily, inquires into our health, and then launches into the details of hers — a recital that takes us from the backs of her burning eyes to the bottoms of her stiffening ankles. Maybe you could drop her a line. She seems a little confused these days. Last night she said something about you being in Halifax. I told her it was Ottawa, and she said of course, of course — Ottawa.

Your mother's dropped in several times — keeping a careful distance — with donations of soup as well as a tall bottle of brilliant green microbe-killer she's invented. "It does wonders for me when I'm down," she said. "A secret recipe."

She always asks how you are and if you've phoned lately. I told her you and I had decided to write letters instead, and she seemed to think this wonderfully quaint. She wishes, she said, that she had time to write letters, and maybe after the Fall Fair.... Implying that I have nothing *but* time — or am I being paranoid? I didn't bother telling her we were trying to trim the phone bill.

Gil Grogan has so far made only one crack about the "turkey trots," for which I am grateful. He's done some shopping for us and even cut our side of the hedge Sunday, said he was glad to have something to keep him busy — a remark I found profoundly sad for some reason. And on Saturday night, when I was feeling my worst, he sat in the corner of our bedroom and read the newspaper aloud to me. You would have been surprised to hear him read — elegantly, without a pause, like silk off a spool. Clunky old Gil. He read it all, sports, editorials, even the letters to the editor. (I'm enclosing one of those letters, which I think will give you the flavour of our little backyard war.)

You asked about Sanderson's. In the last few days I've been on the point of picking up the phone and calling them to see how the job application is coming, but something always stops me. Food poisoning has a way of weakening one's resolve, and then, too, I suppose I'm afraid of hearing negative news or even of getting snubbed by a bloody secretary. (More paranoia?) So I'm holding off, hoping no news is good news. Surely by next week there'll be something.

By the way, have you heard any more about your pay coming through? I've had to pay the furnace people. They phoned one day when I was out and spoke to Greg, politely I imagine, but it seemed he found it a mortifying experience. I suppose the poor kid thinks we're really at rock bottom, when in fact we're only experiencing a phase of what I like to call intermezzo poverty.

But, yes, let's look into cheap fares. Come as soon as you can, darling Jock. I'm sure this continued chastity is weakening to body and spirit.

With love,
Chas

P.S. When I handed the kids their allowances last week Greg shook his head and refused — said he could manage without. I have to admit that this noble gesture of his stung me more than it should have.

4 Old Town Lane
Ottawa, Ont.
Oct. 17

Dear Chas,

You poor sickies! You should have phoned and I would have . . . I don't know — *done* something. Probably a good thing you didn't, I would probably have pawned the family jewels (make that jewel) for a non-charter Air Canada fare, and we must be approaching our Visa limit as it is.

Will I never be paid?

There's to be a big reception in the House of Commons to celebrate the opening of Parliament. Van is going to try to get me an invitation, and I'd love to buy a new something for it. Can you believe this? Nearly two months, and when I go in to the payroll people and ask (read plead), I get these terrible tales about computers and changing categories. It seems incredible. Surely there are laws (there are! — made by the very people who aren't paying me). I'm so frustrated and so *broke*! I still have a few bucks on Amex, maybe I can find a scarf for my silk blouse. I can't believe I won't get some money soon — actually, they've pretty well promised to use emergency funds if nothing is forthcoming by next week. I'll send as soon as I possibly can.

Thinking of you all lying there with nobody to soothe the fevered brows has left me feeling more than ordinarily desolate. This morning a noise like a large splat wakened me and my first thought was, "Oh, it's been snowing!" It was just like that whoosh when a cascade of snow slides off the branches of the Douglas fir by the house and slaps down onto our bedroom roof. Then when I opened my eyes and saw the scabby brown dresser across the room I felt a wave of something indescribably dreary that pinned me to the bed.

The room was freezing cold. I got up, finally, and went to shut the window, but a little drift had blown in on the sill. I went to sweep it off and it didn't *feel* like our snow. I just stood there, holding onto that cold, clammy powder, and I started to cry — I mean, if you can't count on snow, what can you count on? It doesn't even come down like our cheery, fairy-tale, Christmas-card snow. It's brisk, business-like, small, severe, punishing, governmental.

Okay, I was feeling sorry for myself. It's tougher here than I thought it would be. I'm losing my self-confidence (another blooper today), and to top it off I slammed the window on my thumb. I yelled "shit!" and a man down in the street looked up and made an obscene gesture, and I threw open the window and shouted, "Mind your own business!" at him.

I was beginning to think I really was losing it, and then the sun came out and the snow departed, and our hearings were unexpectedly cancelled so Austin suggested a drive up into the Gatineau Hills to see the leaves — still fairly spectacular. We went to Kingsmere and wandered among the ruins and had a little lunch there, although I wasn't hungry. (As usual these days.)

Austin has been carrying a lot of the Commission's writing load, and Van has been looking for a writer to relieve him — someone like Austin who can write prose that "comes alive." (Van says this is going to be one report that isn't going to languish in the archives. Vance is pretty dedicated to poverty, although, as Jessica so often mentions, he doesn't practise it.) He has hired a very nice man named George O'Reilly, who isn't Irish but is (believe it or not) *French*. At least, his parents are French-speaking, but having been brought up in Ottawa, he is *complètement bilingue* — slips from one language to the other with absolute facility, although he has this eastern mannerism of ending every other sentence with "eh"? In fact, he's an ex-English teacher. Quit to do some writing, and although his first novel got a lot of critical acclaim, he only grossed two thousand dollars from it, and so he began to do some speech writing for various ministers and thus came to Vance's attention.

I must say it's pleasant to have someone more or less my own age — he's a bit younger, but not that much — whom I'm not somewhat leery of. Yes, I might as well admit I'm cautious with Van, what with those dumb innuendoes in the press about his extra-curricular activities, though even Jessica dismisses them as so much horseshit. He's never made anything that could even remotely be construed as a pass at me, but he's so obviously aware of his own tremendous attractiveness. And he's so rich. And capable. And brainy.

I guess that's why I'm enjoying George. His family life is a lot like ours. His wife sells real estate, and their kids are teenagers too, and his son sounds just like Greg. After the hearings yesterday George and I had coffee together and I told him about Greg's sudden surliness, and he said, "Do you think it might have something to do with the changed role models?"

I said no, that I've always worked (outside the home, I'd better train myself to add that when Jessica's around), at least since Greg was quite young.

"Maybe," George said, "he can manage his mother in a secondary role, eh? But not in the breadwinner's shoes."

Good Lord, I thought. Our children would be much too enlightened for that, I mean, remember when we got Mia the truck for Christmas and gave the Cabbage Patch Doll to Greg? Remember the disbelief — nay, outrage — on the faces of The Mothers? (Remember — oh Lord — how fast truck got traded for doll?) Society's expectations again — with the added weight of not one but two dedicated grand-mothers. (An unfortunate turn of phrase, given the girth of our Dear Ones.)

Anyway, food for thought, don't you agree? (Eh?)

Devastated about the salmonella, you poor, dear, neglected family. If money comes I'll phone.

Beaucoup, beaucoup d'amour,
Jock

P.S. *I* feel guilty about *your* salmonella. Why?

29 Sweet Cedar Drive
North Vancouver, B.C.
18 October

Dear Jock,

You shouldn't have phoned last night, but thank God you did. It raised our group morale twenty notches, and even Greg seemed bucked up. I'm looking forward to your letter but thought I'd scribble a quick note to tell you about today's rather bizarre phone call.

Needless to say what with our *après*-turkey malaise, I didn't get to the Creative Connections class this week. And, as a result, I received a phone call from Davina Flowering herself. At first I didn't recognize her voice — all the bump and thunder had gone out of it. "You weren't at class this week, Charles," she said. Whispered, really.

I explained. I had been the cause of severe food poisoning in my family unit and was now taking the rap. (Why, I thought, need I explain all this?) I didn't tell her the truth — that I was thinking of dropping her course. And a good thing too, because the next thing she said (whispered) was that she hoped I wasn't planning to drop the course.

A short silence followed, also some embarrassed har-rumphing on my part.

"I really hope I didn't scare you off by that first assignment," she said.

"Oh, no," I told her. "In fact, my poem was all typed and ready to go when illness struck."

"Well," she said, "only three people showed yesterday, and so I got a little worried and all, and I was just wondering — "

"Maybe the demonstration in support of the unions . . ." I started to say.

"Do you really think so?" She seemed childishly eager to believe this. "I suppose that could be the reason."

"Oh, I'm sure that's got to be it," I said, asking myself why the hell I felt it was my responsibility to reassure her. "Next week everyone'll probably turn up."

"Well, I hope so," she said, "because if we don't get at least six registrations the college has the right to cancel the course."

"Really?" said I.

"Really," said she. "I think it's dumb myself, that kind of bureaucratic slaughter. I mean, small groups work best with this kind of dynamic. Intimacy, trust, that's how workshopping gets its energy. If you see what I mean."

I didn't see, and so there was another small silence.

"The thing is," Davina continued, "I only teach this one

course. I mean, I like to leave the rest of my space for writing, so I've opted for just one course, and that's, well, more or less how I sort of keep myself in bread and marge. If you know what I mean."

This time I did know what she meant, but I was surprised. I remembered all those books of poetry she'd published, and those prizes she'd won — evidently the prizes were not financial in nature. I hung on to the phone weakly. The cramps were reasserting themselves, bands of steel across the lower abdomen. I promised her I'd be in class next week.

"That's great, Chuck." Feverishly.

"I'm usually called Chas," I said. Stuffily.

"Chas?" She sounded incredulous. "Anyway, Chas, be sure to bring your poem."

"Well, I don't know if you'll think much of it . . ." Mumble, mumble, mumble.

"I'll like it." She was booming again — I could feel her coming back. "I respect all forms of sincere communication, I really do. It's just feeble-minded bullshit that makes me want to vomit."

"I'm afraid I have to go," I told her.

"Great, Chas. See you Monday. We'll be moving into the real stuff on Monday, how we feel, how we touch one another, the real guts of — "

"Honestly," I said, "I have to hang up right now." And I did — without a goodbye, I'm afraid. The bands of steel immediately receded, but I was left with the feeling I'd somehow been manipulated. Ah well . . .

We're all much better. Mia actually went over to Laurie's this afternoon. Look forward to your cheery words!

Love

Chas

29 Sweet Cedar Drive
North Vancouver, B.C.
21 October — midnight

Darling Jock,

You were wonderful. No, you were superb. When Hana
Gartner fixed you with her glittering eye and put that question
to you about wages for housewives, I thought you responded
magnificently. That little pause (thoughtful, theatrical) and then
the clear and steady way you set out your case without any
stumbling around or bullshitting. I had to keep asking myself if
that was really the woman I sleep with. (Used to sleep with.)
That elegant creature with the seductive throat and the expres-
sive hands and the curving cheekbones (for God's sake don't lose
any more weight — I don't want to lose another ounce of you).

The kids missed it, damn it. Mia was at the movies with
the Finsteads and Greg was "out." I kind of liked having you
all to myself. Me and five million others.

This is not a fan letter, lovey. This is a love letter.

Chas

4 Old Town Lane
Ottawa, Ont.
Oct. 23

Sweetheart —

Thank you, thank you, thank you for those kind words!
Yours is the only feedback I've had — Vance missed it and I
think Jessica is miffed. Van was supposed to do it, but some
family matter in Montreal came up, something about
Catherine and the curse of *la vie politique* — anyway, he

phoned me a *bare two hours* before the interview and asked me to fill in — Austin was in Charlottetown, and Van didn't suggest Jessica and neither did I.

I asked him if it was really suitable, I mean, I'm just the counsel and not on the Commission, but he got all hurt-sounding and said, "Jock, have we ever treated you any differently from the rest of us?", making me feel ungrateful and cavilling. So there I was, two hours later, trying to appear serene while Hana Gartner asked me all those tricky questions from Toronto and I tried to focus my eyes as instructed on her pretend chair in Ottawa.

Dear heart, was I really clear and steady? Am I fishing for compliments? I should get an Emmy award. My heart wasn't merely thumping, it was bumping and grinding out of sync, and I was enormously surprised when actual sound (rather than squeaks) came out of my constricted throat. Did you *really* like my response about housewives' wages? "Would it apply equally to house-husbands?" flashed out of me before I could stop it, I suppose because you are never far from my thoughts these lonely days — and, on a less romantic note, because I couldn't help thinking how helpful it would be if you *did* get wages right now. Anyway, I'm relieved that you think I sounded reasonably coherent.

Thanks, too, about the praise for the elegant *maîgre* creature I'm fast becoming. Was the Duchess of Windsor right, do you think, that you can never be too rich or too thin? I'll never know about the first, but I still don't feel like eating and so may find out about the second.

Your letter and note, through some quirk of the postal system, arrived simultaneously. Sorry I've been too busy to write properly, but will very soon.

Much love,
Jock

P.S. I hope to God you remembered to let Mother know about the TV. She'd never forgive us.

P.P.S. Greg will no doubt give you a bad time because you didn't record it. Haven't you figured out how to work the VCR yet?

P.P.P.S. NO MONEY yet!

29 Sweet Cedar Drive
North Vancouver, B.C.
31 October

Dear One,

Well, it's happened. Today was N-Day, and all the nurses in the province and some *teachers* — in support of the nurses — have walked away from their jobs. Even sitting here in a relatively quiet and ordered house, we can feel the seismic shudder. Everyone is so *mad*. I think the level of anger has actually frightened people — it is somehow so un-Canadian. No one ever prepared us for so much concentrated social rage! Inevitably some people are already crossing the picket lines, and a prof from the medical faculty at UBC very nearly ran down six students who were demonstrating on one of the campus drives. The students, interviewed on TV a few minutes ago, were shaking, and not just from indignation. The professor, also interviewed, was impenitent, though he came within an inch of injuring the lot of them. Jesus!

Remember the peace demonstrations we used to go to?

— how, even at their most hysterical, there was a kind of gaiety about them? Not this time, not in B.C. There's no merriment here, no sense of holiday. It's deadly serious, and the seriousness is more than political. Sue Landis — yes, our own Sue of the mops and pails — had a letter to the editor in yesterday's *Province* pointing out that something has happened that's unique in democratic society: the teachers who've gone out have decided to risk their material possessions and even their livelihoods to fight for a matter of principle, mostly to support "fellow women" (clipping enclosed, but I would like it back). It's the divisiveness that seems most painful, the families and neighbours who no longer speak to each other or tolerate each other's views.

Which leads me to confess that I had a royal dust-up with Gil Grogan yesterday over the whole mess. Like a couple of *hausfraus* we were sitting in the kitchen (ours) having a cup of rosehip (I've almost succeeded in giving up coffee), and he was carrying on in his tiresome, tuneless way about the deficit and misguided idealists and their embarrassingly inflamed passions, saying that when you counted up the real victims all you got was a handful of losers who probably had it coming to them anyway.

That was too much for me. I pointed out, rising to my feet and striking the table, that I happened to *be* one of those victims, one of those so-called losers he was blithely writing off, and I wasn't going to stand in my own kitchen and listen to that kind of crap.

Oddly enough, Jock, it was the first time I've perceived myself as a bona-fide victim. It was seductively, and dangerously, comforting. I also felt that I should damn well be out there marching and yelling and not sitting around shooting the breeze with crusty old neighbourhood fascists. I didn't exactly ask him to leave. I just said I felt the need of a brisk walk in order to cool off. "If that's the way you feel..." he said, the old Neanderthal.

I slammed out the back door — goddamn rain, I'd forgotten about that, of course — and walked all the way up to that nice spot where the creek goes into that little patch of cedars (you remember the spot) and sat on a wet log and contemplated the insanity of the universe and other weighty themes to be filed under existential angst, meaninglessness of life, the solitary self, and the loneliness of the soaking-wet victim.

I also composed, as I sat there, the opening lines of what will be my second poem for Creative Connections (haven't read them the first yet), and to my surprise the words sprang into my head without the least urging or agonizing.

> *Each day now is an open mouth*
> *Heated with anger and yawning time*

Luckily I had a pen in my pocket and also a scrap of paper — the receipt from the furnace folk, stamped "Paid in Full." An omen maybe.

The irony is that by next week I will no longer, strictly speaking, *be* out of work. A letter from Sanderson's arrived yesterday — at last — offering me two days of work a week.

I didn't phone you, Jock, because it's a bit of an anticlimax. They regret that the work will be rather routine — just drafting, in fact — but they hope they'll be able to offer me something "commensurate with my abilities" before long.

Naturally I read the letter to the kids — I especially wanted Greg to know about it because he seems so hangdog about our being in the poorhouse. I thought the news would relieve his worries, but he went into this crazy tailspin.

"You're not seriously going to take it, are you?" is what he said.

"Most certainly I am," I boomed back.

"Drafting?" he said. "You've got to be kidding. You're supposed to be an architect. You're not a draftsman for crissake." His language has deteriorated as you can see.

"All architects know how to draft," I informed him. "It's the first thing we learn."

"If I were you I'd tell them to stuff it." He actually said this, Jock.

"It's money," I said. "Regular money. A cheque twice a month. Not a large cheque, but something. Now what's wrong with that?"

"Are we poor?" Mia asked at this point.

Greg looked sick. "You're crazy if you take — "

I held on to my temper and gave him my Father-Knows-Best look and made a short punchy speech about honest labour, cogs in wheels, fulfilling society's needs — not a bad little off-the-cuffer.

"Couldn't you hold off a little longer?" he asked. "Something's bound to come along if you wait — "

"I can *not* afford to wait," I said.

"We must be poor," Mia said. "I didn't know we were poor. It feels weird."

Greg said, "I'm going out." I said, "No you're not, it's dinner time." "I'm not hungry," he said, and slammed out the back door. Nice kid. Reasonable.

Sanderson's want me for Tuesdays and Thursdays, which suits me fine. I can keep on in Davina's class and maybe get a little work done on my plans for the living room. As soon as I get a set of drawings, I'll mail a copy off to you.

Afraid I have to cut this short. I want to get another line down before dinner. I asked Davina how long a line of poetry should be. "About as long as a piece of string," she said. Hmmmmm.

I see your Vance Pierce is in hot water with the press. Hope he's thick-skinned. And his wife too.

Love, profane and otherwise,
Chas

P.S. Don't know if I'd have applauded the teachers' courage if I'd remembered the kids would be home. The three of us are going to have to formulate a plan so we don't murder each other.

P.P.S. I start at Sanderson's next Tuesday. I guess I can't reasonably expect a paycheque before the 30th. However have found that 7-Eleven takes Visa, although groceries are about double the price. Beats starvation!

Ottawa,
Thursday

Dear Chas,

Too bad Sanderson's can only give you two days a week, but at least it's an opportunity to get out of the house (know the feeling) and bring home a few bucks, and surely things will start to improve in B.C. I suppose all the labour unrest has slowed the economy. When I see how dependent these women out here are on the social-support systems I get mad as hell at the cutbacks. Glad you can keep on with your class anyway.

Your new interest in poetry inspired me to get one of Austin Grey's books out of the library. Imagine, that beautiful poetry! Out of such a grey man!

I have wandered by night and seen black forms
And touched things colder than moonlight on a still spirit.

Imagine that kind of passion lurking beneath the good grey exterior!

Wouldn't your Davina be bowled over if she could meet him! The Commission *could* come to Vancouver! Van hinted at the possibility yesterday!

Sorry my letters are on the short side lately, but I have so damn much *reading* to do. Can't believe I know so little about poverty, especially when I think of myself as having spent the larger part of my life in it. And still am. (I've given up asking.)

Love and loneliness,

Jock

29 Sweet Cedar Drive
North Vancouver, B.C.
4 November

Dear Jock,

Do you believe in synchronicity?

Can you believe that I too have just finished *Moonlight on a Still Spirit*? A gift from Davina after the first class — at which we had an adequate turnout, by the way; she must have been busy on the phone rounding us up. Everyone listened with grave respect while I read that parody about Bill Bettner, though the respect may well have been kindled by my grey hairs, for I am the oldest by far in the class, Davina being a possible exception — but she is so raddled and scarred and creased with *feeling* that she might be thirty-five or fifty-five. I think you'd like her, and I'm pretty damn sure she could provide a case history for your Commission — if holes in sweaters and mismatched socks are any indication. I thought the Canada Council supported all these types in style?

There were exactly six of us in class, the minimum number, according to Davina, if we are to continue our existence. ("I hope," she said, fixing us with a flinty gaze, "that there will be no further class drop-outs.") There is Bob, about twenty-five, a police constable, hideously shy, who bites his nails. Janet is a breathy fat girl with thick glasses and a Cowichan sweater. Stan is your standard criminal type, the kind of dirty, spikey kid who possibly sets houses on fire as a form of recreation. Melanie (or is it Melody) is a nurse who "adores" poetry, and Tracy is the token black, token baby boomer, and token feminist all rolled into a quite magnificent body. (Forgive me, I couldn't help noticing.)

We were, Jock, so solemn. The respect with which we listened to one another's drivel was extraordinary. Melanie / Melody read in one of those holy voices — you know the kind — as though each word were floating in sauce upon a golden plate. Stan barked his way through a forest of fucks, pricks, cunts, and farts — all directed at the government — and this sparked a rather interesting discussion about whether politics and art should be addressing one another. Davina said yes, Janet said no, Bob said well sorta if ya kinda know what I mean. I don't know what I think. To tell you the truth, I've never thought about it before.

Afterwards Davina grabbed me and invited me to the cafeteria for a cup of coffee — my first in a week — intoxicating. She is the first person I've ever seen to take seven sugars in her coffee — could this be reverse diabetes or is she just hungry?

"Well, Chas," she said, stirring her sludge, "I thought your poem was terrific."

"Really?" I said, but sniffed a qualification.

"Yeah," she said, "but I had this funny feeling that your total self was definitely *not* involved in that poem."

I told her how I happened to write it, about Bill Bettner retiring from the firm, what an exceptional man he had been, and a little about the farewell dinner where I read the poem.

"So he was a great guy," she said. "And you really loved this guy?"

That stopped me. Love? "Well," I said, "love maybe isn't the word. You'd have to know Bill."

"And you really *knew* him?" she pressed.

Stopped again. I offered to buy her a bran muffin. She accepted. I think she *is* hungry, despite the girth.

"Listen, Chas," she continued. "Poetry, if it's going to sing, has to be a slice right off the primordial soul." She applied butter to her muffin like a professional plasterer. "I mean," she said, "your poem was great stuff. There's nothing wrong with funny bits and a good vigorous rhyme scheme — I'm not doctrinaire about these things — but you have to ask yourself when you finish a poem, 'Is this what I really mean?' Otherwise it's crap."

"I see," said I. "Well, I've been working on something new."

"Lemme ask you something," she said. "Have you ever read Austin Grey's stuff? I mean, that man *delves*. He *gives*. It's cloth of gold with Grey, every inch of the way. Hey, I made a rhyme. May the god of prosody forgive me."

I started to tell her that Austin Grey was on a commission with my wife, but she interrupted by pulling a little book out of her voluminous, not very clean, army bag. "Here, Chas. I'm going to lend you my copy of Austin Grey's latest book. It's called *Moonlight on a Still Spirit*. Great title." She handed it over like a holy object. I received it like a holy object.

"It'll give you an idea of just what words can do, how far they can go if you ream them out."

"I really appreciate — "

"What Grey does is write about what matters to him, the most important thing going on in his head. What's the most important thing right now in *your* head, Chas?"

She took me by surprise. "Being out of work," I said off the top of my head. I think it is true, next to chastity.

"Okay," she said. "Let's have a poem next week about where you're at, headwise. Joblessness. Worklessness. Are you on?"

"Slice off the old soul?" I asked.

"You've got it."

I now have the first six lines, two of them from the cedar grove and four of them that I composed the next day and reworked this morning. Can you imagine a grown man spending an entire morning writing four lines? My God, the self-indulgence of it! But what little beauties they are, and they *don't* rhyme. I read the Austin Grey book last night, and I can see what Davina means about him. Some of it's surprisingly brutal, but it's never limp. He might be the one to lend a beacon of reality to your commission. What's he like anyway? Headwise? — as Davina would say.

Your mother has gone to bed for a week to rest up from the Fall Fair, probably taking one of her hot lemon and brandy cures. This is the first week she's failed to come around and check up on us. *Our* first week without an eggplant casserole, something of a relief to tell the truth.

As for *my* mother, she's gone a bit drifty and I'm taking her to the doctor tomorrow. She keeps losing the thread of conversations — of course, she was never what you'd call focused — and has asked me twice when you're getting back from Halifax. "Ottawa," I tell her. "Oh yes," she says vaguely, "she's enlisted. Now why would Jock go and enlist when she didn't have to?" Do you think it could be the beginnings of hardening of the arteries?

Oh God, I dread old age. Everyone softening up or else going rigid like Gil Grogan.

Love,

Chas

P.S. First paycheque so miniscule it scarcely covered the milk bill. Any news?

Old Town Lane
Ottawa, Ont.
Nov. 12

Darling Chas,

God, it was wonderful! In spite of the downpour and the fog, who cared? Oh I was lucky to get that flight — I didn't realize how desperately I needed to see you. When Vance first mentioned that he might be able to get me on a minister's jet heading for Vancouver my heart did a handstand (very athletic, my heart). I couldn't trust myself to believe it and so laughed hollowly and said, "I can just see the headlines: 'Commission Counsel Takes Freebie'."

Jessica said, "Oh Christ, Jock, come off it. The Establishment owes us. I hitch any chance I get." (A visual impression: Jessica standing on a dirty cloud at ten thousand feet with her thumb stuck out.)

"One must be scrupulous, of course," Dr. Grey — Austin — chimed in. "But remember, the seat would be empty if you didn't go. When I went to Charlottetown — also as a hitchhiker — I was assured that my additional weight would add a mere cubic centimetre extra of fuel, for which I could be billed roughly fifty cents if I wished. In your case I would hazard an estimate," he cocked his head and eyed my boney frame, "oh, twenty-five cents, give or take a penny either way." (They all tease me about my appetite — they should have seen me demolish your week's supply of 7-Eleven groceries. Hope the Visa isn't at its limit. Has the refrigerator door recovered?)

Anyway, it was Wonderful, Wonderful, Wonderful! When I walked in the door everything seemed strange, so familiar and expected and yet almost as though I were seeing my own house for the first time — it seemed so huge after this little apartment. How I miss it!

I keep hating myself for getting into that peculiar little snit over your drafting table in the kitchen. What on earth was the matter with me? Of course you should work where you want — especially when I'm not there — but somehow it seemed to change the character of a place that I had thought of as uniquely mine and no one else's. I can't believe myself! Possessive about a kitchen! I hope Jessica never gets wind of that. I guess I must want things to stay exactly the way I left them, sort of a security blanket.

And to fly away from barely yellowing leaves in Vancouver to snow, snow, snow! Nobody stays home here because of a little snow. If they did they'd be in all winter. Instead they warm up their cars and slither and slide until the temperature gets so low the snow isn't slippery any more. And they carry shoes with them in little bags, and on Parliament Hill they cover the cement steps with wooden boards. It came to me as a mini-revelation that I've never spent a real winter in Canada, even though I've lived here all my life. No wonder we're alienated on the West Coast.

The Commission may come to Vancouver! Yes, there's a good

chance! With all the uproar over the cost of studies and commissions in general, Van has been getting more than a little
jumpy — after all, our commission doesn't exactly rate a
morning round of applause in the boardrooms of Canada.
It could become a sacrificial lamb. So he's been fulminating about taking us on the road and thus speeding up the
process. Wouldn't it be fun if we could manage some
sort of "do"? Our rainforest hideaway in the middle of an
Ottawa winter!

I've just reread all your letters. It was that or *Pensions in
the 1990s — A Demographic Forecast*. But even if the choice had
been between you and Alice Munro I'd have read you. And
it struck me that all during our lovely, lovely weekend
we still didn't discuss the ramifications of celibacy —
probably because celibacy was the last thing on our minds.
By the way, I doubt if our remaining celibate season will
be a problem for me, although I don't know why I'm saying
this when I've had spells of base longing. (Probably because
I'm temporarily but thoroughly satiated.) And after all,
we'll see each other again at Christmas (I can hardly wait,
have already started the annual panic). Will it be harder
for you, do you think? (Not Christmas. Celibacy.) Men
pride themselves — if that's the right word — on having
more intense sex drives than women, although I suspect
that's an old husband's tale. But do you think "it" will get
to you?

Which reminds me (although it shouldn't) I did *not*
take to Mrs. Finstead — Marjorie — Mia notwithstanding.
The way she dropped by the *minute* you went to the store,
she must have been watching. She just *loves* Mia, so good
for Laurie, and she hopes it doesn't bother me that she is
providing the little she can in the way of — you know —
feminine guidance at this so vulnerable stage in Mia's life.

(It doesn't.) Oh, but perhaps that nice-looking young woman who comes over every Tuesday? — "The cleaning woman," I said frostily — Oh of course, she should have known, but her own cleaning woman is, you know, such a *frump*! She just never thought.... (She's not kidding.)

Then you came home and she started that awful commiserating with the poor little house-husband left alone to cook those big, dangerous, poisonous turkeys. And that coy sally about leaving such a handsome man all by himself with no one to keep an eye on him (easy prey for cleaning women and other neighbourhood sexpots is what she meant). I don't know how I looked, but when I forced a grin I felt as though my teeth were great white fangs hanging over my bottom lip. It was a good thing we had to leave for the airport at that moment. I was touched, by the way, when Greg ambled out and said he guessed he might as well come along for the ride, not much else to do. And I can't even think of Mia cuddling up to me all the way without getting weepy.

I'd better get off that.

When I phoned to say goodbye, your mother sounded miffed that we hadn't come to dinner. I don't recall her asking us, do you? (For which I'm thankful, I didn't want to spend a moment of time away from my own lovely house.) Otherwise, she sounded fine, except for asking about the weather in Halifax. I think Mother was a bit hurt, too, that we didn't spend more time with her. I'll write and smooth things over.

I *must, must* start reading *Pensions*, etc. I thought I was doing fine in the job, but lately I'm a little scared that I'm not focusing. I screwed up today, and Jessica yelled, "Christ, Jock, is the weight loss spreading to yer brain?" Worse! George O'Reilly hauled his fat paw over and patted my hand. Understandingly.

Wish a million times over that you were here (and could bop George in the nose).

Much, much love,
Jock

P.S. There's some talk about my going to Montreal for a long weekend of French immersion. I suppose it would be a good opportunity but hate to go alone, although Van assures me that Catherine is dying to have me over to dinner. I don't feel too excited by that either. I'll probably do it.

P.P.S. I think I've finally figured it out. The government has stumbled on this Magic Deficit Cure: don't pay employees!

Ottawa,
Nov. 15

MONEY enclosed! Sending this special delivery.

I felt so rich I treated Jessica to dinner. She ate, as Greg used to say, with gusto and her teeth. Even I ate with gusto — now that I've actually been home and know that you are all retrievable, I've lost that iron gate in the centre of my gut that clanged shut after the third bite. In some panicked corner of my unconscious I must have thought I'd never see any of you again.

Oh boy, money! Off to Montreal and dinner at the Pierces. Will tell all after.

Jock

P.S. Tell Greg and Mia to have their Christmas lists ready. I'll phone if I get a chance to shop in Montreal.

29 Sweet Cedar Drive
North Vancouver, B.C.
15 November

Dearest,

The rain is raining, the furnace is faltering (again) and Gil
Grogan is peppering us with anti-union propaganda, but the
remembrance of Remembrance Day weekend is keeping life
profoundly sweet. Say what you like about the pleasures of
the mind, there's nothing like a few hours in a double bed to
refresh the spirit. Celibacy — you did ask my opinion on
celibacy? — was surely invented to whet the appetite. It can't
serve any other purpose but to show what depth of pleasure
lies on the other side. And say what you like, too, about
Marjorie Finstead, it was a christly stroke of good fortune,
the Finsteads' taking Mia off for a cookout Saturday afternoon. When they rolled up with their portable barbecue and
hamper of red meat I could have kissed their wholesome
ruddy cheeks. Oh, God, you were lovely (burn this letter),
and how I've missed your skin, just the feel of it. You asked
me if I thought you were too thin. Sweetie, you are perfect. I
wish I could say this in a fresh and original way, but I can't, so
here goes: it was like the first time. Yes, it was. (Davina
Flowering maintains that the writing of passion has been pre-
empted by Hallmark and Madonna — she is probably right.
You can't even say the word ardour or kiss without shuffling
your feet and saying, "Aw shucks, ma'am.")

As you know, my dad stayed on in the navy after the war
— much to Mother's chagrin — and one of the first things I
remember was him coming home, and how Auntie Jude
whisked me over to her place for the weekend, wink, wink. I
suppose I must have wondered why. Suddenly, forty years

later, it all swims into comprehension. *They* must have had *their* manic hour in the double bed, too — though who, seeing Mother today, would ever believe it? (The doctor has given her some pills and advised rest, as if she's done anything *but* rest in the ten years since Dad died.)

My only regret is that you had to go back on Monday night instead of Tuesday. I don't want to bleat, but on Tuesday, Jock, we could have used your maternal presence.

I woke up at seven sharp, defying that widely believed myth that the unemployed sleep in till noon, and found myself hummingly alert to the revised draft of my unemployment poem. I could actually see the words printed in the air over the bed, afloat in little white balloons, the perfect lines that said what I wanted to say without yelling. I scribbled them on the margin of a newspaper, which was all I had at hand, and then made my way down the hall to the bathroom. The door was locked, and when I banged, in my gentle way, Mia called out that she would be out in a minute or two.

I waited. And waited. "You'd better use the other bathroom," she called finally. I hollered back that I wanted a shower and could she please get a move on. There was more silence. I made some coffee and read the *Sun*. Fifteen minutes went by and she was still in the bathroom. "I'm out here in the hall waiting," I hollered, "and I think you've been in there longer than is strictly necessary."

I could hear her snuffling through the door.

"What is it?" I yelled. By this time Greg was up and wanting a shower too. "Maybe she's sick," he said.

"What's the matter in there?" I bellowed. "Are you sick?"

"Maybe she's locked in," Greg said.

"No, I'm not," she yelled back, only we could tell she was crying. You know how her voice moves up an octave and does that rubber-band trick. She was doing it.

"We'd better go in through the window," Greg said at that point. "Maybe..."

"Maybe what?" I said.

"Well," he said, "maybe, you know...razor blades — "

"We don't have any razor blades," I pointed out. "And anyway, that's crazy. She's a kid — "

He shrugged. Why do I find it so maddening when he shrugs? "You never know," he said.

"Mia," I said through the door, "I will give you exactly three minutes, and if you're not out here by then I'll — "

"You'll what?" Greg asked me. A direct challenge. *High Noon* again.

"I'm counting," I called to Mia. "Three minutes and you'd better open that door." My God, Jock, against all logic I suddenly felt swamped by thoughts of kids swallowing bottles of aspirins and going into comas.

I paced. Greg paced. We timed her for three minutes, then gave her another thirty seconds. She was crying — we could hear her — so at least we knew she wasn't comatose.

"I can't come out." She was wailing like a puppy.

"Sixty seconds," I said.

"Or we'll break down the door," Greg added.

"My God," I said. We sounded like a cheap movie.

The doorbell went just then and scared the hell out of us. It was Sue. She had a coalition meeting, she explained, and figured she'd come earlier than usual and get the house cleaned by noon.

"You look sick as a dog," was what she said when I let her in. "God almighty, you haven't been eating rotten turkey again?"

I explained about Mia.

I have to hand it to her. As calm as you please she sailed over to the bathroom door, rapped sharply, and said, "It's

Sue, the charlady, and if you don't let me in this minute I'll wallop you."

The door opened. We saw Mia's hand but nothing more. Sue marched in, waving us aside, and shut the door firmly. I could hear the lock click shut.

We waited in the hall. Greg's face was the colour of drafting paper, and mine probably too.

A minute later the door opened and Sue poked her head out. "Do you have any Kotex in the house?" she asked us.

"What?" I said. Stupidly.

"Sanitary napkins. Do you have any?"

My heart leapt. Greg sent me the queerest kind of slipping smile, half embarrassment and half something else. Lord knows what.

"Do you or don't you?" Sue said, sounding cross.

"I don't think so," I said.

"I'll go," Greg said after a moment's silence. "The 7-Eleven should be open." (If I had had even one drop of Mediterranean blood in my body I would have kissed him.)

Sue waited in the bathroom with Mia. I could hear them talking through the door, a dull murmur. Greg was back in seven minutes. With that familiarly shaped parcel in hand.

I knocked on the door again. It opened. Sue stretched out a hand, received the parcel and said, "We'll be a few minutes. Why don't you go scramble some eggs or something?"

Greg did the bacon in the microwave and I got the eggs going. Greg set the table, making a half-decent job of it, and I reheated the coffee and cut up some grapefruit.

Ten minutes later, looking a little pale and somewhat shaky, Mia was sitting at the table shovelling in eggs. We all were. When have I last eaten like that? Sue kept making toast and it kept disappearing, half a loaf gone before you could blink. I wondered what the hell we were celebrating. It wasn't just the old mythic deliverance from girlhood, though that may have been part of it. It was deliverance from razor blades (even though we don't have any) and pills and panic and all the things I didn't even know I was scared as hell about. What do we really know about the secret life of our kids anyway? I think we were all tucking into our bacon and eggs because it was the only way we could think of to propitiate what Sue calls the black frenzies.

By the time we finished breakfast Mia was telling us a string of knock, knock jokes. (Seems they're back in style.) She gave me a hug before she set off for school. I told her she didn't have to go, but she just gave me a womanly look. Sue, while stuffing sheets into the washer, gave me a dramatic rundown of *her* first time (age eleven). It was a more detailed case history than I might have chosen to hear, but interesting nonetheless. Curious, isn't it, that half the world is involved in a ritual of which the other half is ignorant? It makes you wonder how many other mysteries there are that are guarded by one sex against the other. My sense is that there are areas of exclusion as wide as soccer fields and that they won't go away overnight, not even with a hundred royal commissions — but who knows.

Nice to have the kids back at school, but everyone here fears that the settlement between the government and the nurses is temporary. Sue says the nurses have been royally screwed — not quite her words, but close — and that they're all numb with shock. We'd been geared up for war and what we got was a swift, overnight resolution. Anticlimax has a way of getting in the way of analysis (another of Sue's observations), and we're left not knowing whether we won or lost. But there's plenty of bitterness around, some of it pretty close to home. Our own RESTRAIN GOVERNMENT sign was stolen off the lawn last night. Three guesses

who did that. And little newspaper clippings praising the
government come slipping through our mail slot — again
three guesses. If it weren't so petty I'd hang a blanket
on the kitchen window. No wonder, Jock, you clung to
those curtains.

I'm a little worried about Greg. About what the hell he
does every evening and where he goes. I suggested the other
night, after my first real paycheque came through (GREAT to
have pockets clinking cheerfully again), that the three of us go
off to the Fishnet for a bang-up dinner. "No thanks," he said.
"I wouldn't waste a whole night sitting around some snotty
restaurant."

I ask him where he's going and he just says, "Out with the
guys." But I haven't seen Pete or Stu or Ben or any of his
other friends around here for ages.

But, God, it's lovely to have a little money coming in
again. Sanderson's is a fairly keen-paced shop. Jobs come in
and out, lickety-split, and you'd never know we were still in a
recession. Greg was right about one thing, though. There *is* a
basic take-that humiliation about sitting in a big, windy drafting room where the carpeting leaves off and where the coffee
comes round in styrofoam cups — *pace* the environmentalists
— but, hell, my mind is full of other things these days. I'm
rewriting my jobless poem after taking in the class reaction.
Bob said, "Wow, that's right on," and Janet said she was
"moved but wanted definitions," and Stan said, "Ya gotta fuck
the bastards harder," and Melanie/Melody said (surprisingly)
that I should get tougher, and Tracy said I'd missed the point,
and Davina said to go back and rethink my anger. So that's
what I do while hunched over the drawing board and watching the clock and chewing on styrofoam — I rethink my
anger. If only I'd had more experience with anger. It seems
rather late to start learning.

I went to the liquor store to get Sue a thank-you bottle of wine and ran into — guess who? — your mother with her arms full of gin. She was having a party, she said. Some old bridge buddies. She chided me a little about not chiding *you* about writing to *her* more frequently and so on, and I said I would definitely mention the fact in my next letter. Shall we consider it mentioned?

I'm marking off the days till Christmas.

> With love from your semi-employed
> spouse, also your recalcitrant son
> and your newly initiated daughter,
>> Chas

The body speaks unearned melodies
and the heart keeps score.
> Austin Grey

> 4 Old Town Lane
> Ottawa, Ont.
> Nov. 18

Dear Chas,

Your letter came this morning (Canada Post is speeding up), and I've been in the most peculiar mood all day — a disagreeable feeling in the pit of my stomach that pushes me into frantic running about, and then stops me, suddenly, remembering. Grief — it seems too strong a word, but I don't know how else to describe it. I loved Mia's childhood, loved her baking cookies at Christmas with such earnestness, loved watching her long brown legs as she roller-skated down the street, loved the plays she and Lucy (remember Lucy?

brown curls and braces?) used to put on and charge us a quarter to see. And now it's behind us. Yes, grief! And then there's the maternal sense of being cheated out of an important event. And sorrow for Mia too, on whom such a nuisance is inflicted, such a curse as Mother still calls it. And beneath it all the familiar *sotto voce* guilt for not having been there — although honestly I did put a box of napkins in her dresser drawer and mentioned it to her, but I guess in the shock (it is a shock) she forgot.

I felt the need to talk to someone about it and happened on Austin in the Reading Room peering through his specs at a volume of Auden. (Was he avoiding George? George has become a bit of a nuisance for Austin, I suspect. George can't write a line of his immortal prose without tearing over to Austin, eager brown eyes sparkling with self-congratulation, with some trumped-up question such as whether "gender" and "sex" are interchangeable. Pity his wife if he doesn't know that.)

I don't see Austin as merely grey the way I did at first. Would you believe he's only two years older than Van? Why does he seem older? Especially since his hair isn't nearly as white as Van's (the Man from Glad, Jessica's new sobriquet for him). In fact, when I really looked at Austin I realized that his hair is sand-coloured and not grey at all. Wonder why such a pleasant man never married?

He glanced up then and caught me staring and smiled and we went to the cafeteria for coffee.

"Discouraging words from the West?"

Austin's so damn perceptive! But then I suppose that goes with the territory if you're a poet. Your letter was in my purse and I read him the bit about Mia and tried to explain my own queer reaction. He laughed at your description, but he did seem to understand. He talked about the mythic proportions that menstruation took on in primitive societies, and says there's a story in *The Golden Bough* about an Australian aborigine who found out that his wife had lain on his blanket during her period. He killed her, and then he himself sickened and died within a fortnight. Woman as the other, the witch, the feared object, the unclean vessel of death — part of what you were talking about in your letter, the closed mystery of the unknown sex.

Yes, sometimes it seems to me that men and women advance through time along parallel lines that obey the laws of geometry and never truly intersect. Am enclosing a letter for Mia.

Went by train to Montreal Friday night — only a two-hour trip. Sat in the first-class compartment where they actually served me dinner, airline style. (Way to go.) The train comes right into the centre of the city, and it's the shortest ride imaginable to McGill, which is also right in the centre of the city. (Vancouver could learn a lot from Montreal.)

The room in the residence was spare but adequate, and a printed sheet of instructions advised me of a get-acquainted gathering at nine o'clock. About twenty in the class, but the only one I talked to (was cornered by) was a fifty-year-old Revenue Canada senior tax assessor who had just acquired the bewildering information that "chartered accountant" in French is *comptable agrée*. At the class the next morning, when we gave our names, he said, "Ju swee Mon-sooer McBride, and ju swee comp-tabel agrayay avec Revenue Canada." The French teacher (fresh from Paris) said, *"En français, s'il vous plaît,"* which broke everyone up.

Why does Mr. McBride have to be such a stereotype? In truth he turned out to be rather a nice person whose hobby is

bird-watching and who was quite disappointed when I was
unable to tell him how many varieties of mudhen nest in the
Fraser Delta.

The class was fun, although M. Beauchemin did not
bother to conceal his low opinion of the French-Canadian
accent. One would think the noblest aspiration of the human
race is to be *parlezing français* in the accent of Tours (did
you know it is the most pure?). As for Canadian nationalism:
quel provincial fantasy. Finally a sweet little grey-haired
woman (who turned out to be a very sharp little grey-haired
woman and whose French is very good) said, as nearly as
I could tell, "We are interested in learning to speak French
in order to communicate with our fellow Canadians who
speak French." M. Beauchemin received this information
with obvious shock and was dispirited for the rest of
the day.

As for the main event, the dinner at the Pierces' in the
modest three-acre Westmount battleground that Van and
Catherine the Formidable call home, I'll write more later.

Oh my God, *not* the furnace again. Maybe he didn't fix
it properly?

Must to bed. After rereading *Moonlight on a Still Spirit*.
How does Austin Grey know all that?

Jock

P.S. I can understand your paranoia, dear one, about Mia
razor-blading and aspirining, but crying in bathrooms is
something adolescents *do*. How well I remember — and we
had only one bathroom.

P.P.S. Why don't you ask Greg straight out where he goes?
And insist on an answer. On the other hand, we don't want to
hover. Do we?

29 Sweet Cedar Drive
North Vancouver, B.C.
22 November

Dear Jock

My God, you'd hover too if you were right here in the middle of Real Life instead of idly voyeuring it up in the land of Hollywood/Westmount. I *worry*. I can't help it. Mia spends most of her time over at the Finsteads baking cookies and making Christmas-tree ornaments out of papier mâché. What's wrong with her own home? (A little voice in my head asks this question from time to time). Is it just that I don't know the recipe for papier mâché?

Yes, you're right, I will have to have it out with Greg, especially since he's out every night, sometimes till midnight or later. I would have put my foot down long ago if his marks had been slipping, but you saw his last report! I guess what really bothers the hell out of me is that he seems to have plenty of money to jingle. Where does he get it, anyway, and do I actually have a right to ask? Drug dealing? I know it sounds ludicrous, but stranger things have happened.

When he was out the other night, I set aside all my pious beliefs about respecting kids' privacy and did a thorough search of his room. I looked everywhere, under the mattress, in the back of the closet, and through his incredibly cluttered drawers. What I found was one girlie mag of the less-disgusting variety and about forty rolled-up unwashed socks. That's all. And a letter to you, half written, dated September 30. "Hi ya, mom, how's things in the nation's cap?"

Sue seems to think my problems are political and last night dragged me to a meeting of the Solidarity Coalition, on the grounds that as an unemployed person and a single father (neither category exactly fits, but…) I should *segue* into the political front that is busily out there fighting on my behalf. The turnout — in a rented hall on Commercial — was small. As Sue says, you'd hardly know we'd been through a thirteen-day strike in B.C. People seem to have buried the whole thing so quickly it might never have happened.

The forty or so people there laid plans for two demonstrations, one to defend tenants' rights and one to speak out for the handicapped in the province. We signed a few petitions and listened to a few speeches and afterwards Sue and I went out for coffee with the angriest young woman (friend of Sue's) I've ever seen, a single mother whose rent has just gone up 15 per cent. She couldn't have been more than thirty, but rage had done terrible puckery things to her mouth and to the skin around her eyes. Furthermore, her neck was not quite clean and her glasses were smudged. I wanted to reach over and remove them and polish them on a paper napkin, but didn't. She couldn't speak without yelling. I thought we'd get pitched out of the café, what with her thumping the wall and reviling the government. And men. Men are scum. Men are shits — so she informed the happy coffee sippers in every corner of the room. Men are not ready or willing to surrender their power and so it has to be wrested from them.

Did I feel threatened by this? (I can imagine your asking me.) Yes. But I also felt dismayed at all this wasteful fury. What does it bring in the end but ulcers and facial craters? Sue insists — this was later — that anger is the fuel that's going to bring about the revolution. I wanted to say, "Now which revolution is that?" but resisted. These days I'm feeling out of joint with the times and a little unsure about what is permitted.

Today is the 22nd — one more month and you should be winging your way home. Any word on dates?

Love,
your Chas

P.S. I'll definitely get on the Greg thing this week.

4 Old Town Lane
Ottawa, Ont.
Nov. 27

Dear Chas,

At last a breathing space so I can sit down and tell you all about my *très étrange* evening at the Pierces'. *Mon aventure*, if you'll pardon my French.

Van insisted on picking me up, in spite of my feeble protests that I could easily take a cab — feeble because during the short ride from station to university my life passed before my eyes several times, and when another cab cut in front of us I learned some interesting French that is probably not spoken in Tours.

As you know, Westmount is right in the centre of the city. Great arrangement! A *maid* opened the door and took my coat, and then Van steered me up three or four steps, through a hall into which our living room would fit with a metre to spare, and into a room with a thick, sculptured Chinese rug — magnificent lotus flowers bursting from a white background — white velvet chairs, and a fire blazing in a lovely marble fireplace. (The *den*.) The maid hovered briefly while I ordered Scotch, and then Mrs. Pierce — Catherine — sailed into the room the way the *Britannia* used to steam into

Vancouver harbour. She is a big woman, not in the sense of fat, but in the sense of solid, *très formidable*, and nearly as tall as Vance. She was draped in a flowing printed-silk hostess gown that billowed behind like a spinnaker sail. She wears her thick yellowish hair wound in big loops around her head and secured by combs, and she is good-looking in the Maggie Thatcher sense, peaches-and-cream English complexion and good bones. Ageless. What Father used to call "a fine-looking woman." Rather startling green cat's eyes. (I found myself wondering what shade of turquoise their children's eyes must be, crossing his blue with her green.)

She boomed, in an accent I first thought was English and then identified as William F. Buckley, "The Senator has spoken of you so much — delighted you could come, Mrs. Selby."

I checked the impulse to curtsy.

"Oh, please call me Jocelyn — "

"Call her Jock," Van said flatly, sinking into a chair.

Catherine ignored him. "Jocelyn," she said. "Charming name. And you're studying French I hear. What a bore! I suppose the Senator talked you into it."

"Not all Canadians share your antediluvian views, Catherine," Van said. "Jock may have some interest of her own in understanding the other official language."

"Poof." Catherine waved a dismissive hand in Van's direction. "One need not backslap in the patois in order to parade one's loyalty. I've lived here twenty years and I have never, at any time, felt the slightest need to speak anything but English. If those with whom I deal don't speak English, that is their problem. I neither intrude on their lives nor do I expect them to intrude on mine." And having disposed of the vexations of bilingualism, she fixed me with an unabashed appraisal that took in my good blue silk dress — thank God I wore it — and pumps. "Now," she went on, "if you, Senator, will stifle your impossible habit of speaking for others and let Jocelyn tell her own story, I should like to hear what she has to say."

I attempted to placate them both by saying that it was an opportunity to learn a second language. "And it fills up a weekend. Without my family my weekends are sometimes a bit barren."

"You have children?" From the enthusiasm in her voice I could tell that children were a Good Thing, so I rushed in to enlarge on my maternity. "Two teenagers," I said, as proudly as if I'd just given birth.

"In school, I suppose?"

Where did she think they'd be? "Oh yes," I said.

"Shawnigan Lake? A number of my friends have children there."

I couldn't have felt more rustic if she'd caught me squatting in our rainforest sending messages by tom-tom. I confessed that the children went not to private but to public schools. At that moment the blessed maid brought drinks, and I fortified my quaking soul.

Catherine wondered, then, who looked after them. "A housekeeper?"

"Their father."

"Their father?" Incredulity. I could tell she thought it was the usual broken-family situation and in my rush to rescue our marriage I babbled, "Actually he's managing very well. I was able to go home last weekend, and it was almost a blow to my pride to see how well they managed without me."

"*Last* weekend?"

I was a bit taken aback by the intensity of her interest, but I acknowledged that it had indeed been last weekend, the November eleventh holiday.

"You mean, you're in Ottawa merely to serve on the Commission?"

"Why yes, except I'm not actually *on* the Commission, I'm the legal counsel."

"If you listened occasionally, Catherine," Van broke in, "you wouldn't have to subject our guests to your infernal cross-examinations. Pay no attention, Jock." But I could see that I'd passed whatever test of Catherine's I had been put through, because she smiled with sudden (surprising) warmth and said, "You must be lonely. Senator, why on earth haven't you brought her here for a weekend?" (Perish the thought.)

I was saved by the sound of the doorbell and Van said, "Oh, that must be Austin," and got to his feet. I was immensely relieved to learn that Austin was joining us.

As soon as Van left the room Catherine motioned me to sit down beside her and said, rather hurriedly, "I hope this miserable press the Senator has been getting isn't an embarrassment to you."

I was astonished. You'll see what I mean from the enclosed clipping of Valerie Cerise's gossip column in the *Montreal News*:

Who would have thought our very own Senator Blue-eyes Pierce would become a dedicated feminist! So zealous in his pursuit of equality that he spirited (at taxpayers' expense) his rising young assistant all the way to Halifax! What better education than to accompany our fleet-footed Senator through the twists and turns of the pork-barrel polka at a Liberal convention? Senator Pierce makes his home in Montreal. He is married to the former Catherine Nesbitt-Holmes, heir to the Nesbitt-Holmes cookie fortune. They have two children at school in Switzerland.

Of course I knew then what Catherine's interrogation had been about and I blurted, "Even Jessica says the media are way off base on this one."

"Jessica?"

"Yes, Jessica Slattery, you know — "

"I know perfectly well." Catherine strode to the fire, grasped the poker, and hammered the smouldering logs roundly. (The few glowing embers flared up into a respectable flame.) "You have my sympathy, my dear."

Well now, just a damn minute, I thought. I cleared my throat and said, "I've come to have a good deal of respect for Jessica. She has a strong social conscience and she is willing to fight hard for the causes of women."

"Jessica Slattery," Catherine said, fixing me with her cold green eyes and speaking slowly and precisely in her proper Boston accent, "is a royal bitch."

At which point Austin and Van came into the room, and Catherine rushed to Austin with cries of greeting and he stood on his toes to buss her on both cheeks. Evidently no stranger around the place.

"Ah, Jock," he said, and then turning to Catherine, "You did well to invite Jock. It doesn't cost much to feed her."

"I never diet. A faddish capitulation to style," Catherine said firmly, and guided us into the dining room. After we were seated she asked Austin what he was writing.

"I'm not getting much done these days, what with the Commission and all."

"I call that a waste. I have severe reservations about this commission and its mandate. The Feminization of Poverty." She made it sound like a disease. "Pretentious-sounding." She sniffed. "*Is* there a great deal in Canada? I doubt it."

I felt my face growing hot but Austin merely smiled and looked quietly around the immense dining room. "It isn't too visible, is it?"

The manservant (*not* a hired caterer. Would he be the butler?) removed the oysters — better than the ones we gathered last year on Hornby Island — and brought salad, and Catherine said, "I've always been wealthy and I make no apologies. I can't even say that I *prefer* being rich, since I've never tried anything else. The Senator has, of course, and he didn't like it."

"And I still don't." Van was slurring his words slightly. "That's why I'm trying to alleviate it."

"You did alleviate it," Catherine answered. "You married me." With which she burst into a loud guffaw. Austin smiled slightly, and I buried my head in my lettuce.

"Really, Catherine, you'll give our guests the wrong idea."

"Nonsense. Austin, are *you* getting the wrong idea?"

"No, my dear, I'm not, but anyone who doesn't know your sense of humour might be — shall we say — mystified? My own recollection of Vance in those days is not of a poor boy in rags. In fact I seem to remember him striding across the campus at Harvard looking for a tennis partner, and very well turned out he was too."

"Thank you, Austin." And, turning to Catherine, Vance said, rather aggressively, "You did *not* rescue me from the gutter, my dear. By the time you fastened yourself on me I was quite comfortably off."

"There's a difference between comfortable and rich," Catherine said flatly. "Rich is what I have always been, and what the Senator hasn't always been. Scholarships don't buy rare burgundy, do they, Austin?"

Before Austin could answer Van got up, with great deliberation, and made his way carefully to the other end of the table, where he knelt before Catherine, ceremoniously took her hand, and kissed it right beside the Hope diamond she wears on her ring finger. Then he turned her hand over and kissed the palm.

"My dear," he said — now get this, Chas, he said this,

almost whispered it, in such a caressing voice you would have thought they were in the midst of a *grande passion* — "I would like to invite you to reciprocate by kissing my ass."

Fortunately, he said it in French.

Unfortunately, my weekend of immersion took that moment to pay off and I understood every single *mot*! I felt my face flame to the roots of my hair and I bent so far into the lettuce I could have passed for Peter Rabbit.

"Oh do get up and don't be such a fool," Catherine said, sounding a bit flustered, but pleased. "And you know it's very rude to speak French when I don't understand it."

As Van lurched back to his chair I risked raising my eyes and unfortunately met the servant's eyes. He looked as though he was about to choke. He disappeared abruptly, and another servant-clone came in and took away the salad plates and the white wine glasses, replacing them with another set for the red wine.

"Jocelyn seems to be quite taken with Jessica," Catherine said. "Has she improved?"

"If she has it isn't noticeable. I had to get the carpet cleaned after she tossed my best burgundy around," Van said.

"While dressed in rags, no doubt, and holding forth in tones of holier-than-thou. Well, at least I have more pride than to live off the avails of poverty." She signalled again, and we were served Beef Wellington and beautiful little carrots and potatoes and asparagus with hollandaise sauce. (Don't worry, Chas. I won't let the glitz and glam corrupt me.)

I launched into the tale of how Jessica had taken up Jean's cause — did I ever tell you the rest of that story? You remember Jean from the group home, who quit her lousy minimum-wage job because of the manager. Well, good old Jessica — without Jean, and without Jean's knowledge — sailed into the offending restaurant and confronted the lecherous manager and threatened him with a sexual harass-ment charge, so that when Jean went in later for her separa-tion certificate, all was sweetness and light.

Austin laughed and Van toasted "fat ol' Jess," and Catherine said, "And this Jean didn't know that Jessica was interfering?"

There's nothing worse than having to explain a good story, but (in my innocence) I assumed Catherine didn't know what a separation certificate was and so had missed the point. "No, Jean — " I began, but was cut off.

"Do-gooding," Catherine said flatly. "Sticking her nose into other people's business without so much as a by-your-leave. Typical of Jessica. Butting into other people's business."

My jaw went slack, and not just because of the tirade but because I saw in it an uncomfortable grain of truth. Middle-class morality, as Eliza Doolittle's father would say. Maybe Jean would truly have preferred that Jessica keep her nose out.

"Catherine, my dear, I would never have tagged you as a civil libertarian," Austin said gently. Ever the peacemaker. Probably a good thing that he cut off one of my Jessica-inspired feminist diatribes. (J. has either raised or lowered my consciousness, depending on your point of view.) And then the "servant" — the original one — distracted me with a twelve-layer French torte filled with wonderful fattening goo (which I couldn't finish).

One more tête-à-tête with the redoubtable Catherine before I left. She inquired if there were others like me work-ing with the Commission.

"Just George O'Reilly, who is a writer."

She sighed, seeming suddenly tired. "Secretarial help?" she asked.

"Oh, of course, Yvette — Vance's secretary."

"Pretty?"

I nodded. "She does a lot of work for us," I offered.

"I'm sure she does. Shall we join the others?"

I tried to question Austin when he drove me back to the university. "Why does she hate Jessica?"

"Need you ask?" Austin said with a smile. "They'd be bound to tangle. Catherine's not just another wealthy socialite, you know."

"No? What is she then?"

"A historian of some repute, has periodic bouts of bestowing her insights on McGill, which, being rather beholden to her in more material ways, is quick to praise. Actually she's a very good historian, although her conclusions wouldn't be my conclusions — as to the cause of the rise of communism and the effect of mal-distribution of wealth for instance. In between academic bouts she breeds horses."

Who with? I wondered (but didn't ask). "Did she mean all that, about Van's having married her for her money?"

"I'm afraid she did. But don't judge her too harshly. She's definitely a barker and not a biter, and she's had her disap-pointments. Or so rumour has it."

"She's really rather rude."

"The very rich often are." Which is as definitive a judge-ment as I'm likely to get out of Austin.

As I was getting out of the car he patted my hand and said I'd brought a breath of western freshness to the Commission.

Also he likes my jokes. Pass it on.

Beaucoup d'amour, encore,

Jock

P.S. Wish I'd had a doggie bag at the Pierces' and could have mailed you my uneaten torte. Heavenly!

P.P.S. Glad you've decided to tackle Greg.

29 Sweet Cedar Drive
North Vancouver, B.C.
6 December

Dear Jock,

This has been a busy week. For some reason my social life has boomed. That is, it's gone from zero to a quiet buzz, though not quite in the same league as Montreal dinners *avec comédie domestique* (as you might say; as you *would* say).

Tuesday night I actually had a choice of invitations. Sanderson's held its annual Christmas bash at the International Plaza, and on the same night, as luck would have it, Davina decided to invite the whole class to her apartment for an end-of-term get-together.

It's hard to believe we're already halfway through the course and all I've written is half a poem that I am thinking of chucking. Half a poem, though, is more than Bob (the policeman) has produced. He is suffering from writer's block — get this: he's never written a word in his life but he's blocked. I would expect Davina to be exasperated with Bob, but she's deeply sympathetic and is advising hypnosis, which seems pretty drastic when you consider that no one knows what will be unleashed when he does come unblocked. A diversion, sorry.

I mentioned to Davina that I had a conflict on Tuesday night, and such a look of rejection and vulnerability came over her face that I instantly told her I would arrange to be there. "Can you bring a hot dish?" she said, recovering speedily. "And *plenty* of wine?"

I thawed one of your mother's eggplant quiches and, feeling only moderately ashamed, bought a jug of plonk, the likes of which you and I haven't seen since our poorest and earliest married days. Mia enthusiastically pressed my old blazer and both the kids waved me off.

Davina and her three cats — a trio of neutered males — live in that cluster of greyish, low-rise apartment blocks at the bottom of Burnaby Mountain, you remember the area. It was the first time in years I'd been in an apartment where there was no real furniture, just large lumpy "shapes" draped with Indonesian cotton. Davina herself, smiling and slightly drunk when I arrived, was also draped in Indonesian cotton. Somehow it suited her. "I knew you wouldn't let me down," she said, and gave me a smokey hug.

The seven of us sat about on floor cushions — try it and see what it does to your back muscles — and ate baked salmon and chili and eggplant quiche off paper plates and drank my godawful wine out of thick coffee mugs.

At first I felt hideously old. I felt I was inhabiting someone else's scaly, antique skin; but two mugs of plonk later I was persuaded I'd chosen the right party after all. Bob loosened up and told us about a transsexual bank robber he once chased down Broadway, and Melody smoked a joint and told us why vitamin E was not a part of her belief system, and Janet said she absolutely agreed, and Tracy read our palms (a romantic catastrophe ahead for me), and Stan fell asleep under Davina's weeping fig, and then Davina read us a few of her poems, which are mostly about blood and hair and the brittleness of bones. Janet cried and Tracy looked as if she was going to, and so I said I had to be on my way — teenagers at home, heh, heh — and bounded out to the car like a man reprieved and headed over the Second Narrows Bridge. It was one of those rare clear nights with the temperature just at the freezing point, and the lights from the North Shore seemed, more than usual, to beckon. I knew then that I had chosen the wrong invitation. What I should have done was stay happily at home and work on your Christmas present — no hints forthcoming.

Two more weeks. Mia is marking the days off on the kitchen calendar.

With love,

from your Chas

P.S. Much as I love your letters, could you ease up on the French phrases. Jesus, lovey, it's like an invasion of fleas.

4 Old Town Lane

Ottawa, Ont.

Dec. 11

Dear One,

A quick note before good old Noël (sorry, is that French?), when home I come — and not a moment too soon, by the sound of it. Where are all our *regular* friends? The Chapmans and Clarkes and Ticknows, our upwardly mobile (shudder at the phrase) Saturday-night cronies who have put Indonesian cotton shapes firmly behind them and are working their way up to the velvet-covered goose-down of Shaughnessy — don't they ever call you? Or are they saving us for Christmas?

Speaking of goose-down (eastern species), a small update. I didn't see Jessica for a few days after my Montreal weekend because she took off on some mysterious errand, but Monday when I got into the lounge adjoining the hearing room she was already there reviewing the morning brief. I hurried over and told her I'd been to the Pierces' but she didn't even look up. "Fuck off, I'm busy," she said. Vintage Jessica.

I swept up my copy of the brief and wheeled around, but before I'd taken more than two steps, Jessica (as I knew she would) stopped me. "Oh shit, I suppose I have to hear it some time." She pulled out a cigarette and struck a match on her jeans. "Pull up a couch and let's have it."

"Listen, Jessica," I told her, "you don't have to hear anything you don't want to."

"Come on, Jock, don't get in a snit." She yanked a chair over beside her. "Sit. Spill. I'm actually all a-twitter. Tell me the worst. You loved Catherine."

"Not exactly," I said, letting myself be mollified. "She's a mite — you know — overpowering — "

Jessica yelped. "Jesus, Jock, you shore do get an A for acumen."

"She doesn't care that much for you either."

Jessica reared back like a shying horse. "Why? What'd she say about me?"

"She offered me her sympathy for having to work with you. I thought that was kind of perceptive."

Jessica started to turn a dull brick red, but I couldn't keep a straight face and when I started to laugh she turned back to her normal colour (mottled) and said, "Okay, cut the crap and let's have it. What lies are the Wimps of Westmount disseminating?"

I gave her a quick run-down. "Austin said he hadn't realized Catherine was such a civil libertarian."

"Austin was there, was he?" She leaned back in the leather armchair and lifted her decrepit boots onto the coffee table, making black marks on the brief she'd been reading. "So Catherine would like me to mind my own business, would she? I guess I've actually managed to rattle her cage a couple of times. Does she still hate the French?"

"Mmmm — not hate, exactly. Lives and lets live."

"In a pig's eye she does." She started to remove her boots from the coffee table, and I remarked that Catherine and Van didn't seem that happy together.

I could see by the glint in her eyes as she settled back and inhaled a lungful of smoke that the news didn't exactly displease her. "Yeah?" she said. "In what way?"

I told her how Catherine kept hinting that Van had married her for her money — "Real insight," Jessica snorted — and how she'd pumped me about Yvette — "Poor old Kate. You can buy the goods but you can't get a guarantee" — and how Van had told her, in French, to kiss his ass.

Jessica exploded, whooping and inhaling smoke.

If you'd been there, Chas, you would have accused us of gossiping, and we were. It felt wonderful — made me realize how much I've missed Beth Ticknow, and Margie and Gwen, and everyone at home, our lunches, our good long jabbers on the phone.

Jessica and I were in full swing, but then Austin came along, peering at us over the funny little half-glasses he has perched on the end of his nose.

"God, I'm glad you went on that immersion course, Jock. I wouldn't have missed that for the world." Jessica yanked her feet off the table, attacked an ashtray with her cigarette, and stuffed the brief into her tattered briefcase. "Come on, it's damn near ten. Hey, Austin, have fun in the *haute monde*?"

Austin took off the glasses, wiped them carefully, and recited:

> *While I sit here a-skimming this brief,*
> *The Poo-bahs of Westmount are coming to grief.*

Must run. Only twelve more days! (And nights.) I can hardly wait!

Love,
Jock

P.S. You're *making* my Christmas present? Remember the time I did that, made stuffed kangaroos with cookie-filled pouches for our friends' children? And the foam stuffing leaked, dribbling out slowly for two months afterwards? Claire Chapman said she relied on the kangaroo to help her keep track of the children.

Me

29 Sweet Cedar Drive
North Vancouver, B.C.
15 December

Dear One,

It's a little crazy to be writing you a letter tonight — you'll be here in exactly eight days and seven hours (I picture you swirling through the doorway in a crimson cape for some reason), but my pen itches in my hand. Or rather, the keyboard begs to be caressed. The tree is on the patio "relaxing" and the goose is in the larder — or rather the turkey is in the freezer. (Do you know what the robbers at Safeway want for a goose?) The Christmas pudding, courtesy of Marjorie Finstead, is sweating with booze in a "dark cool place." (*Her* instructions, so urgently conveyed that I didn't have the heart to tell her we can't abide the stuff.)

I've just finished the Christmas shopping. I went ahead and got the up-market guitar for Greg. Sue helped me pick it out — just finding the right one took all day Saturday — but I'll have to leave Mia's present until you get here. What do I know about up-scale T-shirts? As for you, your present is just about ready, and I can't wait to see your face. Ah, lovey, it's perfect, what you should have had all along.

I wanted to buy Davina Flowering a copy of Austin Grey's new book, but it isn't available out here. Do you think you could pick up a copy? It's called *Circle of Water*, published by something called the Sweet Onion Press. And could you have him autograph it for her? It would mean the world. For your mother I got a six-pack of Beaujolais, not very original, but well targeted as they say in the business world, and for my mother, a dressing gown (which she will of course call a wrapper), suitably fuzzy and in a vague shade of pink. And for Gil Grogan I got a copy of *The Diefenbaker Years* — took a bit of searching for, that one.

You'll be amazed to hear that Gil and I are once again on speaking terms. As of today, our quarrel, whatever the hell it was about, seems more or less patched up. A note came slipping through the mail slot early this morning. I witnessed this incursion as I went to pick up the newspaper. Little white card in little white envelope, just like one of your mother's everlasting hospitality notes. Saying: "Would you care to join me for lunch today at the Vancouver Club? 12:15. Gil Grogan."

You know my feelings about the Vancouver Club. And I know yours. But he did not proffer the option of an RSVP. The old dinosaur just assumed I'd grab at a free lunch.

At 11:45 I stood at our living room window and watched him back out of his driveway. At 11:46 I backed out of ours, tailing him all the way to the Lions Gate Bridge. Did he wave a cheery hello? — no. Nor did I. We nosed through the noonday traffic like zombies. Once over the bridge I followed him through Stanley Park (bitter and brown-looking at the moment, dusty shrubs, splintery trees) and down Georgia. I even followed him straight into the parking lot and pulled up next to his waxy old Olds. We opened our car doors simultaneously, then shut them with a single bang. "Well," he said, as though bowled over to see me, "how've you been?"

"Not bad," I said, avoiding his crafty eyes.

He had a table for two reserved by the fireplace. The first martini went down so fast I hardly noticed it.

We discussed the weather. We discussed you and how you were coming with your French. (He was bowled over that you would learn French. Disapprovingly bowled over, that is.) We discussed the Lions and, after, the Canucks. Treasury bills are now a good investment, he informed me. We ate lumps of veal in sweet cream, then a dish of strawberries. A bottle of good wine glided by. The waiters were soft-footed and kind. I told him about my Creative Connections class and asked him if he knew the work of Austin Grey.

"Who?" he barked politely. He mentioned his daughter from San Francisco who won't be coming after all for Christmas. He mentioned his gall bladder and, God help us, his prostate. I discussed the work I was doing at Sanderson's and the chance of being taken on permanently, should the economy improve. "Humph!" he said, and that was as close as we got to politics. He related a not-bad shaggy-dog story about Clinton and Yeltsin — you'll have to get him to tell you at Christmas (I invited him for dinner), and then he signed the bill. We went out to the parking lot, shook hands, and did a repeat of our earlier journey, only this time with him tailing me. A few minutes ago he waved amicably from his window and I waved back, all rather surreal and comic.

One of the most frustrating things about this bloody separation is not being able instantly to replay happenings for you. What do people who are *truly* separated do with their prize experiences — bury them? make light verse of them? stew them up for supper? Oh God, I do need a wife and no substitute persona will do.

Hurry home, libidinous one, and I'll deck you with holly
or whatever else in the universe you desire.

Your

Chas

Dec. 21

JOYEUX NOËL!! Dear ones — can hardly wait!
MOM

4 Old Town Lane

Ottawa, Ont.

Sunday, Jan. 5

Dear Chas,

I'm still so upset I don't know if I can write this letter,
but this is the fifth time I've tried, so this one goes no matter
what. Something has to be said. I know that perhaps what
should be said is "I'm sorry," and yet I can't bring myself to
say anything so simple when the truth is far more complex.

Of course I'm sorry for the way I acted — bursting into
tears in your very own home whose every corner you've
mopped, scrubbed, painted, and loved, and whose interior
reflects your soul just as faithfully as the clothing you wear
and the shade of your lipstick — I can't go on.

To walk into a place you've longed for every day for four
months and to find that it has disappeared, overlaid by a jumble of two-by-fours and plastic sheeting that barely keeps the
gale-force winds at bay — God, you'd have cried too if you
hadn't been the creator/destroyer. Sorry.

I still can't talk about it without wanting to wade out into the snowdrift on my balcony and hurl crockery onto the frozen wasteland.

Oh God, you must have worked day and night, and so I'm also coping with a tremendous load of guilt that keeps tempting me to say forget it. Certainly I was emotionally upset after the hectic work-load we waded through in order to break on time for Christmas. I'm tempted to say that after I got used to it I loved the changes, that you certainly know best, that of course you needn't consult me when you knock out walls — after all, you're the architect, the specialist who has some right to impose his view on the uninformed.

But I *can't*. I can't be that dishonest, *I don't feel that way*. I suppose it's my problem and I have to work it out — no, that's not true either. It's your problem too. *We* have to work it out.

There are no marriages that don't go through times of stress, and I suppose we've been unbelievably lucky to have had so few real crashes. Maybe that's why I'm more astonished than I should be that this thing could have built into something so major between us that we couldn't even have sex in *ten whole nights*. Something I thought only happened to other people.

The anger kept surprising me, welling up and grabbing my brain and making the accusing words swell my tongue until it burst and boiled over. I couldn't help myself — when you put your arm around me all I felt was an icy stillness. I've never had anger I couldn't deal with before — at least, not since the early frustrating days of diapers and playpens. I tried to hide it and contain it and not cringe and I thought I leaped into bed with a fair show of enthusiasm and turned to you with real pretence of passion, but it seems I didn't make much of a job of pretending. Then when you failed to rise to the occasion (not funny, I know) I was at first shocked and then freshly angry. I felt as though a huge red vaporous cloud, something like the pictures *Voyageur* sent back of the surface of Mars, was hovering in a giant ball just above the bed and descending slowly and capturing my brain cell by cell. That was when I started to accuse you and say I'd always heard impotence was a sure sign of infidelity, and who was it, Sue? Davina? the worshipful Marjorie? I don't blame you for turning your back.

Underneath I know I love you very much, but the Martian fog is blanketing and smothering everything so that I can't move into the areas of my head where I love and care about anyone.

Can we work it through?

Jock

P.S. Where is the *money* for the addition coming from? I mean, as Mia said, it's weird, we're poor. *What* government loan? My job will probably only last till May or June, given the political climate. Sometimes — especially since George came — I wonder if they really need me anyway.

29 Sweet Cedar Drive
North Vancouver, B.C.
5 January

Dear Jock,

Every day I get up and say to myself: today I've got to sit down and write a letter to my wife, Jocelyn, in Ottawa, and every day I put it off. It's not because I haven't thought about what I want to say. Ten times, twenty times, I've written that letter in my head — mainly in the middle of the night when I'm up dosing myself with Maalox-Plus and looking in the mirror and thinking that this whole business of your going off to Ottawa was a grisly mistake. Jesus! — what a couple of

fools we were to welcome this Commission as an "opportunity." What in God's name did we think we were doing?

What gnaws at me — and I mean this literally, see above
— is that we threw away our calm and relatively happy married life, our family life too, for mere *money*. Am I right? — is
this what we did? We had other options, the most apparent
being that we could have hung in there a little longer. The
Sanderson thing opened up just weeks after you set off for
glory and greed in the east, and it's almost certain they'll be
taking me on permanently in the spring. Or we could have hit
your mother for a loan. God knows she's offered often
enough, so often, in fact, that I can see the words bubbling
up on her lips when she swings her car into our driveway
with yet another nourishing casserole to place in the arms of
our three-person refugee unit. So that's what's burning the
angry little hole through my stomach wall, sweetie: *We could
have managed.*

I am as confused as I am furious and sad. Who exactly
was that forbidding woman who stalked in here the day
before Christmas and screamed, loud enough to send the
poor cat running for his life, "*Mon Dieu!*" and who, in front of
her husband and her two puzzled, silent children, shrieked
for ten minutes straight about the violation done to her
house, the desecration, the outrage.

It's strange, but all these years I've persisted in the belief
that this was my house too, our house, the somewhat sterile
and poorly built compromise dwelling we chose together
because (1) it was what we could afford, (2) it had a magnificent view and a cedary smell, and (3) it had excellent possibilities for improvements, which some day, when we had the
time and cash, we would make. A solarium, you said *at least a
hundred times in my hearing*, would turn this place into par-
adise. You pictured it, you said, full of tropical plants, a fig

tree in an earthenware pot, a bird singing in a bamboo cage; and *here*, you said — so many times I've lost count — here you would drink your morning coffee and read your newspaper and find true serenity.

In the days (and nights) I spent working on the renovations I paused now and then, looked up, and imagined you coming in the doorway at Christmas. There it would be — what you've talked and dreamed so often about. I pictured your surprise, your lit-up face, your cry of delight. I never in all my imaginings counted on that wild screech of "*Mon Dieu*" and the ten-day attack on my judgement that followed.

Maybe (ah beautiful hindsight) I should have consulted you, as your mother kept battering away at me to do. But where then would have been the surprise? Christ, there are so few surprises left when you get to this age, and how we need them. At least I need them. You apparently want every knife and fork to remain in its hallowed place, and while you're at it, keep the old husband in his place too. (A bamboo cage?) And the skylight in the kitchen — didn't we always say we had to do something to bring more light into the eating area? Maybe I dreamed up those times when you and I sat turning the pages of *Architectural Digest* and saying, yes indeed, a skylight is just what we need. Maybe that was a different woman altogether. What have these last four months done to us?

I know that you and I grew up in a rather quaint period when it was considered a tad crude to discuss the price tags on Christmas gifts, but I could tell you were concerned about what the solarium cost. And when your mother murmured her "It might have been better to wait," I knew she thought I'd been extravagant at a time when I couldn't afford to be. So let me break with tradition by explaining that I got all the windows at the wrecker's lot out in Burnaby. Those three big triangular windows came from a fast-food place on lower

Lonsdale, that place that went broke; and the rectangular ones came from a house that burned down out by the university. The little stained-glass piece came from a church — four bucks. The trick was to design the structure around the available materials, and I think even you will have to admit the concept is unique. Now that the panels are actually in place (since yesterday), it's fairly breathtaking. The skylight too is recycled — someone ordered it and then changed his mind — and it was (almost) given to me (almost) free. I did have to get a small home-improvement loan for the rest of the materials. Low, low interest and, as you know, the labour was donated. Donated? — is that the word? A labour of love was what I almost wrote.

I agree that the house was ridiculously cold for the whole holiday, but I think it was a little unrealistic of you to blame me for the weather. I already told you that I had hoped to have it completely done for Christmas, but the windows needed a special sealer that was suddenly and inexplicably unobtainable west of the Rockies. I also thought it was extremely generous of Gil Grogan to offer us his portable electric heater, and I believe he was hurt, as well as mystified, by your "*ça ne fait rien*." He's a bit of an old goat, but the poor guy is lonely and now he's got prostate problems. God, I look at Gil sometimes and think: Is this what we struggle through life to become?

I'm not prepared yet to live a disappointed life, and I guess that's why I want this letter to be as frank as I can make it. But it's hard to be honest as well as kind. If only we had had time to talk more when you were here. My theory is that the sex thing (or the non-sex thing) that happened over Christmas made us both so tense and frustrated that there didn't seem a way to think about what was really happening.

What more can I say? Can I put it down to extreme anti-climax over the solarium? Was I afraid to go to bed with a woman who has faced-off with Hana Gartner on national TV? Or was it first-time jitters, the kind of jitters that come from going to bed with a stranger.

Because in a way you were a stranger. You're thinner and somehow quicker and seem to have a new set of expectations. As a result I felt slow and lumbering and overwhelmed. I hope to hell I'm not being overly expository about all this, but Sue says the best thing to do is thrash it out before it goes cold. Thrashing, of course, is something we've never been all that good at, and it's no wonder when you think of the families we've come from. Can you imagine *my* parents airing their sexual differences? I'm sure their night-time fumblings were never translated into words. And as for *your* mother…

A new year. I still can't get used to the sound of it and can't imagine what it will bring. Here I am, halfway through my life and living in a half-dismembered house. I've got half a job and, for the moment it seems, half a wife. Is it any wonder I'm feeling severed? I keep watching the mail, hoping for a letter from you that will say something about the future, something positive.

Keep writing, lovey, and let's try to keep this ship floating along. (It's a good old ship.)

Love,
Chas

P.S. Greg has decided to return the guitar after all. Thank God I was able to find the receipt. And you already know Mia returned the T-shirt. She's bought another one in its place, a punky thing with no neck or armholes.

4 Old Town Lane
Ottawa, Ont.
Jan. 7

Dear Chas,

Our letters crossed — is it significant that we wrote on
the same day, do you think? Anyway, I'm glad they crossed.
An article in the weekend *Journal*, "Is Your Relationship Out
of Sync?", advises both sides to spell out their real feelings
after a blow-up. So — as Davina would no doubt say — let's
let it all hang out.

Your logic as to why we bought the house in the first
place is, of course, unanswerable. All your logic is. Jessica
says that men have always swamped women with logic, that
they've taken something that was supposed to be a tool and
changed it into a god, and that in their eyes anyone who fails
to worship Cartesian clarity is either a fool or a woman. I
wouldn't go that far, but there's a speck of truth there.

Logically, we did choose the house because it was the
best we could afford, but illogically we — but mostly I —
lived in it day and night for fifteen years and *I* learned to care
for it and nurture it. Is it any wonder I came to think of it as
belonging more to me than to you? (Possession is nine-tenths
of the law, remember.) No, I don't want every knife and fork
in its hallowed place, nor husband either — that was a cheap
shot — but — oh, what's the use. I can't explain what I
don't understand.

Perhaps we could have discussed it like the rational crea-
tures I once thought we were, if it hadn't been for Christmas
dinner. And Mother. She didn't help, did she? Of course she
spotted my gloom at once, but I could have killed her when
she marched in and said, "I told you, Charles, didn't I? I
said, don't do it without asking her. Jocelyn has always been

strong-minded, and you could never please her if something wasn't exactly what she wanted." And then her rotten aside to me: "Some women would consider themselves in heaven to have a husband that cared that much, not to mention looking after everything while they're free to pursue a career." If it hadn't been for the presence of Gil and your "charlady" (with *enfant terrible*) I'd have told her...I don't know what I'd have told her.

Okay. Sue. I don't think we ever got around to discussing *why* you asked her. Certainly I wasn't prepared when I answered the door on Christmas Day to find a skinny redhead — in jeans — who looks more like a teenager than a woman. I was even less prepared for the six-year-old she was dragging by the hand. When she said, "Hi, I'm Sue," I suppose I looked as stunned as I felt. "You know, the cleaning lady," she said, and I managed a smile. The only one that day, as far as I can remember.

In retrospect I can see that she was mightily embarrassed, but I wasn't in a forgiving mood. "Chas invited me for dinner," she said. "I hope he didn't forget to tell you?"

I could hardly tell her you and I weren't communicating, so I mumbled something — didn't I? — and invited her in. Now that I've written all this down I feel pretty awful. I acted like a shrew — it's tough to be civil in the face of creeping hypothermia. Bloody furnace!

Good old Mother! She always has the sauce to retreat into when there's tension. I thought she was going to drift away on the fumes of that ghastly Finstead pudding, and I even debated about withholding the brandy sauce on hers. As for *your* mother, when she turned to me and said, "Jocelyn, dear, tell me all about Halifax," I could cheerfully have chucked my mashed potatoes at her. Would have if it hadn't been for Mia and Greg.

Not that Mia appreciated my restraint. All she seemed to think of was the Finsteads who might come early for the eggnog you so hospitably invited them to consume, and could we please put another bundle of wood on the fire? As if a measly little fireplace could counteract the ocean gale blowing through the open wall of the dining room, with its festive covering of heavy plastic, and the Vancouver temperature actually below freezing.

Sue did her damnedest, I'll grant her that. She was actually interested in, *and knowledgeable* about, the Commission. She knows plenty about the problems women are coping with in the work-force, too. Her own case, for instance, having to do cleaning to keep studying. She told me about the courses she's taking at Simon Fraser. In other circumstances I know I would have liked her, but at that point I suspected everyone of being an aider and abetter to the Big Renovation project. I admit it was nice of her to offer to help me clear the table, and not so nice of me to refuse, although I suspect she was partly motivated by the need to escape from Marjorie Finstead (so was I) in her gorgeous silk shirt and matching skirt. (Must have cost the moon.)

Marjorie was clearly no more Sue's type than she is mine. "Oh, I do hope you'll give Mia's room the Laura Ashley look — Laurie is so crazy about hers that she spends every available minute in it." What exactly is the Laura Ashley look? Is that why Mia and Laurie begged to be allowed to leave our house immediately after dinner and rush back to the Finsteads? Or did they just want to thaw out? And as for the "hubby" — Gus — he seems to regard Christmas as an unfortunate commercial break between hockey games.

I don't know why Marjorie Finstead drives me up the wall the way she does. The *Journal* article claims that we project the failings we dislike most about ourselves onto others — perish the thought.

Good for Greg, at least he suffered it through until the bitter end, even tried to be sociable and play with Sue's little monster. Okay, okay, unfair, she's only six, and Christmas makes the best of children whiny and unmanageable. It can't be easy being a single parent. As I suppose you are these days. I guess you and Sue must have a lot in common.

That session after dinner when we sat in the freezing living room with our icy egg-nogs and rapidly cooling coffee will go down in my personal history as the LOW moment of modern times. The neat piles of plaster where the wall between the living and dining rooms used to be, the thunderous booms of the plastic covering the former wall as gusts of wind crept around its edges, the clear evening with the moonlight glinting off the distant ocean (which should have cheered me after Ottawa's drabness but didn't), the crazy mix of people — Gus Finstead droning on and on about the Canucks, Marjorie burbling about Laura Ashley, Sue grim-faced and silent, the child whining, Mia and Laurie communicating in repressed hysterical giggles, Greg trying to discuss with me the work I'm doing and the impact of the briefs, you sitting there trying to pretend that you weren't upset (I didn't know how upset until bedtime) and leaping up every five minutes to throw another piece of our forest on the fire, Mother declining egg-nog and polishing off the Christmas bottle of Bristol Cream, your mother contributing her occasional insights ("My dear, Halifax harbour has never been the same since the explosion, wouldn't you agree?"), and then Gil Grogan lecturing us on the need to pound some sense into the heads of the unions before the province goes down the tube, with Sue rearing up as though stung by wasps but checking whatever retort she was about to give in deference to the grim-faced lady of the house (me). Let's stick that in the annals of never-to-be-repeated Christmases and try to forget the whole sorry mess. And on top of everything else I'd forgotten what a hell of a nuisance it is to cook and clean up — expecially in a welter of saw-horses and disconnected tubing.

Oh yes, and Gil Grogan attacking the French on the cereal boxes. I forgave Sue's little girl everything when she said, *"Oh Monsieur Grogan, est-ce que tu ne peux pas lire le français?"* I was the only one who laughed and then of course I couldn't translate because it would have embarrassed Gil. (Good for Sue's ex, sending the kid to French immersion.)

Jan. 8

I've just read this over and I realize I overreacted. For that, I'm sorry. And for being short with Sue. We did start to have rather a good chat about the trouble she's having going to college and keeping body and soul together, but then Marjorie Finstead butted in with an inane comment about how handsome you looked brooding before the fire with that melancholy expression, sort of like Leonard Cohen, and Sue said, "Sure, okay, if that's what you like," which would, normally, have made me laugh but instead made me jealous. (I suppose part of it is that I feel some resentment that's she's in my house more than I am.) And then Sue looked at Greg and said he was going to be a carbon copy, and Marjorie said, "Oh, we always call that the spitting image," and laughed uproariously.

Speaking of Greg, where on earth do you think he was on Christmas Eve? I was still awake — dry-eyed, virginal, and mad — at two a.m. when he came in.

Well, as Mother murmured countless times into her

glass, troubles always come in threes and everything goes wrong that can go wrong at the same time. (That woman had a good mind once, straight A's at Queen's. I found her marks at the bottom of an old trunk — symbolic?) But she's right, everything went wrong that could go wrong. The unusual cold snap, even though it was clear and beautiful — but for us warm and raining would have been better. Mother's double messages and your mother's vagueness — is it possible she puts it on? At one point she was wandering about in what used to be the kitchen, getting in my way, when suddenly she turned to me and said, "Men just don't understand what a house means to a woman. You have to weigh that." I almost cried, but then I fell over the stove, and she smiled vaguely and drifted out of the room.

Well, Chas, perhaps that's enough said about Christmas. I think I have, for better or worse, let it all hang out — and some of it, I admit, doesn't bear close scrutiny. Still, I think we're secure enough — aren't we? — to be able to turn over a few stones and have a look at the grubs. In fact, I was surprised by the tone of your letter, which seemed to put our marriage at some sort of risk because of a little separation. Darling Chas, we've only been apart four months. Mother and Dad were separated four *years* during the war! — and if our roots aren't any better lodged than that — well.

What we have to do is think it through. I know you must have been miserably disappointed that you worked that hard to surprise me and I hated it. I do understand that. What I don't understand is how you could have lived with me for twenty years and not known that completely uprooting my kitchen without so much as consulting me in any way, not to mention the living room and dining room, would injure me, *grieve* me — maybe we don't know each other as well as I thought we did.

And as for our choice — the Commission has been — I don't know quite how to say this without hurting you — it's been the most tremendous experience of my life. I wouldn't give up these last months for the world, the people I've met, the things I've learned, the insights I've gained, the self-confidence. I suppose I *am* different, as you say. It wouldn't be possible to pack all the experiences I've had into such a short time and come out the other end unchanged. All my nerve endings are working. I'm alert in a way I've never been before. Oh I know what people say about royal commissions, that they're a waste of public money, just a delaying tactic, but this *feels* like authentic work, and I feel, maybe for the first time, like a legitimate person who has serious work to do. Yes, I do — I feel *legitimate*.

What I really want to say, without screaming, is that *I think you should be as excited about my changed life as I would be if it were you!*

Love,
Jock

P.S. George O'Reilly and his wife invited me to dinner last night. (Not Indonesian cotton and not goose-down. Imitation black leather.) When I told them (humorously) about the house renovations, Esther reacted with unexpected fury, making me feel vindicated in a small way. She said that George had once painted the whole house pale purple when she was away. "I still haven't forgiven him," she said. All George said, turning sort of tight-lipped, was, "I worked my butt off, but never again."

P.P.S. What do you mean, *Sue* says we have to thrash it out? Surely you haven't told her?

29 Sweet Cedar Drive
North Vancouver, B.C.
9 January

Dear Jock,

I admit I made a mistake about inviting the Finsteads in afterwards. But they've been embarrassingly good to Mia since you left, taking her on all their wholesome family outings. (Didn't we used to go on family outings? When did that stop?) And I guess I feel sorry for Marjorie Finstead. She seems always to be so nervously desperate, as I guess I would be too if I were married to someone with a personality like the back wall of a handball court. (He actually asked me what kind of running shoes I thought were best.) Dopey Marjorie, in her dizzy way, has her head screwed on, at least. She has a great belief in the "intact" family and says that making a "pleasing and attractive refuge" for her family is a serious responsibility. Well, damn it, it *is* a serious responsibility. Mia, as you saw for yourself, loves to be over there, so I can only assume that she's in need of a refuge. She sure as hell covets Laurie Finstead's canopy bed. That's all I hear about these days.

Now why didn't I make Mia a canopy bed for Christmas instead of . . . ? but here we go again, and I don't know if I'm up to it.

I had a good case of the shakes after mailing that last letter to you, thinking I just might have gone and thrown away the best part of my life, namely you. What in hell did I write to you anyway? I can't remember, I was in such a blaze of fury. Unstrung. Unfocused. Uncentred, as Sue might say, and often does, as in, "Don't mind me this morning, I'm not quite centred yet."

Seems to me what I wrote to you was one long blubber, the defensive male rampant. What can I say now to explain myself? That, one, I was more than a little alienated by what I perceived as the New You? Two, that I was feeling decidedly castrated and not just metaphorically? Or, three, that I was knee-deep in a bad case of anticlimax following several weeks of non-stop work on the bloody house? Three out of three probably.

And something else, too, though I hesitate to mention it because I don't put much stock in *delving*, as you know. But I'm sure I had before me the family story of Dad going off to Halifax during the war. He wasn't drafted, you know — he was too old, thirty-nine, I think. The poor guy sat twiddling his thumbs for the first two years of the action and then woke up one morning, banged a fist on the kitchen table, and told Mother that he was bloody well going to enlist and she could scream blue murder if she liked. She did scream. She felt Dad had deserted her. In a sense, I think, she's still screaming.

No, lovey, I do *not* think *you've* deserted me. And I *am* "excited about your changed life" as you put it. But can you blame me if I got a bit wobbly, thinking you'd become some-one I hardly recognized — and wasn't sure I liked much. (Can I risk this? Yes. You are the one who said we had to be open.)

And then along came your letter today, and I knew you were still my own lovely Jock. You're right, of course. Our roots do go deep enough for us to shake them up occasion-ally. But please, let's shake gently, for my sake if not for yours.

Yes, I did talk it over with Sue Landis, but of course I told her that it was *friends* of ours who were having a dry patch. As you know, Sue's taking this family studies course at Simon Fraser. Sue says that any kind of separation puts a relationship at risk. The absence of one component, she says, forces the other component to adapt — *stretching*, it's called. This stretching either encourages growth or leads to debilitation, and, contrary to what we've always been told about the human personality, people do change — and change very rapidly — under pressure. Even a few months can make a difference.

Sue also says that sexual dislocation is almost inevitable after a separation because the components of a relationship bring to bed with them their so-called stretch marks, which they're both proud of and frightened of — if you see what I mean. (It all made perfect sense when Sue said it, but I'm having trouble getting it right in this letter.) Maybe I should go back to the roots metaphor and say something about plants in small pots getting root-bound and needing trans-planting, etc. Or maybe I should just shut up.

Sue's daughter, by the way, the fact that Sue *has* a daugh-ter, was as much a shock to me as it was to you. When I asked her yesterday why she'd never mentioned her, she said, a little testily, that she hadn't felt it was relevant when she applied for the job. Anyway, Molly lives with her father in some com-mune on Vancouver Island and only spends holidays with Sue. I wonder what he (the father) is like. Sue says he mainly sits on the beach trying to learn what the waves have to teach him. She did it too for a couple of years, but all the waves ever said was, "Here I come again, and again, and again," and finally she was driven to "re-engage," as she put it, with the world. She's still hoping the Child Abuse Team will be rein-stated, but meanwhile she's picking up some new options at Simon Fraser and cleaning houses to pay her tuition.

Am off to do some shopping — the fridge is stripped bare.

Love,

Chas

P.S. I'm enclosing Greg's Christmas marks. With marks like that, how can I legitimately complain about his going out every night? What do you think?

P.P.S. Have you had a chance yet to show my poem to Austin Grey? Any comments would be appreciated, even negative ones.

P.P.P.S. Where do you buy sequins?

4 Old Town Lane
Ottawa, Ont.
Jan. 12

Dear Chas,

Thank God for these letters. I have read and reread yours, and love and longing are definitely stealing back into the big space recently occupied by anger. Maybe I really *will* like the solarium. When will it be finished? Send me a picture.

Neither of us mentioned one aspect about Christmas that may have been partly to blame and unfortunately may have a lasting effect — the disastrous visits with all our old friends. (Although maybe you've discussed it with Sue — is she studying psychoanalysis?) As I suspected, the friends saved us for Christmas and that gave us too little time to sort things out. And neither of us was in the mood to be sociable night after night. I think we were a great pair of wet blankets. Will they ever ask us again?

The funny thing — somewhat disturbing — is that I didn't much enjoy seeing them, and yet I used to love to go to parties, especially those New Year's bashes at the Ticknows. I found myself being rather bored — the talk seemed dispiritingly shallow and self-centred. British Columbia is *not* the centre of the universe, and all those pitying allusions to my tremendous sacrifice in going to *Ottawa* (you'd have thought it was Siberia) made me feel somewhat alienated. Living in lotus-land is all very well, but it's no wonder the rest of the country finds us a mite chauvinistic.

I came back to a feeling of urgency, almost panic, on Van's part. He thinks the PM will call an election within a couple of weeks and that we have to wind this thing up fast. Therefore we're off to the North West Territories on Saturday, and when we leave there we'll be going to Alberta and Saskatchewan, then back to Vancouver for a week. Should be the week of the 26th. I'd *love* to have a "do" for the Commission on the Saturday night if the holes in the house are filled in that is. We could have it catered since I'll be working all week and won't have any time. And we'll really talk — I promise not to seem different.

I think what you said about plants is right on, that transplanting must have been exactly what I needed, I *was* becoming pot-bound. Remember when Grant and Mia were about to go into a growth spurt, how they would eat anything and everything they could find? I feel as though that's what has happened to me, that I've developed a voracious appetite for changing the social milieu for women, and that it *is* leading to growth. I definitely do *not* mean that I've *outgrown* anything, dear Chas. I think — hope — there's room for it all. My stretch marks are definitely beginning to grow to include the solarium, and may soon encompass the kitchen.

Sorry this is so short. Thrilled about Greg's marks, and agree it's difficult to complain. But where the hell *does* he go? You'd better find out. Perhaps a discreet phone call or two to friends' parents?

Love,

Jock

P.S. Do you think Sue was fooled for one minute by your story that it was friends who were having problems? I'd rather we kept it *entre nous*.

P.P.S. Austin says my anger re the house changes is because the unconscious speaks in symbols, and that a house may be the mind's symbol for the self. He says that when he began to write poetry he used to dream that he was discovering new and wonderful rooms in the house he'd been living in for years — great floor-to-ceiling windows of paned glass and exotic plants winding about the rooms and hanging from the ceiling — and in the dream he'd be astonished that he hadn't explored them before. And that he hadn't even known they were there. Interesting (though bewildering).

P.P.P.S. How would you have felt if I'd traded in the *car* without telling you?

29 Sweet Cedar Drive
North Vancouver, B.C.
15 January

Darling Jock,
    Your letter has just come and I've read it three times, the third time with an erection the size of a — well, never mind, I won't set myself up as part of the macho enemy. Dear Jock, it has, to tell the truth, been hell waiting to hear from you, but at the same time I'm grateful for once that the mail in this country is so bloody plodding. Why? — because I've needed these last few days to mellow out — as Greg would say. Or to let it all hang out, as you say in

your letter. (At least you didn't say it in bloody French, thank God.)

Yesterday Sue brought a contribution to the solarium (yes, it's finished and beautiful if I say so myself). A little fig tree she's had for five years, that she raised from a cutting. Gil brought over a great line-up of miniature geraniums, and Marjorie has donated a feathery thing that looks like a palm. Your mother joined in by presenting a bizarre cactus four feet high with flat unreal-looking flowers stuck to its spines. And my mother gave us what looks like a pepperonia with a case of the bends. Mia has propped it up and is nursing it back to greenness. All in all, we're looking fairly tropical, and I think we should have things in good shape by the end of the month for the Commission bash. I can't help feeling that you'll have a change of heart when you see the room in its finished state. Sue think it's the most attractive part of the house and that, if we were to sell, the solarium would be the selling feature.

I should confess that there's something else that's prod-ded me into my present state of "temporization," as your mother calls it. Or some*one* rather — Davina. I told the whole story to her the other day — well, why not? *you* seem to tell all to your pal Austin — and she took a few royal stripes off me. "You fool," she said. "You bovine. You idiot."

We were having lunch in the cafeteria before class — God, that woman stows away the starch: a plate of fries, two bran muffins, and then a chunk of apple pie. Since she hadn't seen our house, either before or after the renovations, I felt I could trust her to be impartial. I told her the whole story, beginning with How You'd Always Wanted a Solarium and How I Wanted It to Be a Surprise.

"Enough, enough," she cried.

She said I should be garroted, chopped to mincemeat, and strewn on the grave of Ezra Pound. She said, or rather shouted, that anyone who dared move one ashtray in her apartment without consulting her would be immediately dismissed from her life. She would consider it a subversive act, a belligerent act. Her husband — apparently she was once married, since she refers now and then to this being — took her Woodstock poster off the bathroom door while she was out and *folded* it. For Davina this seems to have been the apogee of betrayal. Violation of one's immediate domicile is unpardonable. (These heightened legalistic phrases drop out of her mouth like briquettes, but she's ferociously sincere at the same time.)

Furthermore, she continued — and by now we had the attention of several other tables — surprises constitute a cruelty, an outrage, including surprise disclosures, surprise visits, and especially surprise gifts. These almost invariably misfire. The human personality is not constructed to accept the element of surprise, which is really a form of concealed aggression. (I am quoting more or less directly.)

Well! With all the spirit I could muster I argued in favour of surprises. (I tried whispering, hoping she would too.) Surprises — I wracked my brain for a metaphor she'd like — are the candy of life.

"The arsenic-laced candy," she said. Loudly.

I told her I bloody well hoped there were a few surprises left for me, or what's this miserable life all about? (I abandoned whispering. In fact, like poor old Dad, I found myself pounding the table.)

But Davina (by now into the apple pie and cream) had more to tell me. What she said was this: when one expresses a wish to *have* something, it doesn't necessarily follow that one actually wants it. For example, she once, feeling kittenish, told a lover of hers that she'd love to have a cat, and the fool went out and bought her a cat. Now she's stuck with the damn thing — the lover's gone off to Prince George — and it (the cat) pees regularly on her prayer rug so that every day when she does her breathing exercises she's reminded of her rash plea.

But this is a fantastically beautiful solarium, I told Davina. Show it to me, she said. So after class I drove her home to have a look. As a matter of fact she stayed for dinner — Mia made one of her smoked oyster omelettes — and afterwards Davina said, well yes, the solarium was beautiful all right, breathtaking in fact, but the crime of territorial invasion precludes gratitude. "Though personally," she said, looking around with a bright eye, "I could live quite happily with all this."

And she had an interesting suggestion for the solarium. She thinks hanging panels of coloured glass would make it more dramatic. She's got a good friend who does stained glass and she offered to ask his advice. We could get a sort of prism effect, she thinks. I don't know why I didn't think of it. I guess it's been a long time since I've done anything at the wild and curly end of architecture.

Christ, I've just read this letter over and note that I've used the word bloody three times. No doubt you're getting the impression that I'm in a bloody-minded mood — which I was before your letter arrived. I suppose I'm feeling a mite harassed. Tonight is Parents' Night at Greg's school, which for some reason I'm dreading, and before I go to that I have to pick up Mia from her bloody ballet class — I'm getting bloody again — and I want to get a start on my new class assignment for Davina. She's asked us to do prose poems for next week. "What is a prose poem?" I can hear you asking from Ottawa. Well, you take all the lines of a poem and squeeze them into a paragraph, God only knows why. (I see your Austin Grey has written a few of these contraptions. By the way, did you ever show him my out-of-work poem?) On top of all this I have to go to work two days a week in order to keep the good green dollars rolling in.

When I told Greg I was working on a new poem he said in his snarlingest voice, "What for?" I couldn't formulate a fast comeback, or even a slow one. Why indeed? Have I gone a little off my skids lately? (I'm tossing down a little Al Purdy before going to sleep these nights.) Can you imagine telling the Ticknows or the Chapmans, especially Jim, that I'm sitting on my butt these days writing poems? (Real men don't....)

You might be interested, by the way, in my theory about why the Ticknows, Clarkes, et al, have not exactly been showering me with dinner invitations this year. Because I am no longer, as it were, a couple. Couples only see couples, it seems. Singles are obscurely threatening and may lead to lop-sided, confusing evenings in which everyone gets uncoupled or recoupled or extra-coupled. Singles can only be trusted to mix with other singles. Davina says this is an old story, that her married friends never invite her over for an evening, though she likes nothing better now and then than a good down-home bourgeois gathering. At any rate, I'm phoning the whole damn bunch — Ticknows, Clarkes, Middletons, Chapmans — and inviting them for the big bash at the end of the month. (We'll show your eastern effetes what western hospitality can be!)

And now, Jock, let me end this letter with a few solemn promises to you. No more surprises ever, I swear. Also I give you my word that the house will be in great shape for the party. All the major work is now done and it's just a matter of a little cleaning up. Sue's got an exam the day before the party, but I'm sure the kids will pitch in. And I've picked up your idea of having the party catered. After checking around I finally found a caterer who isn't out to rob me. So relax, lovey — it's going to be a memorable *soirée*.

Love always,
Chas

P.S. Have discovered my stomach problems are caused by *trop de* lentils.

P.P.S. Trade my car! Be serious!

Yellowknife, N.W.T.
Jan. 20

Dear Chas,

Your letter came just before we left for Yellowknife and I didn't want to read it until I was alone and now of course I can't sleep. I've even been crying a bit — which is, truth to tell, rather a relief. I had begun to fear that my entire emotional spectrum had congealed into an immovable, impassable lump of rage — actually, something happened today that sort of started the brain-clearing even before your letter.

The hearings here in Yellowknife are light-years away from the kind of thing we do in Ottawa, where we usually meet in the Railway Committee Room and Van, Jessica, and Austin sit behind a formal-looking table and question the groups presenting briefs about the issues they raise. I usually sit at the end of the table and make notes of legal points that may need checking, passing them to Van if necessary, and George is supposed to sit in the first row of chairs, although lately he's taken to sitting beside me and taking an interest in my points. (A bit pushy, George.)

Here in Yellowknife we meet in a community hall, draped with New Year's Eve's somewhat forlorn red and green streamers. When we first walked in the chairs were all pushed back against the walls. I remember Mother telling about dances in the little prairie towns, how girls sat around the walls on display and the awkward powerful men grouped at the end of the hall shifting from foot to foot, eyes craftily averted, and elbows on alert for the telling nudge. "That's how I learned humility," she always ends up, usually tossing off a quick glass to seal her point. (Could anything so silly still bother her, do you think? Or is it just her penchant for quick glasses.)

The mayor and the two aldermen who'd met us at the plane moved the chairs out from the walls and lined them up in neat rows facing the stage, but Austin suggested that the commissioners move their chairs back down onto the floor, which we did. Then our hosts took us to the back room of a nearby café and bought us coffee, and when we got back about twenty people, mostly women, were already assembled there. Mothers, white and Inuit, had brought children bundled in parkas so that only the eyes peeped out, and the occasional burp, fart, or gurgle added a definitely non-Ottawa flavour.

One Inuit woman attracted my attention right away. She had a round-faced black-eyed baby with her and two other little ones who were unbelievably good. But the thing I noticed about her even before she began to speak was her face. Her skin was smooth, but the stamp of despair was so deep, so unmistakable, that I found myself wondering what terrible sorrow could possibly have been afflicted on one so young.

When it was her turn she rose and moved closer to us, and spoke rapidly in her own language to the children, and then faced us and told us she was a widow living on welfare. "My husband, he made a good living," she said, in a deep melodious voice whose faint slurring of syllables was the only hint that the Queen's English was not her mother tongue.

"He was a good man. One summer I go to visit my mother, and when I come back he has made me a new kitchen with an electric cookstove and many counters." She said this with such pride that I felt tears stinging my eyelids. Van leaned forward and asked her very gently (there is this side to Van, he isn't, as I've often said, just another macho pretty face), "What happened to your husband?"

"He died. In the autumn, after I came back and was full of great love for his kindness, we lived in much comfort through the beginning of the cold. And then it was time to go to his traplines. When the morning came, even though the air was clear, I felt the shadow of the thing that was coming. 'Don't go,' I whispered, but he laughed with the sureness of men and started his Skidoo and I watched him until there was no mark left on the horizon and I felt the darkness that followed after him. In the night I wakened in my bed and heard the wind begin, and it blew for three days and three nights, and then I felt the space beside me in my bed grow cold and I knew he had gone." I saw Jessica's lips tighten in a fierce line and Austin took off his glasses and began to polish them with his handkerchief.

"I cannot pray now," she finished, in a soft voice, "because we have no spirits any more, and I do not believe your God lives here so far in the north."

The words stripped me bare. I felt as though an electric shock was ricocheting through my addled brain, and for the first time since Christmas the anger was zapped right out of my skull and the way I saw what happened to us suddenly turned around ninety degrees. I'm not sure I can explain it, but it was mixed up with the very real grief I felt for that woman.

Austin says that if anger is more ferocious than it has a right to be, you must dig deeper for the cause. I don't know if mine has been more ferocious than it should have been, everything considered — I only know that for the last while I simply haven't been able to recognize that there are things more central in our relationship than the design of our house, and now, thanks to an Inuit woman, a little crack of light is opening.

I do love you, Chas. I'm even looking at plants for the solarium. Can hardly wait to see it.

Yours,

Jock

P.S. Stay off Skidoos.

P.P.S. You haven't mentioned Mia. *Or* Greg. What did his teacher say?

29 Sweet Cedar Drive
North Vancouver, B.C.
23 January

Dear Jock,

I must remember to tell your mother *good* things come in threes too! First of all, the sun finally came out and the prism in the solarium was everything Davina said it would be. Then your soul-restoring Yellowknife letter (I will, I will stay off Skidoos, especially in the rain). Then I was given a sort of commission. Our very own Gil Grogan, after seeing our solarium, asked me if I would design and supervise the construction of something similar for him. I said no at first, thinking the old bugger was dispensing alms to the demi-employed, but he insisted it was a straight business deal. We've signed a contract, sealed it with half a bottle of Scotch, and I'm suddenly full of ideas — for the first time in what seems like years.

Going into Sanderson's two days a week has become something of a chore. I am finding — don't laugh — that it tends to cut into my time. Did I really once manage to go to work five whole days a week? House-husbandly chores take up part of the time, of course. It's taken me a while to master lentil soup (also to be able to eat it), and I'm now deep into minestrone. (Sue's lent me a vegetarian cookbook she swears by.) There always seem to be errands to do. (Did you used to do all this running around, picking up dry cleaning and buying postage stamps? Without thanks?) And then there are The Mothers to visit. Both mothers have done the dutiful thing this week and had us to dinner. I won't go through the menus — you can, I'm sure, imagine what they were. Mia prefers dinner at *my* mother's because she actually likes canned pears for dessert, and Greg prefers your mother's table because there's always something new to try — smoked lamb last time, superb! We were given the leftovers to take home. Your mother's only reference to the solarium, after downing a bottle of good wine, was, "She (you) will probably get used to it in time." I bloody well hope so.

Greg has actually been dragging some of his pimply-faced pals through the house to see it. Which reminds me, when I was in the bank yesterday I had my passbook brought up to date. What a surprise to find two thousand bucks just sitting there. At first I thought you might have made a mail deposit, but when I asked the teller to check, she went all flustery and said she'd made a mistake and given me Greg's account instead of my own. That's impossible, I told her. He only, as you know, gets fifteen bucks a week for looking after Gil's yard, and it takes a helluva lot of fifteen bucks to make two thousand.

Now this is my quandary: do I pretend I never blundered into his bank account or do I demand that he level with me about where all those big bucks came from? Sue's in favour of levelling, but I think of my own dad who had faults aplenty, but who at least never pried into my personal affairs — not ever. He never asked where I spent my time or who I spent it with, which is why I'm trying hard not to hound Greg on this. He's touchy as it is.

Time to give the minestrone a kick. Only one more week!

Love,
Chas

P.S. Any idea what your crowd likes to drink? I thought we'd have a punch, but for those who don't like punch I should lay in a few bottles of hard stuff. And sherry. Your mother is dying to meet the famous Austin Grey.

4 Old Town Lane
Ottawa, Ont.
Jan. 26

Dear Chas,

I know I'll see you Saturday, but wanted to get some rather odd experiences on paper before I forget.

Ottawa actually seems balmy at minus two. When we left Yellowknife yesterday the air was so cold it almost hurt to breathe, and even though it was mid-afternoon it was eerily dark. Two slashes of dull red on the horizon glinted off the smooth sheets of snow, and when we climbed into the welcome heat of the little jet the steward helped us out of our parkas and Van handed him a bottle of rum. By the time we'd reached cruising altitude everyone was holding a nice fat mug of hot buttered rum.

These little jets! The time would have nearly doubled if we'd had to go on commercial aircraft. Hours and hours over frozen tundra. I think I really understood for the first time the vastness of Canada and the audacity of a civilization that would try to capture and change it. It's all very well for Britain — scepter'd isle...precious stone set in the silver sea, etc. — but to bring Shakespeare to the Inuit?

When I posed this question to the group, Van drawled, "Damn near as nutty as bringing Jessica to them." At which Jessica lumbered into the aisle and, holding out the end of her heavy old sweater, launched into that funny song from *Kiss Me, Kate!*, the "Brush Up Your Shakespeare" one. On the last "Odds Bodkins!" Van and Austin jumped up too and, linking arms with Jessica, ended it with very passable harmony. George and the steward and I applauded, and Yvette (yes, Van said he needed a secretary along) looked somewhat bewildered but applauded anyway.

"Where did you pick that up?" I demanded. George tried to let on that anyone with more than a passing interest in musical comedies could do the same, but I held my ground and finally they admitted that the Harvard Glee Club had put on *Kiss Me, Kate* the year they were all there at the same time.

Jessica? At Harvard?

"Quit gawking, Jock." (I hadn't realized it showed.) "I had to get a bit of education, otherwise Van here wouldn't've let me be on his Commission. Course I wouldn't be chosen to head it, that could only go to a man."

"The PM isn't that foolhardy," Van said. Jessica glared; George hooted.

I asked her what she'd studied.

"Oh, lotsa helpful things. Anthropology. A smattering of economics and social stuff. English lit."

I guess my mouth was hanging open because Jessica got a little belligerent. "What's yer problem, Jock?"

I blurted out before I could stop myself, "Why do you talk the way you do, Jessica?"

"What way?"

"You know damn well what way. As though you'd dropped out just after kindergarten."

Sometimes Jessica surprises me with her candour. "It's better in the work I do. You don't spout Jung at women who've been physically abused and mentally brainwashed, you talk to them in their own language. Van and the silver-tongued cliques hate it, hey Van? That's why I need qualifications. If you've got a coupla PhDs you can tell them to stuff it."

A couple? I did my best not to look astonished, and even George, who has taken to calling Jess "the bag-lady from Hades," couldn't come up with a put-down.

When we got to Edmonton we disembarked and had dinner, then got back on the plane. But a winter fog had rolled in and we had to wait until nearly ten o'clock — midnight, Ottawa time — to take off.

Everyone was beat. Those little planes don't have any room to lie down, although there is one couch at the front for the minister (in this case Van), but he gallantly (?) offered it to Yvette and took the seat next to her. Everyone else had a double seat to themselves except George and me, who, not being commissioners, had to share. But there was lots of leg-room and we tilted the chairs back as far as we could and the steward handed out blankets and switched off the cabin lights.

Hurtling through the dark still night wasn't very much like sitting around a camp-fire, but that's what it reminded me of. Primitive cave dwellers gathered closely for warmth and safety. We settled back, lulled by the steady roar and a very slight gentle yawing that must be peculiar to this breed of small jet.

Much later I woke up rather suddenly and looked out the window. An enormous moon glinted over the endless snow and one small light twinkled in all that vastness. Who would live there? I shivered and turned back to our spaceship, and as I did I felt something waft over me — a warmth, a closeness — I can't describe it exactly. It was as though the little plane was the outer shell of a single organism and those of us in it as necessary to and as much a part of one another as, say, my stomach is to my heart. It was as if the boundaries of separateness had dissolved between us, the way I'm told men in the trenches feel towards one another.

But that wasn't all. There was something else, an overlay like the pressure before a thunderstorm but almost tangibly heavy and sweet, almost cloying, and then I recognized it as sexual.

I edged away from George, although I didn't think that was where it was coming from. (He was snoring slightly.) Then I saw that Yvette was sitting up — dark hair tousled, eyes wide and frightened — with a blanket pulled up to her *bare* shoulders (they hadn't been bare before), saying something in rapid French which sounded like *J'ai peur, j'ai peur.* (She hates flying.)

Then I heard Van's soothing voice. I couldn't make out the words (he was using *tu* rather than *vous*, that's all I know) and I felt the sweet density of our common air stir in me. The silence, the softly murmuring voices in their unfamiliar, caressing tones — again I was transported to the dying camp-fire and the primitive men and women reaching out for comfort.

I looked at my watch and saw that it was three a.m., and remembered times when we, you and I, have rolled over in the heavy darkness almost as if on cue and held one another with an unquestioning mutual need, the incomplete becoming complete. Sex seeming merely incidental to wholeness.

The spell was broken abruptly by — who else? — Jessica. She heaved herself up and squinted around the darkened cabin, and suddenly she bawled, "Hey, Yvette, take this, yer need is greater than mine." Peeling off her tattered black sweater she circled it over her head and sent it flying toward the front of the plane where it settled neatly over Van's head.

Van swore softly (in French) and belted the sweater back at Jessica. George and I pretended we were just waking up and hadn't noticed a thing. Austin stirred and got to his feet and started down the aisle to the washroom. The steward brought coffee. Austin, returning, zipped open his bag and brought out — unlikely treat — a bottle of Tia Maria and spiked our coffee, and we chatted until Ottawa at five a.m.

I don't know why the strange feelings in that nocturnal trip affected me so much. I felt as though I'd had a close look at the thinness of the veneer of civilization. Austin pointed out the other day that the first city-states existed about seven thousand years ago, and that if a person's lifetime is the biblical three score and ten — seventy — seven thousand years spans only a hundred lifetimes. As a race we're not very far away from our beginnings.

I'm greatly excited about the "do" on Saturday, but I have some disappointing news — I have to leave Sunday morning. Van is pushing it so hard that we are going to get into Vancouver a little before noon on Friday (instead of for the three days originally scheduled), work Friday afternoon *and* evening (I may not even make it home Friday night; he's taken to working until one and two in the morning), then finish up Saturday morning. Big deal — Saturday afternoon off! Good thing you got a caterer.

I can hardly wait to have you meet everyone. How many are coming? I kind of envisage a rather relaxed evening, don't you? With some really good (maybe even scintillating) conversation.

Love,
Jock

P.S. Greg has two thousand dollars in the bank? I don't know what to think.

P.P.S. Jessica and the group-home groupies are throwing a skating-party on the canal tomorrow night. Should be interesting.

Ottawa,
Sunday night, POST-BASH

Chas —

Sorry I didn't wake you this morning to say goodbye — honestly, I tried, and you did sit straight up in bed and mumble, "Be right with you," but then you fell back, and I knew we didn't have time anyway, so I planted a regretful peck on the stubble before I got up. (You did smile, sort of a drooling upturn at mouth-edge.)

I crept down the stairs at the crack of dawn into the salubrious atmosphere of stale cigarettes and spilled beer, the whole mess highlighted in glorious technicolour with a kind of Hitchkovian flavour, thanks to the stained glass. In fact, I was more than a little startled to see a blood-red gash splashed across the sprawled body of a woman — but it was only Sue.

Rare to find one's caterer passed out on the sofa. Well-positioned for an early start, anyway! (Couldn't repress a sneaky satisfaction that it wasn't going to be me cleaning up.)

That was quite a party, was it not! Thank God the Ticknows and Clarkes and Chapmans went to Maui *en masse* (is there some new Vancouver penchant for group vacations?). As for the Sandersons, just hope they entered into the (carnal) spirit of the occasion. Do you still have a job?

After Van told us *our* jobs would be on the line if we weren't at the airport on time — and after I had so regretfully levered myself out of the still-chaste marital bed — guess what? The only one at the airport — besides me — was Austin. He had no news of Jessica or George, but he did say that Van's black eye was hurting and he was going to try to get a ride back on a government plane to avoid the media. *What* black eye? I know Jessica didn't do it, because she'd stomped off into the night just after Mother left. Was it Sue? I saw Van following her about — who didn't? Maybe Yvette got mad enough to punch him? (I thought Yvette was consoling herself sufficiently with George.) Or — note the many ghastly possibilities — was it the ebullient Marjorie? I saw her disappear into the rain, shoeless and near to sightless, still regaling us with her rollicking rendition of "Roll Me Over in the Clover," with variations.

I was a bit worried about Jessica, but Austin said she was probably okay. Seems she got in some sort of row with your famous Davina (who wouldn't go along with her coda that all men, but especially Van, are insensitive, arrogant SOBs), and she got so mad she just took off. Van and Austin spotted her hitch-hiking along the Upper Levels in the pouring rain, and Austin had to give chase along the side of the road to get her into the same cab as Van. Rather inopportunely, a police car hove onto the scene and Austin had quite a bad moment when Jessica seemed about to lay a complaint of sexual assualt against them both, but fortunately she relented and got into the cab and the officer let them off with a warning about acting their ages. (As Austin recited all this, the guy in the aisle seat between us couldn't stop laughing. Hope he didn't recognize Austin. Wouldn't the media make sushi with this?)

Oh, by the way, Austin admires the house changes. (I don't think he was just saying it; he knows I'm still coming to terms.) I gather you asked him about your poem, and he made me promise to show it to him. Did you give it to me? And he found Mother charming, he said. (Hope he wasn't being patronizing; I don't think he was.) When we got to Ottawa he offered to buy me dinner, but all I wanted to do was to hole up in my safe little retreat and hide there for the rest of the winter. Or until the hangover abates. (It has, two aspirins and a glass of warm milk.)

I have to laugh at myself — now that I'm feeling well enough — about the "cultured" evening I'd thought we'd have. I suppose it was because when George and Esther entertained the Commission they included some very stimu-lating friends. Not that Davina, Sue, Marjorie Finstead, Gil, and that toothy creature from your Creative Connections class aren't stimulating. In fact I'd say they out-stimulated the O'Reilly crowd by a country mile.

What I'm trying to say — admit — is that I think it was good for me. I'd been putting the Ottawa crowd on a bit of a pedestal, somehow had gotten it into my head that they were a cut above our sneaker-clad yokels. But although the intel-lectual level last night was on a par with the Ozarks, it was the easterners who out-Ozarked the westerners by about two to one....

Much (platonic — sigh) love,
Jock

P.S. Greg came in to that shambles at two a.m. *Where* is he until that hour? Isn't it time you found out?

P.P.S. Yes, the solarium is lovely. Odd, though — I feel quite detached about it. Maturity? (I hope.)

29 Sweet Cedar Drive
North Vancouver, B.C.
2 February

Dearest Love,

This is being written in rather a rush since I want to get down to the hospital to visit Gil Grogan, and the visiting hours are over at nine.

I was sorry — I can't tell you *how* sorry, and for more reasons than one — to wake up on Sunday morning and find you'd gone. (I think it's possible I had one too many cups of Gus Finstead's Maple Leap Surprise Gin Punch, because I didn't wake up until noon.) I couldn't help remembering how you and I used to lie in bed in the morning after our parties and compare notes — the post mortem always seemed to me to be more interesting than the parties themselves. Remember those wonderful spaghetti smashes we used to throw, and the time Tiny Wiglow fell on top of our new glass-topped coffee table? And that disastrous Open House when we tried to mix the unmixable — architects and lawyers — and the result was one party on the deck and a separate party in the living room? And the dinner parties where sometimes everything (and for no discernible reason) seemed to hum — the food, the talk, the warmth of it all?

I think you'll have to agree that Saturday's party was one of our best ever, in spite of that little set-to in the kitchen between Gil and your golden-boy, Vance. (By the way, the good news is that Gil's jaw isn't broken, only dislocated.) From what I gathered later, Vance, parched from pursuing Sue, stumbled into the kitchen and asked *in French* for a little "*soupçon de cognac dans son café*," and Gil, joking of course, asked Vance if he had a "little frog" in his throat.

I have a feeling that your pal Vance has very little sense of humour, and no doubt he richly deserved the poke in the eye he got. Gil maintains that Vance shoved him against the refrigerator and he had no choice but to defend himself. (Evidently they don't teach the young lads of Westmount not to attack the elderly.)

I got all this later from Sue who came running from the living room when she heard the sound of glass breaking. (Don't worry, only *one* of the crystal glasses got smashed, the rest were cups and saucers.) Sue was the one who managed to get Vance calmed down before she drove Gil over to Emergency. And you know what Emerge is like on a Saturday night — packed — which is why the buffet supper was later than we'd originally planned. But who at that point cared?

And you have to admit the food was worth waiting for. As I explained — or did I? — Sue volunteered to do the catering, but then got tied up in a rescheduled exam, and everyone pitched in and helped. It reminded me of those terrific potlucks we used to have when we lived in Kits. Your mother's eggplant crêpes were sensational, though we seem to have a thousand left over, and Davina's yam and yogurt casserole was a hit, at least while it lasted. Melody — did you meet Melody? — brought a blueberry cheesecake, but in the confusion it somehow got left in the fridge (we had it this morning for breakfast). Gil's Greek salad could have been better — he can't digest black olives *or* feta cheese — but at least he made an effort, and I think it was Marjorie's raspberry mousse and not the salad dressing that gave us all a slight case of the bends the next day — or else it was the insidious Maple Leap Surprise.

Speaking of the effects of the punch, I don't know when I've seen your mother more lively and flirtatious. She was so enthusiastically engaged in conversation with Austin at one point that she knocked the sparkling spectacles off his nose, and they flew half way across the room, landing on Davina's lap — rather a thrill for Davina who, until that point, had been too shy to introduce herself. The two of them, Davina and Austin, had a great old literary chin-wag later in the evening, and Davina was over the moon to learn that Austin had read her book *Wild Bores and Other Whores*, which won the Southwestern British Columbia Poetry Prize last year. I asked him if he'd had time to read my poem and he said he didn't know I "wrote verse." That's what he called it — "writing verse." Davina's eyebrows shot up at that. He looks more like a banker than a poet with his polished specs and gleaming breast-pocket handkerchief. By the way, he does not share Davina's belief that the flame of poetry burns in each of us. They had quite a cheerful little row about this that was on the point of escalating when Jessica came along and loudly commandeered the conversation.

Now what can I say about Jessica? That she is a mite over-whelming? Certainly it is the first time in years that I've been slapped so hard on the back I began to cough. "If you're the famous Chas," she said — we hadn't met at that point — "I want to give you my congrats." Naturally I asked why. "Because you're not a godamn phallocrat like the rest of the pigs I run into." Phallocrat? I learned it was French for male chauvinist, and that I was being congratulated

not for my solarium, as I had thought, but for volunteering
myself as house-husband for a year and not making a
goddamn martyr of myself. I warmed to her, hearing this. I
warmed even further as she sang *your* praises. What can
be higher praise than being called a brick, as in "Jock is a
good goddamn brick"? (I could tell she too had been to the
punchbowl.)

   It was interesting to see how Davina and Jessica got
along. (They had met once before, apparently, at a feminist
conference in Toronto.) Their girth was remarkably similar,
but their approach to feminism was radically different —
or so they both seemed eager to inform me. Jessica, for
instance, can easily imagine a world without men, something that Davina finds unthinkable. They were about to go
at it hammer and tongs when Yvette came along — what
a coy little mouse she is — and said that George had acci-
dentally locked himself in the bathroom. (You'll remember
we've always had trouble with that lock.) I went to look
for you, but you were in the den wiping up the wine, and
so I went out to the shed — by now it was raining — to
get the step-ladder. And who should I encounter but
Marjorie Finstead, semi-unclothed, dancing on the lawn
and singing what seemed to be an original new version of
"Roll Me Over in the Clover" — all to the delight of your
buddies Vance and Austin, and my boss, Talbot Sanderson,
who were cheering her on from the carport. (And you
thought Marjorie was a wet blanket.) Gus, apparently, was
less than amused, and went home early in a huff — that
is to say, 2:30 or so — which is why Marjorie stayed
overnight, making herself a little bed out of cushions
and curling up in a corner of the solarium beside your
mother. No doubt you tripped over them on your
way out.

All in all, I would call it one of our more interesting parties, and I was glad the dreary Ticknows, etc., hadn't come. Naturally I grew increasingly large-headed during the evening hearing the comments about the solarium and skylight — even you seemed pleased with the final effect, though we didn't have much chance to discuss it. And the good news is that Talbot Sanderson phoned this morning saying he and Joy had a ball at the party and that they liked the solarium so much they'd like me to design one for them. (How's that! An architect's architect!) Needless to say, I didn't bother telling them that the design for ours had been dictated by what was available at the wrecker's. So as soon as I finish the plans for Gil, I'll get busy on some ideas for the Sandersons — Talbot says they're willing to put twenty-five thousand into it, so I'll have a lot more leeway.

Poor Gil. He'll be in the hospital for a couple of weeks, since the doctor decided they might as well "do" his prostate while they're realigning his jaw. Do you think you'd have time to drop him a get-well card? It would mean the world — he's worried that you might have taken offence at the rabbit joke he told. For the moment, at least, I've managed to talk him out of bringing charges against Vance. I don't suppose you could get Vance to drop him a little note of apology? It might help soothe the old self-esteem feathers.

It's taken us all of two days to clean up after the party, but it was worth it. The kids pitched in and helped. Mia slept through the whole bash — ah, youth! — and Greg's comment as he came in at two o'clock, dodging Marjorie in the yard, was, "I can hardly wait to be an adult."

When did you go to bed? — it must have been early. Between your early retreat and my sleeping in, there wasn't much hope for our getting together. Do you think we could

manage a weekend soon — before I go crazy? What about
Winnipeg? I've always wondered what Winnipeg had to offer
in February.

My darling, my lovely brick, I send you love and kisses,
Your,
Chas

P.S. Thanks for the fax number. Sanderson's doesn't object to
our using it for emergencies.

FAX
3 FEBRUARY

MY POEM ACCEPTED FOR PUBLICATION BY CAPILANO
REVIEW. PAYMENT FIVE DOLLARS. THIS IS ECSTASY.
CHAS

4 Old Town Lane
Ottawa, Ont.
Feb. 5

Dear Chas,

After I read your letter filling me in on the missing parts
of the Selby orgy, I had a few second thoughts — wondered if
maybe we had shocked a few people — but Austin laughed so
hard over your description of how Van got his black eye that
he had to wipe his spotless glasses. Then when I read out a
few other selected episodes from your letter, such as the bit
about Marjorie Finstead's dance — which, by the way, he

thought was one of the most exhilarating spectacles he's ever seen — he grabbed a pen and in the space of three minutes dashed off a poem "To Marjorie":

> Under the boughs of the hemlock tree,
> Minus her bra danced Marjorie.
> I cheered and clapped, old foolish satyr,
> And when the bra fell, though I'd hoped they'd be fatter,
> I hid my chagrin and stepped forward to pat 'er.

I don't think I'd appreciated before how bizarre the whole thing must have seemed to somebody like Austin. I told him it hadn't been quite what I'd expected either, how I had envisaged a civilized and more or less intellectual gathering rather than a brawl, but he pointed out that civilized and intelligent people can't be counted on in a confrontation with Maple Leap Surprise Punch.

And here's something that'll rock you — Austin *wasn't* being patronizing about Mother. Mother reads all the literary criticism she can get her hands on; you know how the apartment is always awash in *New York Times Book Review*, *Commentary*, the *Saturday Review of Literature*, etc. Well, according to Austin, she has "very well thought-out insights and a singularly sophisticated grasp of the nuances of the modern poets." I'll be damned.

Odd, isn't it? Here I've always gone around feeling superior to Mother's "fuzzy thinking," and putting her love of poetry down to retreating, the kind that could be expected of women of her generation.

As for Austin's ability to write poetry, I just thought it was an amusing sort of secondary talent that ranked behind his truly important achievements in statistics and economics. But he says not. Being a poet is more important and more difficult for him than those other "computer-brained" skills. He says poetry is what distinguishes a man from his calculator and — get this, but don't let it go to your head — he says your designs are "poetry materialized."

Yes, he *loves* the skylight and solarium. He says the creative urge is like a bubble of helium in the bottom of our heads that tries and tries to rise to the surface, but can't make itself heard for the incessant babbling of the legalistic layer of the brain. (Only he didn't mix his metaphors.) And that if anyone were to ask him what is the meaning of life — and evidently the odd freshman still does — he would have to say that it is bringing into consciousness those ancient and primitive stirrings that are the building blocks of creativity. By doing so one gradually realizes the self, and that is the purpose of life. (All this has left me a tiny bit bewildered. I don't have that kind of mind, and I don't even know if I know what he's talking about. I find all the fulfilment my brain can handle in the logic of law, and the last time I was creative was when I made the stuffed kangaroos that leaked.)

I wonder if any of these insights could be brought to bear on *our* problems? I agree we need something brought to bear before we both die of near-celibacy (especially if it's fatal, and sometimes I feel as though it might be). Sorry about the lack of opportunity in Vancouver — I hadn't expected to have to work right up until the party. Speaking of lack of opportunity, why in heaven's name did Greg come storming into our bedroom hunting for dental floss at four-thirty in the morning? His timing was impeccable. *Where* is he till those hours? FIND OUT!

Why, you may ask (probably are), is the Commission so frantically busy all of a sudden? Because Van thinks the Prime Minister will call an election, and he's worried about the future of his report. If the election were called before the

Commission is finished, what would become of all our work? A sorry waste. Austin says it could all go down the drain — to hell with the poor in Canada if they get in the way of political expediency!

Van is being pressured to run for the presidency of the Liberal Party, and I can't help wondering if I might be appointed to fill the vacancy. I've got a lot of background now. You know, Chas, I'm kind of surprised — now this is going to sound conceited, perhaps — but I've discovered something quite unsuspected about myself. I'm really good at this job! I guess I hadn't really believed I would stack up this well in the Big Time, but tonight it hit me, I do stack up, I do! I honestly believe I'd be an A-one commissioner! (What do you think of that?)

But of course they might want a man. George could be a possibility — if that happened, I'd be pretty miffed. On the other hand, it would mean extending the contract and being away from home another few months. These things have a way of stretching on, as you know.

Anyway, Chas, our schedules are being pushed forward and it does look as though we'll be in Winnipeg toward the end of the month. As for what Winnipeg is like, the reports aren't great, but Ottawa's no great shakes in February either. If we can afford it — with these new solarium commissions of yours — do you think you could come and spend the weekend with me there? I'll let you know the dates as soon as they're firm. Yes, we do need time together. Alone.

Yours,
Jock

P.S. Mother and Marjorie slept in the solarium? How did I miss that?

P.P.S. I've been trying to phone you but I keep getting a recording about the number no longer being in service. What's up?

29 Sweet Cedar Drive
North Vancouver, B.C.
9 February

Dear Jock,

Question: did you or did you not get my fax telling you about the acceptance of my poem in the *Capilano Review*? I am unwilling to, I *can't* believe that you could have received this news and failed to respond to it. Respond, hell! — not even a comment. Do you know how hard it is to get poetry published these days? (Ask your pal Austin.) Do you know that the *Capilano Review* gets more than a hundred unsolicited manuscripts every month? Do you know how rare it is for someone to get a first poem accepted? And in case you think the *Capilano Review* is a smeary little photocopy passed out on street corners by bulgy-eyed indigents, let me tell you that it is large, glossy, and respectable, and can be found in libraries across the country.

Good God, I know you're busy. I know you're occupied with Jessica and Vance and "what Austin says," but for crissake, we're your family and we'd like the odd stroke now and then. No, stroke isn't the word. I'd settle for a breezy "well done" or even, Lord help us, *felicitations*. (Davina, out of her tiny income, bought me a bottle of *faux* champagne. Your two children took their old dad out for a Big Mac!)

I know, I know — I sound like a big baby begging for attention, and maybe that's just what I am, but I sent that fax because I wanted to share with you the one golden plum that's dropped from heaven for me in the last year. I really wanted you to have a bite of it too. It seems to me you wrote (a few letters back) that you needed me to applaud and appreciate the new "legitimate" you. What about the other shoe, the other foot? Please write. Please tell me the fax got lost, that someone forgot to pass it on. (Actually, the more I think of it, the more I think this is probably what happened.)

Let's change the subject. Things have been more than frantic lately. Last night was Mia's ballet recital, four hours of whirling bunnies, fairies, leprechauns, and autumn leaves, and just as I thought my brain was turning to fudge, in came our lovely daughter as the East Wind and stole the show. The costume worked out fine. Marjorie Finstead must have sewn on about a thousand sequins — maybe you should drop her a little thank-you note or something. Unfortunately the side stitches came out at the last minute and so we had to staple her into it, but it looked terrific. Oh, she was lovely. I'll send snaps as soon as I get them back — I took a whole roll. (Greg had said he'd try to come, but then he pulled off one of his typical no-shows.)

You asked me to find out where he spends his time. I *have* had a couple of showdowns with him, but he is an expert at changing the subject, and I find myself less than willing to pursue it — do I really want to know where he hangs out and with whom? No, no, no. How about writing to him yourself, maybe going at him sideways?

I go over to the hospital to see Gil most afternoons and sometimes in the evenings. I seem to be his sole visitor. (By the way, did you get a card off to him?) He's a little low at the moment, ever since the doctors found something leaky in one of his arteries. They want to keep him in hospital until it's checked out — could be another few weeks. I can't even get him to rise to the government's defence these days, and when I asked him if he wanted anything to read, he said he'd like a Bible. Old Gil, who hasn't been inside a church since his wedding in 1932. I looked all over for a Bible in his house and ours — and in the end went out and bought one. I hope to hell he doesn't want me to read it to him.

Better go. I've got my new poem to solidify by tomorrow.

Love,

Chas

P.S. When I mentioned Winnipeg I was thinking of just you and me — not the goddamn Commission.

P.P.S. Seems I forgot to pay the phone bill. Now I have to go across town to put down another deposit — I'll let you know as soon as we get a new number. Incredibly sticky, aren't they?

4 Old Town Lane
Ottawa, Ont.
Feb. 12

Dear Chas,

Of course I'm pleased about the poem, and of course I got the fax. Look, dear one, I'm sorry if I've been insensitive (and Sue and Davina haven't, lucky you), so send me a copy, I don't seem to have the one you say you gave me. I promise to show it to Austin. I wonder if he's heard of the *Capilano Review?* (Is that all they pay, five bucks!!!)

I did try to phone last night when I got home (about eleven, eight o'clock your time), but guess you haven't paid the bill yet. (I thought there was a three-month leeway? Surely you've paid since I left.) Anyway, Jessica dragged me off to her group home. She thinks I'm a good influence on Jean (remember Jean?), who — it was bound to happen — is tied up with a man who's exploiting her, at least in Jessica's view.

I can't believe that Jean's unemployment pittance would inspire fortune-hunting, and the male in question seems like your standard unemployed tight-jeaned leather-jacketed youth *avec moto*. (The moto is temporarily in hiding in the group-home basement where neither sleet nor snow nor frost of night can mar its shiny surface. He spends a lot of time down there moping over it — moped moping? — and muttering about moving to Vancouver and — get this — looking you up.) Anyway, Jessica seems to think Jean identifies with me as a sort of role-model, and I've been trying to steer her — gently — to the self-fulfilment to be found in a career in dental hygiene (an unlikely vocational longing to which she blushingly confessed).

"I don't dig that dental hygiene crap, Jean, let's you and me get the fuck outta here" — this from Norm, the motor-cycle threat, a viewpoint with which I am not entirely unsympathetic. (Except that he forgets the obvious: Tricia, the baby, who is now crawling.) At that point I had already said approximately three chapters more on the subject of dental hygiene than I cared to say, so, with my blessing, Jean and Norm finally roared off into the night in Jessica's Volkswagen — the motorcycle too precious to be exposed — and Jessica and I put Tricia to bed.

Funny thing, while I was getting some Kleenex for Jessica in her room I noticed an enlarged black-and-white photo of four young people — taken years ago judging by their clothes — arms linked, teeth flashing, and did a double take when I recognized Van on the end, thinner, with his hair black and a tad bushier, but otherwise oddly unchanged. And the smiling girl next to him in granny gown and sandals — I never would have recognized Jessica if it hadn't been for the glasses. It came as something of a shock to realize that Jessica without a double chin was actually good looking!

Beside her was a younger version of Austin, also rather unchanged (is it only women who change? Horrors!) He was conservatively dressed, grey flannels, open-necked shirt, tennis racquet in hand; and of course he was — is — older than the others.

I don't know who the other pretty girl was. Jessica caught me looking at the photo and got in a bit of a huff over what she called my snooping nosiness, so I didn't find out anything except that it was taken while she and Van were studying at Harvard and Austin was teaching. All she'd say was, "Isn't it time I took you home?

"On the motorcycle?"

"Oh yeah. I'll walk you there."

"But it's freezing cold, and anyway why are you safer wandering the streets than I am?"

"I don't attract a lot of guys, and besides I've got a black belt in karate." Too bad Van didn't give *Jessica* the shove at our party. Poor Gil! Yes, I will write.

One reason I tried to phone was that I had to make the reservations for Winnipeg or would have missed the deadline for cheap fares, so I've gone ahead and done so. You won't be sharing me with the Commission, I'm just trying to work our reunion around the hearings to save money. The Commission is sitting the week of the 23rd but is not sitting Friday afternoon, so I thought if you were to arrive Thursday night we could have Friday afternoon, Saturday, and Sunday.

I do hope that suits you. It would cost the moon to cancel, and I only did it because you said you wanted to meet in Winnipeg. We get Thursday night free at the Westin, courtesy of the government, and I think I can get the government rate for us for the entire weekend. Phone at once if you can't make it, but we should try, we have a lot of catching up to do.

                                        Jock

P.S. I had to have a new pair of boots and went and bought *purple* ones. What do you think?

P.P.S. Thrilled about Mia's ballet recital. God, how I wish I could have been there! I've written to her.

29 Sweet Cedar Drive
North Vancouver, B.C.
16 February

Dear Jock,

Hold your hat, Jock, I've got some exciting news! As of yesterday I am no longer working at Sanderson's. I can't tell you what a high it gave me to go in there and put my letter of resignation on Talbot's desk. I confess, it was even more pleasurable to listen to his protests — he immediately offered me full-time hours and more interesting work, but for once I was able to stick to my guns. He thinks I'm off my head to be going into business at a time like this (so does your mother, so does *my* mother), and it *is* a risk. On the other hand, I figure there's not much to lose and maybe something to win. I've already landed two more solarium jobs — one from a guy who was driving by the house last week and stopped in to ask who my architect was. (He lives over in Shaughnessy, has money to burn.) The second client came through the salvage-yard people where I'm getting most of my glass. I've decided

to start small and stay small, strictly a one-man office. (I figure you'll be able to do the books and correspondence next
year, and for the time being I'm doing it myself.) I found a
dirt-cheap office location over on Mountain Highway — just
one filthy room, but wait till you see it tranformed!

My financial backer is — are you ready for this? — Greg.
Your son, Greg. Right away he took to the idea of the business, said it was time I stopped being a draftsman at half-pay,
and he let it be known that he had some money in the bank
that he'd like to invest. How much? I said. A little over two
thou, said he. (I feigned surprise.) I admit I didn't pin him
to the wall and ask how he happened to have twenty-five
hundred, nor did he volunteer any information; the two of us
danced like a couple of boxers over this, but then signed a
proper legal contract with Sue as our witness. (Sue, by the
way, thinks the solarium madness is catching on out here
because people feel confined, politically and spiritually, by the
spaces society has crammed them into.) We celebrated with
champagne — second bottle this week — and tried to phone
you (from pay phone) with the good news, but couldn't reach
you. (I'll get onto the phone bill right away.)

I'll miss the regular money coming in, but in two or
three months we should be seeing a profit. Meanwhile I've
rented our basement room to Sue, who got booted out of her
apartment Saturday — some heartless expropriation order
— and that provides us with a little additional income, plus
free cleaning. (No doubt your Jessica would regard this trade-
off as a choice morsel of male exploitation, but why shouldn't
people buy and sell with their skills as well as their cash?)

Great news about Winnipeg! I'll be there with bells on
(and parkas and mukluks). *All* shed-able.

Love,

Chas

P.S. Who the hell are Jean and Norm?

P.P.S. Of course you're good at your job — can't figure out why you're surprised. From what I've heard, royal commissions aren't too taxing, mentally. You're probably doing twice as much as they expected. I think the last thing you'd want is to actually be *on* the thing.

4 Old Town Lane

Ottawa, Ont.

Feb. 18

Dear Chas,

YOU QUIT YOUR JOB?

SUE IS LIVING IN OUR HOUSE?

Really, Chas, I may be liberated and I think I am, and reasonably trusting, but haven't you got the brains to see how Sue in the basement must appear to outsiders? Especially to the talented sequin-sewer across the way? (God, I hate to be beholden to her, but yes, I'll drop a note.) I *don't want* somebody, anybody, in our basement, and besides, after I'm home, where will you have your drafting table? You can hardly expect it to stay on in the kitchen — where does Sue *eat* by the way?

How could you quit your job *without even discussing it with me first?* When my stint here is over we won't necessarily *have* that extra support base of my income. Lawyers are starving in B.C. in case you haven't heard. Is there enough money in solariums to send two children to expensive universities? A province on the edge of recession probably has only a limited market for frills such as solariums — you may well have tapped the entire market spectrum already. And Talbot Sanderson offered you a good job! — I don't know what to think, but I do know that your breezy assumption that I'd be able to do the books and correspondence made me damn mad. I am, believe it or not, considered something of an expert in my field now — labour law as it applies to women, the effect of the constitutional changes on that field, the application of the Charter of Rights, the rights of children before the law, to name a few — and I haven't discovered in me (or even looked for, for that matter) any real expertise in bookkeeping or secretarial work. What about Sue, whose talents and dedication seem limitless?

We're suffering a communication gap, that's obvious. I'm glad we've scheduled the time in Winnipeg — we have a lot to thrash out.

Jock

P.S. Very strange about Greg, but if he's that above-board about the money he must have acquired it legally, don't you think? A prize at school perhaps? Why don't you insist on an answer?

P.P.S. FIX THE PHONE!

FAX
18 FEBRUARY

UNABLE TO REACH YOU BY PHONE. GIL GROGAN DIED THIS MORNING. FUNERAL MONDAY.

CHAS

Chas —

Gil dead! I can't believe it! I'm staggered, and I feel, I don't know, vulnerable. What I mean is, it's so casual, so sort of accidental . . . almost careless, as though a life doesn't count for anything, as though a man were no more than a beetle. Gil gone! It doesn't seem possible.

I tried to get you as soon as I got your fax, but still no phone. (I'm getting very friendly with that recorded message.)

Austin and I had to work late, that's why you couldn't get me. Austin is doing some revising for George who is away skiing. (George has been more than sweet lately, asking me about legal points and so on — I think I've misjudged him.)

Anyway, after your news about Gil I was so shaken that Austin suggested I come back to his place for a nightcap. How I blessed him! I dreaded the thought of going back to my little apartment alone.

He lives along Bronson within walking distance of the Hill in an old mansion that's been converted into two huge and lovely apartments. His is the upstairs one — a bay window looking onto the city and, at the back, glass doors that lead onto a balcony overlooking the Ottawa River. The apartment is furnished in a rather masculine style — I don't get the feeling there's been a woman in his life, at least not for some time — roomy leather chairs and footstools and books lining the walls, and huge stereo speakers. It turns out he's a Mozart addict, too, and has the same recording of the Fortieth as we do.

I was feeling a little numb, and the music helped. So did a good shot of Scotch. "It's frightening the way it jumps out at us," Austin said finally. He meant death. "Like a macabre jack-in-the-box."

I nodded and stared out at the city lights.

"Are you thinking about Gil Grogan?" he asked. "Or about death?"

That stopped me for a minute. "Death," I said at last, and felt a wave of shame. "I suppose that sounds selfish?"

"Not unless you're aspiring to sainthood."

He went on to say that there's a school of thought that believes all our myths as well as our neuroses are mechanisms for the denial of death.

"More dignified than the Freudian mechanisms," I said, and then asked him if he believed that. He shrugged and said he suspected it was another case of the blind men and the elephant, that all the theories are right and all of them wrong.

Then I asked him something that had been worrying the life out of me ever since your fax came, whether the dust-up with Van at the party could have contributed to Gil's death.

He shook his head and told me I was hunting for reasons. If we can lay blame it doesn't seem so random.

How are *you* coping, darling Chas? I know you'd come to care for poor old Gil — did you worry after the party? Do you think it aided and abetted at all?

Oh, Lord, I feel guilty that I never dropped him that note.

I tried again to phone you last night as soon as I got in — midnight our time — but no phone. I'll be in hearings all day, so will mail this and perhaps you could phone some time this weekend. There's no chance of my getting home for the funeral, I'm afraid. We leave for Winnipeg Monday morning.

Looking forward to our love-in. We need it, we need it.

Love,

Jock

29 Sweet Cedar Drive
North Vancouver, B.C.
23 February

Dear Jock,

Of course I understand about why you couldn't make
it for Gil's funeral. Sweetie, you mustn't blame yourself.
You were tied up (which is inevitable when you sign your
life over to the bureaucracy) so stop tormenting yourself.
Besides, what does it matter? Poor old Gil was a jar of ashes
by that time and wasn't going to know if you were there
or not.

And of course Gil's death had nothing to do with that
poke in the jaw. (By the way, Vance sent Gil a dodgey little
note of apology a couple of weeks ago, very gentlemanly,
very Westmount: "afraid we were all a little heated, etc.")
No, the fact is, Gil died of post-operative heart failure, and it
was something no one could have foreseen, except perhaps
Gil himself, who left me a little letter of farewell.

I'm just sorry I lashed out at you on the phone. The
minute I uttered all that rubbish about priorities and values
and so on I wanted to take it back — proof to me, by the
way, that letters are a better means of communication than
phone calls, more rational, more reflective, somehow fairer.
Which is why I'm writing this c/o the Westin where I'll be
seeing you Thursday night.

What a dreary little procession we made — just Gil's
daughter from California, two or three fellow curmudgeons
from the Vancouver Club, and our family, including Sue
Landis and The Mothers. *Naturally* it was raining. *Naturally*
the wind was blowing like fury. The minister droned on about
God's forgiveness, though Gil's only sin as far as I could see
was his over-subscription to the free-enterprise system —

and we finished off around the crypt with a wobbly version of "Rock of Ages." Back here at the house afterwards there was more joyous fare. (In Gil's farewell message — he must have had premonitions going into surgery — he left me the contents of his wine cellar, also a substantial cheque for the drawing I'd done for his renovation — alas, never now to be executed.)

The house is up for sale already — the California daughter seemed anxious to "liquefy" everything as quickly as possible — and yesterday there were people trooping through all day. God, it's going to be quiet around here without the old bugger dropping in.

When I phoned Davina to explain why I wouldn't be in class, she suggested I try to get some of my thoughts onto paper, and that's what I've been doing tonight, or at least trying to do. But for some reason I can't get a focus on it. I wanted to write a few dignified lines, just a simple lament for a friend, but it's turning into something long and maniacal about how little life boils down to in the end — just a handful of acquaintances standing in the rain and trying to sing an unsingable hymn. (Try it if you don't believe me.)

By the way, I thought you'd be glad Sue was living here. We can use the rent money, and besides we're back on green vegetables again after months of frozen corn niblets and eggplant by-products. Maybe I should have explained that she's only perching here temporarily. There are plenty of apartments available, but the prices have stayed high, and so until her job is reinstated she's finding it tough to make ends meet.

Actually I'm damn glad she'll be here while I'm in Winnipeg, because it was something of a problem to know what to do with Mia. Your mother said she'd love to have her except that she has a heavy bridge tournament on, and

I had grave doubts about sending her over to my mother, who says she can't imagine why on earth I want to go to Halifax in the middle of the winter. She's getting muzzier by the day, and I don't want Mia to have to cope with muzziness. The Finsteads offered to have her for the weekend, but for some reason Mia got a bit squirrelly about that and said she'd rather stay home. Naturally I couldn't leave her here with Greg, since he continues his late-night rambles. Sue's being here suddenly solved all the problems, and the two of them get on like a house afire.

I'm working every spare minute trying to get the new office on Mountain Highway in shape. We're hoping to have an official opening a week today — just a few friends and potential clients. Davina came up with a terrific name: The Sun Spot. What do you think? I've already moved my drafting table over there, so you don't have to worry about it cluttering up *your* kitchen any longer. I never intended that you indenture yourself to the business, though I do think your legal background will come in handy, since most people have to get city permission to build any kind of extension. I've gambled a couple of hundred bucks on printed posters, just a line drawing with a caption that reads, "You Owe Yourself a Place in the Sun." Very snappy, I think. We expect a good response.

And that brings me around again to Winnipeg. Just four more days. Do you know how long this celibate season has been? Yes, I'm sure you do. I liked your joke about abstinence making the heart grow fonder, but think we've had more than enough of that. Until then,

Chas

P.S. If the *Cap Review* turns down my "Goodbye to Gil" poem, maybe I'll try the *New Yorker*.

29 Sweet Cedar Drive
North Vancouver, B.C.
1 March — Sunday afternoon

Dear Jock,

Well, we seem to have arrived at that well-publicized dark night of the soul. (Davina would call this an inadmissible cliché, but have you noticed that all things worth saying seem to come in cliché form? Like "communication gap," "conflict of roles," "crossroads of life," "end of the road," and so on and on.)

All right then, let's settle for something like "an unwillingness to admit that we are drifting (have drifted) apart and all because of this goddamn-Ottawa-job-that-was-thrust-on-us." No, scratch out all of the above and put back "dark night of the soul."

Actually, if truth be told, the dark night of the soul is nothing compared to the dark night of Portage and Main where I cooled my heels Thursday night after trying (and failing) to persuade the dodo manager at the Westin Hotel that no, I was not a member of the Commission, but yes, I was a bona-fide spouse with squatter's rights to the room reserved in your name. Oh, well, you know the whole outrageous scenario and its expensive conclusion. A hundred and twenty bucks down the drain. On top of my plane fare.

And then there were the uncounted quarters I dropped into the pay phone trying to find out where the hell you were. When I finally got through and discovered you'd left Winnipeg and *gone back to Ottawa*, I was fairly stunned. And just because the PM called an election! My God, Jock, what does the merry-go-round of Ottawa politics have to do with our private lives? Christ, what's happened to your sense of priorities? You *knew* I was getting in on Thursday. We'd had it planned for two weeks. Just you and me holed up in the Westin, remember? (Your own phrase.) We were going to have some time together, straighten a few things out, cast off our chastity chains, try to get our lives back on track, maybe even laugh a little and relax — God knows, I need some time to relax after these last few months of mothering/fathering and the strain of Gil's death — an event, by the way, that I don't quite believe in yet.

I've already told you about my miserable Friday in Winnipeg, so I won't bore you with a recital of that. Just let me say that walking the windy metropolitan streets in February (minus 39° Celsius) only half chilled the anger I was feeling. I tried, as I ducked my way along Main Street, to do some of the meditation exercises Sue's been teaching me. (They seem to work at home; I thought I might be getting an ulcer, but it's settling down.) But eastern philosophy and gale-force winds (carrying strange, gritty little bits of ice and dirt) are seemingly incompatible. The snow blowing across the width of Portage Avenue seemed a betrayal. People with their heads and faces wrapped in scarves seemed a betrayal. The Winnipeg Art Gallery, pushing unthrottled German expressionism, seemed a betrayal. Shoppers crowding into The Bay for a "pre-spring sale" seemed *destined* for betrayal. The one decent bookstore in town was closed for inventory — another betrayal. There was betrayal in the chop-suey I spooned up in a Notre Dame cafeteria and more betrayal at the Marlboro where I stopped for a cup of warming coffee.

The only peaceful moment all day came as I sat in a soft swivel seat at the planetarium watching a simulated journey to Mars — in the middle of which I inexplicably fell asleep. But not for long. A cross-looking girl in a blue uniform poked me in the shoulder and asked if I was unwell. "Yes, I am unwell," I told her truthfully, and then dragged back to my eighty-buck room (at least it was comfortable) to fume and glower. (Sue grew up in Winnipeg and loves it; I thought I was going to love it too.)

By the time you got back to Winnipeg on Saturday — and I can't even fathom why you came all that way for one piddling night — I was past the point of functioning, as you know. Also slightly drunk and more than slightly enraged. And what else? Oh, yes, I was struck dumb by the way you teetered across the airport in those purple boots and then delivered a one-ounce peck on the old grizzled husbandly cheek.

Can you begin to imagine how I felt? I felt like a daft old dear who was being showered with a few minutes of his wife's valuable (and chargeable) time. Perhaps you expected me to shudder with gratitude, but I was past the point of shuddering. As a matter of fact, I was past the point of anything as you were soon to discover. And your words of greeting — "You look awful" — Christ! Not exactly a phrase that sings to the spirit . . . or to the hormones.

I'm sending this special delivery because I think it's time we put our befuddled heads together and said, fuck the Commission and fuck this business of living at opposite ends of the country. We're on the fucking path to disaster, for God's sake, and we've got a couple of kids and a couple of dozen years at stake here.

                                 Chas

And fuck the purple boots too.

4 Old Town Lane
Ottawa, Ont.
Mar. 4

Dear Chas,

I don't blame you for being furious. Spending all day
Friday and most of Saturday by yourself in a town where the
temperature was hovering around forty below, Fahrenheit *and*
Celsius — curse the damn cheap air fares and their implaca-
bility! In the end if you'd flown full fare and been able to cancel, it would have cost less than my having to pay full fare for
one overnight in Winnipeg.

I'm truly sorry. How could anyone guess that the Prime
Minister would choose *February* to call an election? And that
Van would go into an unholy panic and cut the hearings short
and drag us all back to Ottawa Thursday? As it is, he blew up
when he found that the reason I couldn't work Saturday night
was because I was returning to Winnipeg.

All for another sexual disaster! And yet I don't think
there's a thing I could have done about it. Remember those
sci-fi stories where the earth goes through bad vibes in space
and everyone's IQ goes up (or is it down?). I feel as though
my life is going through bad vibes in space right now — not
just between us, but everywhere. There's an enormous
amount of tension in the Commission, since everything
hinges on whether Van will or won't take on the Liberal Party
election chairmanship. (He is considered the guru of elec-
tioneering, but unless he resigns from the Commission he'll
have to stay right out of it.)

He rushes into the hearings distracted and half an hour
late and only half listens to the briefs, interjecting the occasional curt, "Get on with it," or, "Your point, for heaven's sake.
Your point!" One woman got so rattled she dropped her

specs and they smashed and she couldn't see the brief and she burst into tears. Jessica jumped up and right in front of everyone said, "Jeezus, Vance, earn your fucking pay for Christ's sake!" and swept down onto the floor, patted the woman on the arm, sailed back up to her chair with the unfinished brief and proceeded to read it aloud very very slowly, "enunciating every word as though holding a marble in the mouth," as old Witherspoon in the Drama Club used to say.

It's become an uncomfortable pattern. Van hurries the questioning along, then, needless to say, Jessica baits him by meandering on and on. When we're finished he shoots out of the committee room and runs (literally) back to his office where there is a steady stream of Liberal heavies waiting to see him, seemingly truly convinced that the party will go down the tube without Van.

The other unsettling thing is that George hopes he'll be appointed to fill the vacancy if Van goes, with Austin or Jessica moving up to chairman. As I said before, that would make me more than somewhat angry. After all, I've been here since the beginning, and George isn't as qualified as I am. (Master's degree in English, lots of political speech writing sure doesn't stack up beside a law degree and expertise in the particular field being studied, do you think? Tell me honestly — could it be that they just don't think I could handle it?)

When I hinted to Jessica that I'd like it she just said, "Jeez, Jock, of course you won't get it. I'm the token woman. What the hell would the male chauvinist establishment appoint two for?" Nevertheless, she's working against George on principle, so I guess she thinks I could do it.

Mind you, Jess isn't exactly disinterested herself. She thinks she should be chair, but Austin is a formidable opponent, and actually Austin *would* be better. His guts aren't in the issue the way Jess's are, but I think a bit of detachment isn't a bad thing, and besides he'd bring dignity to the post, dignity not being Jess's long suit. But I suppose I should support Jessica for the sake of feminism. Reverse discrimination?

Austin is the only one who seems unaffected by all this. He minds his own business, but when I asked him point blank, he admitted that ambition is as potent a driver and power as tempting a goal for him as for anyone else. It's just that he tries to keep the demons in their place, since in the long run they're more likely to destroy than reward their possessor. ("Ask the Macbeths if you don't believe me." Austin.)

He's the only one I still feel the old camaraderie towards — I care a lot for Jessica, of course, but her boiling point is so near the surface right now that everyone has to duck. As an example, when Jean admitted that she isn't as fulfilled by dental hygiene as she thought she'd be, Jessica tore such a strip off her that poor Jean doesn't dare quit.

I wish I could be like Austin, but I can't. It would be exciting actually to be *on* the Commission. And it isn't just power hunger, in case that's what you're thinking. I often sit there and think of the questions I'd like to put to the people who appear before us, and the things I'd like to stress in the report. We're finally zeroing in on the factors that are keeping women out of the boardrooms (except to clean them), and I think I may have uncovered a contributing bias in the tax system. When I pointed it out, Van was actually stopped in his tracks for all of two minutes.

But if I did get the appointment, I know it would mean more time away from home and of course that worries me. But it would mean more money for weekend visits, and — oh, hell, I don't know. I just can't help yearning after it. In spite of what it might do to us. And already has.

I know how angry you are, Chas, and I do hope you understand how helpless I feel. I love my home and miss it, and it goes without saying that I love the children (I'm thrilled that Mia wants to come for school break). When we're back together as a family the rift will heal itself. Won't it? And maybe in the end we'll be closer than ever; maybe our individual "stretch marks" will join up into one great encircling unbreakable rubber band. When Mother and Dad were separated for four years during the war, they must have started over again on faith — surely we can do the same after a mere ten months? Anyway, faith isn't all we have. We had a lot going for us before; surely we haven't changed enough to erase the happiness of twenty years?

I can't say any more for now. I don't know how.

If by chance I *am* offered the place on the Commission, I promise at least a week alone with you before I accept it. And if I did go for it, we'd be able to afford Hawaii with the kids for Christmas.

Oh, I can hardly wait for Mia's visit!

Love,

Jock

P.S. I love you, but I also feel torn in two. Yes, this is a dark night of the soul.

P.P.S. Sorry I made that crack about double-bolting the basement door while Sue is there, but honestly, Chas, how can you be so naive? Get her out, we have enough troubles.

P.S. 3 Just to give you an idea of the level to which rivalry has plunged us, yesterday a woman came before the Commission and analysed her welfare cheque down to the last penny to show why she'd had to go bootless all winter. George leaned over and whispered to me, "Give her the Purple Persuaders, Jock. You won't need them in Vancouver."

29 Sweet Cedar Drive
North Vancouver, B.C.
6 March

Dear Jock,

I'm sitting here in the solarium shaking with disbelief. Possibly you can feel the force of the vibrations in Ottawa. The glass is about to break. All this beautiful glass.

Tell me something, Jock — do you actually read the letters I write to you or do you have your secretary file them away still sealed in their envelopes? (Under H for husband? Has-been?) On March 1st, or thereabouts, I fired off a message to you, a message torn, as they say, out of the breast. If you took the trouble to read it, you would have seen it for what it was: a plea that we stop this celibate stupidity right now and try to get our lives back together again.

But what happens? Today a letter comes from you — I still can't believe it — chattering blithely away about getting a place on the Commission and spending yet *another* year in Ottawa. Christ! Ah, but there is a sop for poor old Chas at home: the promise of a week together, just you and him. (He wonders where you suggest this week of debauchery take place this time — Swift Current? Just so it fits in with the agenda of the Commission.) No, Jock, I will not be bought off with one week of sweetness. It's not enough.

As for Christmas in Hawaii, oh so generously financed by our own lady in Ottawa — I decline. I refuse. I am sick at the thought. *Here* is where we have always spent Christmas. *Here* in the house which we (you and I) bought so that we would have a place where we could celebrate traditional holidays and enshrine our own family ceremonies. *Here together*. Remember together? So for God's sake tell Vance, or Jessica,

or George, or Austin, or whoever the hell's in charge, that
your contract ends in June and that you're coming home.

Chas

P.S. Yes, I know how you feel about Sue living in the basement,
but who else is going to keep an eye on the kids when I'm
over at Mountain Highway? Besides, I can't just boot her out
on the street, especially now that her daughter, Molly, is here.
(Only temporary.) Seems the ex-husband on the Island is up
for some kind of drug charge. Sue says he's not a criminal
type, just a bit thick. Mia, by the way, treats Molly like the kid
sister she's always wanted, is teaching her to ride her bike and
so on — and is spending a lot less time hanging out at the Finsteads breathing in all those poisonous Laura Ashley fumes.

P.P.S. You never said what you thought of the Sun Spot ad.

29 Sweet Cedar Drive
North Vancouver, B.C.
7 March

Dear Jock,

Just a rushed note...I've got a meeting at noon with a
possible new client over in British Properties. Thought I
should warn you that you might be getting a rather weird letter or phone call from Greg. All a tempest in a teapot. Will
write details later. You know how emotional and hot-headed
he's always been. Know you'll take it with a good-sized grain
of salt.

Love,

Chas

PUROLATOR

MR CHARLES SELBY TWENTY-NINE SWEET CEDAR DRIVE
NORTH VANCOUVER BC

MARCH NINE

WHAT TEMPEST IN TEAPOT? AM WORRIED SICK. IS GREG
IN TROUBLE? PHONE DETAILS TOMORROW NINE AM
OTTAWA TIME.

JOCK

29 Sweet Cedar Drive
North Vancouver, B.C.
10 March

Dear Jock,

Got your courier message. Sorry to have left you up in
the air, but I thought Greg would have written. At any rate,
this particular tempest isn't something I felt I could discuss
on the phone. Hence the special delivery.

I do want to let you know exactly what happened the
other night so you won't go leaping to heavy conclusions — if
you *do* hear from Greg, that is. As your mother used to say (or
was it my mother) better to open the window an inch if
you're finding it hard to breathe. Not that I'm suffocating, I
just like to have things out in the open and I know you do too.

So here it is in a nutshell. Davina — remember Davina?
— phoned last Sunday afternoon saying she had good news
and bad news for me. The good news is that she felt very
enthusiastic about the "Goodbye to Gil" poem, and she
wanted to send it to the *Writer's Quarterly*, which, she says, is

a good place to be "showcased," and besides she knows the editor. (The politics of poetry continue to shock me.)

The bad news is that Cap College has sacked Davina. Or, more gently put, they informed her that her course in Creative Connections wouldn't be offered next year. It seems one of the students in our class, a social cretin called Stan (also a mini-gangster and ultimate churl), complained to the department chairman about the course, saying it was unfocused and that it functioned as a therapy play-pen for unstable adolescents and menopausal males (guess who?). None of this would have mattered except that Davina, when asked to explain her teaching methodology, called the chairman a fat-assed shithead, and one thing led to another, with the result that the course has been taken out of the curriculum, for next year anyway.

To cheer her up — and to cheer myself up, too — I asked her if she'd like to go out for dinner at the Fishnet. The house was cold (furnace again) and silent. Sue and Molly were over on the Island for the weekend, Mia was spring skiing with the Finsteads, and Greg was "out," as per usual. Given the situation, a sociable dinner at the Fishnet seemed a not-unreasonable idea, and I felt it was the least I could do for Davina.

I'd forgotten, of course, how crowded that place gets on a Sunday night (you remember how they pack you into that damp little smugglers' bar while they hustle the clientele through their thirty-dollar swordfish steaks). It was nine-thirty before we got a table, and even then we got stuck in a dark corner behind the lobster tank. Until then Davina had been fairly composed. I don't know what it was — maybe the three Deep-Sea Daiquiris she'd had or else the portentous gurgling of giant lobsters — but the minute we were seated at the table she collapsed, all flowing tears and noisy sobbing. (Thank God only the lobsters were within earshot.)

You have to understand that after May 31st of this year

she will have absolutely no means of support. What about her royalties? you'll ask. The fact is, her books bring in about forty bucks a year, that's all. Even if she decided to sell her soul for some two-bit research job, there'd be four or five others ahead of her. The odd waitress job is open, but as Davina said — gasping, sputtering — it's the younger, better-looking women who get those gems. She could apply for a Canada Council grant, but unfortunately she wrote to the council last year and told them to stick it (this after they turned down an application to set haiku to whale music). So here she is, a well-respected Canadian poet in the middle of her life, and she's about to go on unemployment insurance. No wonder she was bawling her eyes out.

You know my feelings about women crying. Swollen eye-lids and trembling chins and blotchy necks do not enchant me. But I confess that on Sunday night I was swamped by sympathy. The world seemed uncommonly cruel, especially when seen through a daiquiri haze, and what I did next I did instinctively. I sort of took her hand in mine and kissed it. Not, I insist, a lover's kiss. It was only a way — and the only way I knew — for one human being to say to another that he knew how lousy she was feeling. Would it sound crazy if I said it was a maternal gesture?

And at that moment I looked up and saw our waiter standing patiently by the table with his notepad in hand. As I said before, we were in an exceedingly dark and cramped corner of the restaurant, and it took me an instant or two to realize that our waiter was Greg. Our son, Greg. The same. And the only thing I could think of to say was, "What the hell are you doing here?"

"What the hell are *you* doing here?" was what he said back to me, and gave Davina a long, cold, shocked-to-the-booties look.

I grabbed his wrist and burbled an explanation about Davina's job and how I was trying to advise her about future plans and so on. But he jerked his hand away and did a fast disappearing act into the kitchen. We waited half an hour but, needless to say, he didn't come back.

I've been trying to explain to him ever since. "I don't want to talk about it," is all he'll say. He hasn't been home for a single meal since last Sunday (though he does come home to sleep — I hear him come in about two.)

At least that's one mystery cleared up — where he spends his nights. Apparently he's been hopping tables at the Fishnet since last October. On our way out of the restaurant — Davina decided she wasn't hungry after all — I asked the hostess about him. "He's one terrific waiter," she said, all a-twinkle. "He's a sweetie." Some sweetie!

What I can't understand is why the kid didn't tell me he had a job. Here I've been lying awake for months, nursing my incipient ulcer and entertaining nightmares about dope rings. I *did* ask him about it, but he seems determined to preserve a chilly (accusing) silence between us. God knows, I can imagine what he thinks. I realize how it must have looked. An intimate late-hour dinner. Tears. And that ridiculous hand-kissing bit on my part. But it can all be so easily explained — if he'd only give me half a chance.

Anyway, I'd better stop writing or you'll think I've gone garrulous with guilt. Which I have not. Emphatically not.

In fact, if I'm feeling guilty about anything, it's this business of appropriating the memory of old Gil — amazing how I miss him! — and making poetic fodder of it. I'm going to phone Davina tomorrow and ask her not to send the poem to that magazine. I've got a feeling that decision will make me feel a little more decent and slightly less corrupt.

Please write, and if you do hear from Greg, which you probably won't, at least you'll know the true story.

Love,

Chas

P.S. I didn't get the contract over in British Properties. We just about had him signed up when his wife piped up with, "I think I'd rather have a sailboat."

Ottawa

Mar. 13

Good God, Chas! Was that all? A hand kiss. Oh, Chas, the relief of finding there was no more than a hand kiss at the heart of this most recent crisis. I'm not sure you can imagine what I've gone through — but never mind, I'm starting to breathe again. I spent several sleepless and wildly imaginative hours Monday night covering the spectrum from car accidents to girl accidents (I never did believe it could be drugs) in anticipation of your early morning phone call, and then after that cryptic, "It's not something I want to entrust to the phone," I put in a whole day of awful waiting. For a *hand* kiss. (Actually, I laughed so hard when I read about the tryst behind the lobsters — call it hysteria, if you like — that Jessica almost succeeded in snatching the letter out of my hand.)

I nearly had *my* hand, or something equivalent, kissed over dinner last night by — guess who? George. Yup, the same George of recent tirades. He asked me to dinner, said he had something important to say, and confessed he'd been unsettled by my coolness lately, had hoped we were friends and wondered what he'd done, etc., etc. He said he'd finally

• 180 •

figured it out when Jessica said to him, "All the muling and puking in the world won't get you on the Commission, Georgie-Peorgie, except over my garrotted bod."

He was obviously sincere, that's the worst of it, and I felt like a dolt, and worse! — an ambitious, paranoid schemer. (Why is it women have trouble scheming ambitiously or accepting themselves in this role?) George says he knows my qualifications outstrip his by miles as well as kilometres, and that he admires and respects my ability, and — shifting gears rather suddenly — did I realize how attractive I was?

Well no, since he asked, not lately. (Especially not lately.) After these sweet words and a bottle of wine my head was turned, I have to admit, which, along with my guilt for having attributed motives to him that he hadn't even contemplated, might have led — well, where things sometimes do lead. I'm rambling, dear Chas, but only because I want to tell you that I do understand how the odd hand gets randomly, innocently kissed. But, objectively, I also can see why it would upset Greg. It's threatening enough to have Mother cavorting about in sin-ridden Ottawa *sans* male protection, without Father orgying it up in lotus-land. Kids' lives have crumbled for less.

And I think I've figured out, too, why Greg didn't tell you he had a job. You know how sensitive he's always been. Well, I think he was maybe a little embarrassed that he was working and you weren't. It touched me in the middle of my heart that he was willing to put up his hard-earned money for the Sun Spot (yes, it's a good name), because he thought you were being exploited by Sanderson's. (Remember how upset he got about your application letter?) I've written to him, stop worrying.

I've been a little worried myself — between hand-kissing crises — about my future with the Commission, not your favourite subject, I'm afraid. I had a long talk with Van the other day about it. Actually, we didn't start off to talk about my future. We were having coffee together, and he asked after the lithesome dancer who entertained us so tantalizingly at the party.

"Marjorie. She's been sewing sequins. For Mia's ballet recital. Chas says she must have sewn about a thousand sequins on the costume." And then I made a somewhat sour remark — I was feeling sour, what with Sue and sundry other unmentionables — about you being well-looked after. "When I'm there *I* sew on sequins and do the cleaning and pay the bills! And hold down a professional job as well." (Sorry about that.)

"A professional job that you are very good at," he said.

My head and heart both swelled with pride, although of course I demurred, pointing out that my expertise would be forgotten by the time I got to Vancouver.

"How fleeting glory!" was all Van said, and then he asked after the glorious redheaded caterer who had ministered so ably to at least some of his needs. "What is her name?"

He hit a nerve. "Sue," I said. Then I sort of shouted (I told you I was upset), "She's well! *Very* well! Why wouldn't she be? She's living in our house!"

"*Mon Dieu!*" Van said. "Now *that's* panache! My hat — all my hats, in fact — are off to your husband."

That made me pretty mad. "It isn't like that, you — you *roué!*" I shouted. "Sue was turfed out of her apartment, she's doing the cleaning to pay for her room."

He grinned and said, "Ah yes. The old room-in-exchange-for-cleaning routine. But if you believe that, my dear, why are you angry? It sounds reasonable to me, especially since it is only a day or two since I heard you worrying about your children."

"It's *not* reasonable. Hasn't Chas got the brains to see

how that looks? I mean, *you* jumped immediately to the obvious conclusion."

"But my dear, I am, as you suggest, a *roué*. A most difficult role in life, but somebody has to do it and it is not without its rewards."

"I can't imagine how your wife tolerates it," I snapped.

"It's quite simple. She has her horses, I have my girls — although for different purposes, at least one hopes so. And our children go to school in Switzerland, where they are looked after well for ten months of the year. When they emerge we try to ensure that we have good help."

"Does your conscience never bother you?" I said (snarled). I was beyond caring by then.

"I have my conscience under control, and I am not about to change — although if I had it to do over I don't think I would be a *roué*. It can be quite taxing, and it leaves little time for other, perhaps more — ah — uplifting pursuits. But you, Jock, you may be about to change."

Before I could ask what he was getting at, he inquired about whether I was enjoying my work on the Commission. I told him I loved every minute of it, and that it is the most ful-filling work I've ever done in my legal career. Maybe even in my life! (This is true, Chas — this work seems to matter in a way that handling divorces or closing real-estate deals in Vancouver never did.)

He then said that, if he decided to leave, he would be more than willing to recommend that I be appointed to the Commission, and that he had every reason to believe that his recommendation would be accepted. "But it would mean at least six months — possibly a year — more in Ottawa."

For an instant I was terribly excited, and then of course I came to my senses. I reminded him, and reminded myself, that I lived in Vancouver.

"Vancouver is a lovely city," he said, "though a bit wet for my taste. However, I doubt that your children would be traumatized irreparably if they were to move. And there are architects' positions about — if you wanted to bring your husband."

"Of course I would want to bring him, why do you say that?"

"It seems so unlikely that one would sacrifice one's freedom — unnecessarily, that is. Catherine almost *never* comes here — but of course Montreal isn't as far as Vancouver." And he sighed rather elaborately.

I told him I didn't think you would want to leave Vancouver. (Of course *I* love Vancouver too — I'm talking temporary.)

"There you are, then," Van said. "I have placed temptation and enlightenment in your path, and you have spurned them both."

"Temptation. I haven't noticed any enlightenment."

"That can come only when you find out what it is you want."

We both got up to go, and then he turned and said — again mysteriously — "I am not an expert on the foibles of human nature, Jock, but it doesn't take too discerning an eye to see that there are wheels within wheels that you aren't yet aware of. As I say, you may find enlightenment — but then again, you may not."

The man talks in riddles. What do you make of it? If anything? But I am excited about the job offer. Not that I could accept it. Could I?

Love,

Jock

P.S. Kiss all Davina's hands you want, but leave Sue's alone.

P.P.S. Austin says you should go ahead and send your poem to a publisher. He says it's a tribute to you and to Gil's memory that you cared enough to write it.

P.P.P.S. PAY THE PHONE BILL!

29 Sweet Cedar Drive
North Vancouver, B.C.
20 March

Dear Jock

Six more months in Ottawa! That is outrageous. What is this guy Pierce up to? Thank God you sent him packing.

This is just a quickie. Off to the salvage yard in a minute in search of glass and then to Davina's place to help her put up some book-shelves. Glad to know you're not thrown by occasional (very occasional) hand kissing.

Greg loved the book you sent and noticed the autograph right away. It was a good birthday all around, though it's hard to believe he's eighteen years old. Sue made him a terrific cake and even left out the carrots for once.

Busy as hell at the office trying to keep up and do some promo at the same time. Haven't even had a minute to work on my new poem.

Cheers,
Chas

P.S. Mia has packed and repacked three times. Will phone after I get her on the plane.

P.P.S. Glad you set the record straight with Pierce. Playing the old enigmatic game — enlightenment and temptation indeed! I wouldn't discuss it with him again if I were you.

P.P.P.S. Expect to get down to the phone company this week and get the phone operating once more. Mia is threatened with excommunication by her peer group.

4 Old Town Lane
Ottawa, Ont.
Mar. 29

Dear Chas,

God, it's great having Mia here! We have a list of things a mile long to do — don't know how we'll ever fit it into one miserable little week. She's greatly excited about the day I've planned in Montreal for shopping (down on the train in the morning and back in the evening). Tour of Parliament Buildings tomorrow. What fun!

Off tonight to Austin's for dinner — can he cook, too? — and to George's tomorrow. Thank heavens Mia's presence is focusing my mind on something besides the bloody Commission! Van *has* to make up his mind soon. The election campaign is getting into full swing and obviously they can't hold off appointing a campaign chairman much longer. Glad Greg liked the book and that you're busy. Will write as soon as I can find a minute.

Mia sends love too, and says to say Hi if you see Laurie.

Jock

Next day.

Finally! Van has, as Greg used to say, made up his vacuum: he
won't be taking on the campaign chairmanship. What a relief!
Now that I know there's no possibility, I wonder why I
thought I wanted to be on the Commission — was it mere
vanity? Probably, but whatever — it all fell away and with not
even *un petit mot de regret. Au contraire!*

29 Sweet Cedar Drive,
North Vancouver, B.C.
2 April

Dear Jock,

Thank God you've come to your senses and given up the
idea of a place on the Commission. Even if it had worked out,
I'm not sure you could have stuck it out with that strange
crew of eccentrics you're with. From Mia's note I gather
that she's less than impressed by your smoothie Senator —
a nit, is how she described him. Seems Allan Fotheringham
shares her opinion. Did you happen to see his last article? I
thought the bit about "silver spoons and honeymoons"
was a rarefied piece of reporting, though the paragraph on
Jessica Slattery was a mite cruel, especially that crack
about her having "heartstrings like cheap piano wire." No
doubt she's tough enough to take it on the chin — which is
round and ruddy with a bit of bristle as I remember. Austin
Grey appears to be the only one our Foth really approves
of or at least thinks is harmless. Is he gay? Don't think you
ever said.

By the way, you may be right about Greg. He seems a little less sullen now that he's come clean about his job. And I

don't know what you wrote in your letter, but you seem to have convinced him that the "Davina Episode" was entirely innocent.

Molly misses Mia dreadfully. Sue's been having trouble getting her to go to sleep at night. Seems Mia usually read to her and no one else fills the bill.

Must go. Love to both,

Chas

4 Old Town Lane
Ottawa, Ont.
Apr. 7

Dear Chas,

Oh, I'm lonesome! When Mia left I felt like throwing in the sponge altogether, getting on the plane with her. But (ever practical) I recognized that "Counsel Flees Senator's Probe" would scarcely further my career (at least not in the law). Nor enhance my CV — which, judging by your plan to freeze or flood slow-paying clients into submission, and judging by the surfeit of lawyers who spend the winter on Whistler as ski instructors, is going to need all the jazzing up it can get.

It's been a heady experience, being able to phone you again, but we must return to the lowly stamp. I don't know whose turn it is, but I'm too lonely to quibble. I *loved* having Mia here. The days flew by and it was such terrific fun doing mother-and-daughter things, shopping for summer clothes, planning for next year, talking about the Finsteads. I get the feeling Mia is fighting disillusionment. She doesn't want to lose the closeness with Laurie Finstead and so she's trying not to notice what she can't help seeing — something like falling out of love and wishing you wouldn't. We talked a bit about Marjorie's preoccupation with "making everything nice." "Do you think it's important, Mom? I mean, Mrs. Finstead says that a man should really look forward to coming home at night, and wives and mothers have to make the house and everything nice and sort of... exciting, too, so that he'll really want to."

Does Marjorie greet old Gus at the door wrapped in Saran Wrap? But all I said was that I supposed it depended on the couple, some marriages were structured like a master-servant relationship with the one spouse working to please the other, and some were more like partnerships where the exchange of feelings and ideas is what counts.

She worked all that over for a bit and then said Mr. Finstead was sort of boring, not fun like Dad, so maybe Mrs. Finstead had to work harder at it. Then she hesitated, and I could see that something was bothering her, and so I asked her what the trouble was.

"When I go over he always pats me on the bottom and says I'm certainly turning into a fine young filly." She said this in sort of a breathless rush and fiddled with the clasp on her watch instead of looking at me.

I was furious. "Tell him you don't like being patted," I snapped.

She got all upset and said she couldn't do that.

"Why not?" I asked. "It's your bottom," but then I realized I was overreacting, so I cooled it and said, "No, I can see that wouldn't be easy when you and Laurie are such good friends, but I'd try to avoid him if I were you."

"Yeah, I try to," she said. "Only it seems like he always tries to find me when I'm there."

I suggested she have Laurie over to our house, but it

seems Mrs. Finstead doesn't think young girls should spend a lot of time in a house where there's no woman to keep an eye on them. "Of course Sue's at our house a lot, but Mrs. Finstead says she doesn't count, she's only a cleaning lady. I told her Sue was really smart and goes to Simon Fraser, but she just said that the people we *invite* into our homes are a bit different from the people we get to *clean* our houses."

"She's a bit of a snob I think, Mia," I said. Calmly. (Perfect control.)

"I know, but she's sorta right too, isn't she? I mean, you probably wouldn't want Sue to eat with us all the time, but Dad doesn't seem to worry about things like that."

Out of the mouths of babes. A bit of a low blow. I guess I *was* a bit dazzled for a while with what I saw as the prestige and glamour of the Commission. Must have shown, for Mia to pick up on it.

I waited for some self-esteem to trickle back, then told her I try to base my assessments of people on whether a friendship would be mutually rewarding, and that as far as I'm concerned Sue seems like the kind of person I might enjoy getting to know. (I mean that. But *not* as a *cave* dweller — have you solved that?)

Rather to my surprise Mia and Austin got along famously, and it was sweet of him to have us to dinner. He's a damn good cook, on top of everything else. The evening at George's was iffy. Mia had fun with their kids, but Esther and George must have had a row. Remember what fun it is when the hosts have been fighting? Remember the time Tiny Wiglow dumped her soup in Jasper's lap? (He was chasing that little blonde sex-pot Gary What's-his-name brought, and Tiny said maybe that would help him keep a lid on it.) Anyway, it was a scaled-down version of the Wiglows. Esther kept calling him

Pudding 'n Pie. Georgie Porgie, get it? She even tossed in "kissed the girls and made them cry. For which I don't blame the girls." Needless to say George is not crazy about Pudding 'n Pie as a nickname (he's lost weight, actually). I must say I think open marriages risk a lot. (Yes, George confided this to me, that theirs is an open marriage. They made that decision early on, after seeing *Bob and Carol and Ted and Alice* back in the sixties.)

Even Jessica managed to unwind a bit, and Mia and I went over to the group home a couple of times, which she seemed to like, what with the kids and the easy-going ways of the women. To my surprise Mia and Jean got quite friendly — Jean keeps up with the latest styles and rock bands — and I had to be quite firm about Mia's not accompanying Jean and Norm out for a night on the town.

Poor Mia, at that in-between age. The descent into hell. The old brain spews out its hormones and commands the body to do the one thing evolution has taught it to do: repro- duce. The poor new brain, which has plans of its own, is called on for the kind of strength it doesn't yet have. Jean was telling me the other night that when she was that age it was as if someone was taking her over and she'd do things she had no idea she was going to do. Whatever was taking control had nothing to do with the girl she'd been, or the woman she became, after she'd had Tricia. She said she hated to look back on that time because it was so scary. "Like, supernatural sorta. Kinda like a ghost driving the car." I suppose that's what most of the myths are about, Adam and Eve, for instance; though interpretation tends to settle on the male plight, men's dark side compelled by the evil seductions of the temptress. (What else is new?)

And now it's Mia's turn. I'll miss her terribly. When the plane left I was close to tears.

I was rescued by Austin from a weepy evening — we went out to dinner and I felt enormously cheered. Austin was full of praise for you. (Mia had given him a copy of your *Capilano Review* poem. Glad she did, I couldn't find my copy.) He really thinks you have the ability to reach down inside yourself for the right words, that the right word is there like a gold nugget in a deep mine, and a poet may or may not find it. It sounds like a matter of luck, I said, but he disagreed. He seems to think of poetry as survival equipment, that there are times in each of our lives when it's the only way we have of touching and coming to terms with hidden and unknown depths of feeling. Times, for instance, of new love or deep sorrow.

You aren't going through one of those times, are you Chas?

Love,
Jock

P.S. Is Mother serious about making a trip out here? I don't know what she'd do with herself during the day when I'm at the hearings, and I never know from day to day what our schedule might be. Try to dissuade her if you can.

P.P.S. And could you keep an eye on Mia when she's visiting the gracious house across the way? Make sure Marjorie's home.

P.P.P.S. When I asked Jess if Austin was gay, she blew. "What the hell has that to do with anything?" she yelled. "It's none of your fucking business."

9 Sweet Cedar Drive
North Vancouver, B.C.
14 April

Dear Jock,

I meant to write as soon as Mia got back from Ottawa —
I *have* missed our letters — but here at home we've been
plunged into a neighbourhood soap opera, and, as a matter of
fact, we're still immersed.

It started last Friday morning while we were sitting happily in the kitchen enjoying a late hot-cross-bun breakfast
(except for Mia who had already fled to the Finsteads and
home-made blackberry jam on home-made h.c. buns.) Since
it was Good Friday the Sun Spot was closed and so were the
schools. Then the calm was broken by a terrific pounding on
the back door, and when we opened it there stood Marjorie
Finstead (with Laurie and Mia in tow, looking frightened) in a
state of mad-woman hysterics. Picture uncombed hair, dressing gown, and rubber boots — our Marjorie transformed
into a Hallowe'en act. And she was alternately whimpering
and screaming.

It was a lucky thing Sue was here. She managed to shoo
Mia and Laurie into the family room and then she made
Marjorie sit down and drink a cup of raspberry-leaf tea,
which she claims is soothing to the nerves. (Try it. It's done
great things for my ulcer.)

Even so, it was a while before Marjorie was able to bab-
ble anything besides, "I hate him. I never thought I'd say this,
but yes, yes, I hate him."

"You hate who?" I asked. This seemed a sensible question
at the time.

"Her husband, probably," Sue said.

That was when Marjorie stopped crying and pulled

herself together for half a minute. "I'm never going to let that man lay a hand on me again," she said.

Gus? I couldn't believe she was talking about dumb old Gus. "You don't mean Gus?" I asked her.

For some reason that seemed to enrage her. "He's ruined my whole life." She was wailing now. "I've always known he was a monster and now the whole world knows it."

You know my feeling about Gus Finstead, Jock, and I know yours. True, the man is a cerebral puppy and a hopeless bore the way he drones on about balanced running shoes and user-friendly ski boots and "Jap" cars and cost-effective grass seed. But...a monster?

"Maybe not a monster," Marjorie told us, calming herself, "but sick, sick, sick."

I pressed her for specifics. What exactly had Gus done? Punched her in the jaw? (There weren't any bruises.)

But she remained (and remains) secretive. With *me* that is. I have a feeling she's told Sue a good deal more. For some reason I'm being spared the details; perhaps they think I'll fall over in a faint or go after him with an axe. They whisper and hint and allude, but Gus's crime, whatever the hell it is, is a mystery. The conspiracy of women, the way they huddle and confide — I don't understand it, and I can't help feeling at times just a little bit elbowed aside.

Especially when it's *our* house Marjorie has moved into (only temporary, of course). She and Laurie have taken over the guest room...just until she can get her head together, she says, and see where she is in terms of options. Sue has found her a good lawyer who's been here a couple of times to interview Marjorie (in the family room with the door closed), and she (the lawyer) says that Marjorie should take a week or two to consider whether she wants to take action (against Gus?). I can only guess that Gus has been running around, as we used to say, or that he's developed some quirky, unacceptable fetish.

To make matters worse, Gus has taken to lurking. At all hours he can be seen skulking behind the cedar hedge and peering at our front door, watching our comings and goings. Marjorie is as nervous as a cat and insists we keep the doors and windows locked. "Morning, Gus," I said to him on Easter Sunday when I was backing the car out of the driveway. He was blocking my way.

"I'd like to talk to my wife," he whispered, looking not at all sinister.

What could I tell the poor bloke? As kindly as possible I said, "Her lawyer will be in touch," and then felt like a first-rate swine.

He looked so harmless and stripped down. "Tell her I'm getting help," he said before shrinking back into the shrubbery.

I passed this news on to Marjorie, but it only made her start to cry again. As you can see, she is in a fragile state and needs the support of friends and neighbours for a while, and I figure the least we can do is give her and Laurie a temporary roof over their heads. And there *is* a plus side; Mia is exuberant about having a "sister," and she and Laurie and Molly had a great time dyeing Easter eggs last weekend.

The Mothers, who arrived for Easter dinner bearing hams, pies, and quivery salads, were divided in their reaction. Your mother, who was instantly admitted to the female huddle, took it in her stride, saying just, "The poor woman, she's been through a lot."

My mother, on the other hand, found the new arrangements irregular and threatening. "There are plenty of hotels they could stay at," she said, going all sniffy. She isn't too keen about Sue and Molly being here either, even though I explained to her about the benefits of free cleaning and fresh vegetables, and the fact that it was only temporary. (Sue has a lead now on a reasonable apartment, though the landlord is ambivalent about kids and sceptical about single women as tenants.)

I have to say it makes for rather a crowd lining up in front of the bathroom in the morning, but I've been getting up early so I can get over to the Sun Spot by eight o'clock. Another new job has come up — not a big deal really, just glassing in an apartment balcony — but we're trying to think of a new approach. The Sanderson job is in full swing and promises to be a beauty. It better be, for twenty-five thou. At this rate I should be able to pay Greg's loan off by the end of the summer. (He's talking about UBC for the fall.)

Better go. We've got the grocery shopping to do. Two carts!

Love,

Chas

P.S. The *Writer's Quarterly* has accepted "Goodbye to Gil." Notice how calm I am about this news.

P.P.S. Came across one of Austin's early poems:

> *My hand, so controlled*
> *Touches your face, your hair, then*
> *Slips its bonds*
> *To the dark source.*

Doesn't *sound* gay.

4 Old Town Lane
Ottawa, Ont.
Apr. 21

Dear Chas,

Good Lord, let me count the people! The three who should be there, you and Greg and Mia, and the basement dwellers, Sue and Molly, and the Finsteads, Marjorie and Laurie. Seven? In a house that felt squeezed with four? And all female, except for you and Greg, as George pointed out when I told him about it.

Their marriage is in trouble, as I suspected. Seems Esther is having an affair with an electronics wizard who commutes between here and Silicon Valley (she met him when she sold him a modest little shack in Rockcliffe). George says that in spite of the open marriage he's having trouble with his anger. He says anger has always been a problem for him since he was a very angry young man searching for a cause, but that when he wrote the novel he thought he'd dealt with it once and for all. But he's having a lot of pain, because Esther is actually in love with this guy who, George says, is nothing but a talking computer. No heart, Esther will get badly winged. So George says his pain is for Esther as much as for himself. (Can anyone be that noble?)

I told George I couldn't handle an open marriage, I'd be too jealous *and* too guilty to carry it off.

George looked somewhat bemused at that and took my hand and said you, Chas, were a very lucky man and he hoped you realized it, and I retrieved my hand and said I thought you did, since I mentioned it quite frequently. (Don't worry, George just wants an understanding and sympathetic audience.)

I asked him if any of his paramours had meant anything to

him, and his eyes got a sort of glazed look and he said that in spite of the freedom that he and Esther had agreed to he'd never actually indulged. He says he agrees with me that you'd have to care for another person, and Esther has been his only anima. He looked so pathetic that I ended up patting *his* hand. (Patting, not kissing.)

Interesting about the Finsteads. I wonder if it has anything to do with the bum-patting Mia was getting? In which case, shouldn't someone be worrying about Mia instead of Marjorie? Wasn't Sue in sexual abuse? Maybe you should check it out.

Love,
Jock

P.S. A warning. Last night I was wakened by a stealthy middle-of-the-night knock at my door. I groped my way downstairs to find Jean and Norm and Tricia heavily bundled in ski jackets and snow boots, the motorcycle plus new sidecar gleaming behind them on the sidewalk. They sidled in rather furtively and waited until I had shut and bolted the door before Norm mumbled, "We can't hack it — we're breaking out." Jean, in a loud stage whisper, explained, "Like, dental hygiene is a very tough course and I don't sorta, you know, like, *relate* — look, tell Jess I'm sorry and I appreciate everything she did. Tell her I'll write when we get to Vancouver." I gave her a hug, and Norm said, "Say, we might look up your old man. Got any messages?" (Sorry about that.) Maybe you can sic Sue onto them.

9 Sweet Cedar Drive
North Vancouver, B.C.
28 April

Dear Jock,

Thanks for your warning — if only I'd taken it seriously.
There I was last Saturday morning, standing out on the front
lawn beating away at the accumulated moss and trying to be
oblivious to Gus Finstead lurking behind the holly, when a
motorcycle with Ontario plates swooped into our driveway.
I asked myself: Now why would a motorcycle carrying two
leather-jacketed human beings (plus strapped-on baby) be
hurtling up our front driveway? It stopped; the engine shut
down; the two human beings removed their dusty helmets;
and suddenly I knew, I knew. Oh God.

Why didn't you give them a false address? Why didn't
you tell them I was a hermit? Why didn't you tell them we
were in quarantine? Why didn't you...?

Just a cup of coffee, they said. That was all they needed.
Then, ahem, they could sure do with a meal. They were a little short on cash — did we know a real, real cheap hotel —
like *real* cheap? You can guess the rest. They're now installed
in the basement between the laundry tubs and the furnace.
Rent-a-Bed brought around two singles plus a crib for Tricia.
Just temporary of course. (Ho, ho.)

One good thing: Norm has finally figured out what was
wrong with the furnace. That valve we had installed last fall
was put in upside down and that was what was causing those
wild fluctuations. He's actually a bit of a genius with converted oil burners, but at this time of year (twenty degrees
today, sunny and fragrant) who's going to hire a furnace
repairman? Until he finds something else, he's been doing
some of the inside finishing on the Sandersons' solarium, and

I might be able to use him on our West Van job — a very nice little free-standing glassed-in gazebo, true fantasyland.

Neither he nor Jean seemed much inclined to shower for the first couple of days, but Sue took matters into her hands and handed them each a large bath towel, saying, "We've taken a vote here and it was unanimous that everyone takes at least one shower daily." Now the water never stops running; I dread the next hydro bill.

Both Norm and Jean assure me they'll soon be chipping in with grocery money. Greg managed to get Jean a temporary job as cocktail waitress at the Fishnet, and she loves it! Says she's found her true vocation. Off she trips with Greg every night wearing her scrap of red satin and black net. Already she looks better.

You may be right about Gus Finstead's roving hands. (By the way, I tried to sound Sue out about whether Mia was in any way a victim but all I got were a few laudatory comments about Mia's maturity.) At any rate, rumour has it Gus is getting counselling. More to the point, Marjorie's case worker, Ruth, has arranged some joint counselling sessions, so perhaps she'll be moving back home before long. Let's hope so. The house *is* fairly crowded, especially *since my mother moved in*.

You know how we've often sworn that neither of us would ever live with our mothers again — but what could I do? Mother arrived here with her suitcase in hand and said she intended to stay until you got home in June. She insists that someone has to "keep an eye on things" and make sure "nothing gets out of hand."

I asked her what she meant by "get out of hand," and she rambled on in her fuzzy way about Halifax and Dad and the dangers of temptation and that she understood better than I did how easily men can go astray and if I wanted to hear the whole story. . . .

I didn't want to hear the whole story. I knew quite suddenly that I didn't want to hear one more word of it. And so she has settled down in the guest room. Marjorie has moved downstairs with Sue (one more Rent-a-Bed), and we've worked out an elaborate housekeeping schedule with everyone taking shifts. Sue does breakfasts and beds, Jean packs lunches, and Norm, Marjorie, and Mother do evening meals. Mia and Laurie vacuum (randomly), and I do the shopping — in fact I'm just off now. Have to stop first at the clinic for Tricia's shots.

> Much love on the run,
> Chas

> 4 Old Town Lane
> Ottawa, Ont.
> May 6

Dear Chas,

A quick note to let you know I'll be coming home *before* the end of June. We'll finish the hearings by the middle of May, but Van wants me to stay on and help George with the first draft of the report. The problem is the new minority government. Jessica says Van is scared shitless (her phrase) that the Commission won't survive long enough to publish if we don't move on it quickly. Van actually thought George could produce it by the end of *May*. ("Haven't you got it on your word-processor, George? What's the big deal?") George looked quite sallow at the thought. I've noticed that, like Dorothy Parker, George hates writing but loves having written. When he attempted a feeble demur Van snapped, "George, I seem to recall a promise from you some time ago that if I would give you advance warning on my decision you would be able to have everything ready to go at the drop of a hat."

Aha! *La lumière!* It didn't take me long to figure out what decision that was. I was conned, the weasly little turnip! And here I was, feeling guilty about being overly ambitious and suspicious, but at least I was above board.

I kept my expression expressionless — with the likes of George it's just as well not to tip your hand — and Van barked, "Bring someone in if you can't do it." George instantly found the strength to bring the task single-handedly to glorious completion if maybe Austin could just lend a moment or two of time at the end for a bit of formal polishing.

To my surprise Austin said no, not the last two weeks of May. He's booked to get away for a couple of weeks to Bermuda, says he's feeling the need of some sun. He *has* seemed droopy lately — I thought perhaps he was avoiding me and must admit I was rather relieved that it was just bushed-ness.

Van had to relent about the deadline; hearings will be finished by mid-May and the first draft (which needs me) no later than the fifteenth of June. Austin has agreed to pitch in as soon as he gets back, since Van's heart is set on putting the final draft in the PM's hands before we get any more bad press.

So — the fifteenth of June is the end for me. But since Mother is bent on coming I'll wait to book my return until I hear her plans. (If you have room to put me up, that is. What is the house count now — eleven?)

Jock

P.S. Very strange about *your* mother, knowing how she loves her creature comforts and has always thought living on the North Shore an affectation. Increased dottiness, do you think?

29 Sweet Cedar Drive
North Vancouver, B.C.
13 May

Dear Jock,

About George, I hesitate to say I told you so, but I did,
didn't I? I just wish someone had tipped *me* off about the
unreliability of gratitude as a human emotion. I don't mean
Norm and Jean — at least they're grateful — but that's a
helluva lot more than I can say for Davina. Two weeks ago I
spoke to Talbot Sanderson about Davina's course being
dropped for next year. As you know, Talbot's on the board at
Cap College, has been since the beginning, I think. I
explained to him that it all came about because of the twisted
testimony of one disgruntled student, and he promised to
look into it. Presto. A few days later Davina got word that
her course had been reinstated. But did she thank me? No.
She says that I should have told her what I was up to, that
she doesn't like being a pawn in the old-boy network. I
suggested we have coffee and I would explain the politics
of the workaday world, but she was decidedly frosty and
declined. Just as well the course has ended. The Sun Spot
is taking up all my time these days, and poetry seems to
have got left behind temporarily. (Why is everything
suddenly temporary?)

Glad to have a date to pin our expectations to. Tried to
tackle your mother on her plans but all I got was a mysterious smile and a "We'll see." I think she and my mother are up
to something, since there are glances interchanged and little
whisperings about Halifax.

Gotta run.

Love,

Chas

4 Old Town Lane
Ottawa, Ont.
May 17

Dear Chas,

I was sorry to hear about Davina. It's baffling — and hurtful — when people turn on you, isn't it? I still feel a sort of sadness over the George episode. Not that any deep feelings were engaged, but just the betrayal of trust. George must know I twigged to his perfidy because he has certainly backed off, although that may be because he and Esther have decided to abandon open marriage and return to monogamy. Seems Esther's electronic wizard departed before coughing up the balance due on the interim sales agreement on the house Esther sold him. He did not return to Silicon Valley — which evidently had never heard of him — and she was left out of pocket and out of lover.

They (George and Esther) invited me to see the famous tulip beds of Ottawa with them, and Esther kept exclaiming how glorious! in a voice that sounded about as joyful as a funeral oration. I have to admit I wasn't much better, because in spite of the bursting yellow and the flaming orange and the unlikely purple effusion of colour my heart did not leap up; I was moved exactly as much by the rainbow array as I was by the dirty mounds of spongy snow still piled in the odd parking lot. I felt as though I were looking through a curtain that blurred the beautiful and the crummy into one dreary canvas of affectless grey — and yet, I kept repeating to myself and them, *I'll soon be going home!*

I don't know what's the matter with me — I'm wondering if I've got flu or something. My stomach feels exactly as it did those first couple of months I was here when I was so homesick — maybe I'm being homesick in reverse for

Ottawa and the Commission? Maybe I can't accept a return
to being nothing more than that hellishly patronizing
euphemism, a homemaker?

I suspect it's a case of cold feet after our disastrous evening in Winnipeg. I seem to be suffering this strange despair.
Very odd, considering all the positives. No more bruises on
my hips from banging the corner of the kitchen table. Being
able to turn around without moving the furniture.

I wish Austin were here — he's good on insights that help
me to understand myself better — but he's off in Bermuda.
And Jessica has been acting quite strangely lately. She watches
me when she thinks I'm not looking, then when I catch her
eye she turns away quickly, seeming almost embarrassed, or
as embarrassed as Jessica ever looks. At the same time she
isn't mad; on the contrary, she seems anxious to include me
in Group Home Gaiety, which I don't feel up to. Does my
despondent mood show?

There's no one else I could possibly talk to. Van has
become almost obsessed with the report and with a redhead
who has appeared on the scene. Yvette's eyes are quite
swollen from crying.

Sorry to burden you with this, but I find the thought of
going back into our ordinary lives a little frightening.

Love,

Jock

P.S. Thank you for the copy of your "Goodbye to Gil" poem.

29 Sweet Cedar Drive
North Vancouver, B.C.
17 May

Dear Jock,

A funny dark moonless night. And it's been a long, dull shapeless day. Hoped for a letter from you, but there was nothing. God, you seem a long way off at the moment. I don't know if I'm fed up with the gazebo job (the centre pane broke during installation this morning) or worried about the future — our future. Probably I'm just spooked by all the melodrama going on around here, but I think I ought to tell you, Jock, that I'm having a lot of trouble remembering what our life together used to be like. What's harder, a helluva lot harder, is trying to think what it's going to be like in the future.

The present is deteriorating too. Sue and I took Tricia in her stroller down by the cedar grove after dinner, and I couldn't believe what we saw there. Bulldozers have ripped up the whole place. There isn't a tree left standing, and that nice little boggy spot with the frogs has been drained and levelled, and there's a big orange ugly sign announcing the imminent construction of something called the Winchester Garden Homes. "For Those Who Care about the Quality of Life." I wanted to cry. I wanted to be sick. Walking back home I tried to imagine what you'd say when you saw it. And I couldn't.

Love,
Chas

4 Old Town Lane
Ottawa, Ont.
May 20

Dear Chas,

Not my cedar grove! Wasn't there something you could
have done to stop it? If you're feeling so out of joint at
the moment maybe we'd better call a halt to all this
penmanship.

Jock

29 Sweet Cedar Drive
North Vancouver, B.C.
21 May

Dear Jock,

Much as I appreciate your attempt to be "fair" and "honest" with me about your feelings of coming home, I'm afraid I
can't sympathize with you about the degradation of "homemaking." For Christ's sake, Jock, think it through. There hasn't
been much homemaking around here for a long time. Or
much home, for that matter. Let's call an interregnum to our
letter writing.

Chas

4 Old Town Lane
Ottawa, Ont.
May 27

Do you remember, Chas, when I was expecting Greg, how one morning you put your hand on my round belly and said, out of the blue, "What would we do if one of us fell in love with someone else?"

I remember it clearly, because suddenly Greg kicked so hard that I didn't know which was making my stomach hurt so, the terrible question you asked or the baby. I remember that I stared at you for a moment with outrage, and that I was so mad I pushed you right off the bed. I shouted at you, threatening decapitation, emasculation, tarring and feathering, if ever again such a thought were to wander through your promiscuous skull. And after Greg was born and I had resolved that I would never let anything mar his perfect upbringing, I worried about you for months.

Never once did I mistrust myself.

Of course I'm not going to send this letter. How could I? I don't even know why I'm writing it. I keep thinking that if only I'd been brought up a Catholic and could have the comfort of the confessional I wouldn't have to write something you'll never read. God knows why I feel impelled to do it — expiation? forgiveness? If so, from whom?

I suppose I do want absolution, which is sort of like having your cake and eating it too, isn't it? — but I don't think that's the only thing behind it. There's something else niggling away in there, some sort of urge to tell it, shout it, show it off. Exhibitionism? — in a way. You don't see me any more, Chas, not the me who's come to life these last few months in Ottawa. But somebody else does, somebody I respect and — care for.

Last night I was moping about and trying to arrange the apartment for Mother's arrival, when the phone rang. It was Austin, home early from Bermuda, and inviting me out to dinner. Yes, yes, I told him. I was longing for someone to talk to, and for the first time in two weeks I actually felt hungry.

My grey mood lifted during dinner, even though Austin wasn't his usual witty self. He seemed alternately preoccupied and uncharacteristically curious — about us, about you and me, about our somewhat fractured lives. Was it the wine, was it the quality of lighting at our table, the lateness of the hour? — I'm afraid, darling Chas, that at that point in the evening I swung into a rather wide confessional mode. At first I tried to keep it humorous, but as I moved through the narrative framework, Christmas, the party, Winnipeg, I found there were tears spilling out of my eyes. He took my hand (of course I flashed to an image of you taking Davina's hand at the Fishnet), and the next thing I knew I was telling him that I was reluctant to go home to Vancouver, that I was scared to death to go home to Vancouver. That there might be nothing there.

He listened to all this quietly, and then suggested we go back to his apartment for a nightcap. When we arrived he opened the door and picked up the mail that had accumulated while he was away. "Good Lord!" he said. "Something from your husband."

He opened it, your copy of the "Goodbye to Gil" poem. He read it aloud. "What a good poem," he said.

We sat down, and he read it once again, commenting on some of the phrases. "Priest of cold disguise," he said, was a perceptive and moving way of describing the undertaker. He asked if I were the woman with "black hair / that thick heavy night-black coil / coloured for mourning / pinned against levity." And then he read the final lines:

I'll bring a beer and I'll spill it
over the sad-faced pansies
and the whispering wild flowers.
I'll try not to forget.

It was strange, but I could hear the exact sound of your voice breaking behind those lines, and tears started up. He put his arms around me and I leaned my head on his shoulder and felt protected and safe, as though I'd been through a violent time. Like the day we were fishing and got caught in the Squamish wind that came roaring down Howe Sound. We were cold and drenched and scared, remember? And then we rounded the corner into Snug Cove, sitting there so calm and friendly, and we knew we'd survive. It was a little like that, the feel of Austin's arms around me. Remember how we crawled up on a rock and the sun came out and we took off our wet clothes and lay there? And remember the doe, how she came down through the trees, and how we didn't move? I remember I felt as though the whole world was bursting inside me and all around me like a giant flower, the trees laced against the light, the doe, the sun, the little waves lapping on the rocks.

How can I explain what happened next? As you said once, all the good words have been co-opted by rock music and paperback romances. In your poem, Chas, the lover has a look "That was like light reflecting / from a thousand crystals / as though the delicate glass / had been sewn, invisibly / and the shining mask / slipped over his face." I've been trying to think if it was like this when we fell in love, you and I, but all I remember is that it seemed to be fitting and that my body said, "It's time," and we were shy and excited and the world was new.

The world is no longer new, far from it, but when I was with Austin last night it scarcely mattered. We took off our clothes as though they were the alien vestments of another life and we embraced again. Lying on that rather narrow little bed of his, we touched one another, and then he slipped into my waiting body and made it whole.

Once when I was ten years old, every night from Hallowe'en to Christmas I prayed for a bicycle, and every night I dreamt about it. In my dreams I flew on it through the astonished streets like a conqueror. Mother was against it. We were broke, it was dangerous, the traffic, child molesters — I persevered, made bargains with God, pricked my finger and signed my oath in blood, and indulged in other ancient rites of witchery. And when, on Christmas morning, the bike was there, festooned with satin bows Scotch-taped to its shiny chrome, it was as though a sudden luminescence backlighted every insignificant object in our little living room. The friendly black cavern of the empty fireplace, the grey wool of the carpet, the battered corners of the sectional furniture, the scarred coffee table covered with nuts and mandarin oranges, the glittering Christmas tree with its all-blue lights shining like haloes through the angel hair — to this day I can see every corner of that ordinary little room as I saw it that morning, with wonder and awe and great joy.

It was like that, Chas. I felt *known* — that strange biblical term. It really does mean something after all.

The early light was reflecting into the room before the world intruded again. Austin was lying on his back. His mouth was open, and he was snoring lightly; the slight breeze through the open window stirred his sandy hair, and I saw a jagged ancient scar, and I thought about how strange it was that I wouldn't have known to expect that. That there were so many things to learn; that I was afraid.

Austin woke up. He said that he loved me.

"I love you too," I whispered. I meant it, I did mean it.

Yet I knew, as I'd known from the first light touch of his hand on mine in the restaurant, that I have another life, a long, solidly packed history with so many separate tentacles and chambers I could never count them all. Austin, on the other hand, so gifted, so perceptive, so *knowing*, a man who floats free — what do I know, really, about him?

Our timing, too, was laughable; in a wink of the eye I will be back on North Vancouver, resuming my life, chafing under its restraints perhaps, but relishing its familiarity, and Austin — he'll be off to Wales, continents, oceans away. Intimacy is a serious business, that's one thing I've learned, and you can't have it at a distance.

"I love you," I'd said to Austin, as though I held in my hand a range of choices.

But why shouldn't I have choices, isn't that my right? Oh God, it isn't easy, Chas. But I do still love you. If you could only see me.

What will I do? What will we do?

Jock

P.S. I'm ripping this letter into shreds so small that even Mother won't be able to piece them together.

4 Old Town Lane
Ottawa, Ont.
May 27

Dear Chas,

Mother arrived safely and has just returned from a swinging evening with Aunt Hilda. Now she's recovering from the dry spell with a well-laced hot toddy.

I was a little shocked when I got her note, but fortunately Austin was back early from Bermuda and offered to drive me to the airport to meet her.

He dropped us here at Old Town Lane, and Mother no sooner got into the apartment than she started in on my weight. "I never knew anyone to go up or down the way you do, Jocelyn, you were like that from a baby, the least thing upsets you and you can't eat. What's upsetting you this time?"

Fortunately, I didn't have to think up an answer before she looked around and wondered how on earth I managed. I suggested she might be more comfortable with Aunt Hilda, but she snapped, "More comfortable but a lot drier. Hilda doesn't approve of a number of things. Speaking of which, Jocelyn, do you have a touch of sherry? I'm quite exhausted from the trip."

I had Bristol Cream but no sherry glasses. No problem, Mother doesn't really care for sherry glasses it seems. "A person spends half the time refilling. I don't know why they don't make them a more realistic size." Then she commented again on my looking peaked and said we'd put some meat back on these bones with lots of fattening French meals out: "My treat. I know you don't have money to squander what with this latest flight of fancy of Charles's." Some things change, but not Mother.

When I told her I wouldn't have a lot of time to live it up with her she said not to worry, she could at least shop and sight-see with Aunt Hilda, and she intended to have a little trek to Montreal. "My old stamping-ground," she calls it. (She worked there during the war when Dad was overseas.)

Love,

Jock

P.S. How is *your* ménage? Dwindling, I sincerely hope and pray.

P.P.S. Sorry about my last curt note. I loved that damn cedar grove.

29 Sweet Cedar Drive
North Vancouver, B.C.
2 June

My darling Jock,

I wonder if you remember a conversation we had shortly after we were married. We were still in that apartment in Kits — the one with the black walls — and I remember you came home from work one day with a new pair of shoes you'd bought yourself. Red shoes with fiendishly high heels. "Here," you said, with a good measure of defiance, pushing a scrap of paper at me, "I want you to see the receipt for these shoes."

You wanted me to know exactly what your new shoes had cost, that they had *not* been on sale. You were so earnest, so insistent. I asked you why. You explained about your mother, how she'd always hidden shopping receipts from your father. And if he ever *did* ask her the price of anything, she automatically subtracted thirty per cent. You'd grown up with a mother, you said, whose most oft-repeated phrase was, "We won't tell Daddy how much this cost." And you were determined that your marriage was not going to go adrift in this kind of deception.

I was, of course, in full agreement. After all, I had grown up with a father who kept his bottle of rye hidden in the coal bin and a mother who kept her age secret, even from the man she was legally married to, for forty years.

Openness, honesty — I was as ready as you to embrace it all.

Mainly I think we've succeeded. But not always. Because there *have* been things I've kept from you. I never told you, for instance, how painful that year of free-lancing was after I left Bettner's, how I woke up at night sweating with anxiety, and how every day was a fresh torment. I pretended to you that it was a liberating adventure, that I was ecstatic to be steering my own ship at last. I even grew a beard and suffered with it through the hay-fever season. I hinted (to you) that I was making important new contacts when I wasn't. I suggested (to you) that new ideas were bubbling up inside me, when really I was walking around feeling half dead. It was a nightmare, and I thanked God (I really did, though not quite on my knees) when Robertson's came along and offered me a job. You didn't know any of this.

And then there was the day you were accepted at law school and I brought home flowers and wine and we stood in the kitchen toasting your success and I made that speech about how glad I was and how proud. But all I could think of was that you were about to move away from me and that our happiness was imperilled. It didn't turn out that way, of course, and I soon realized we were into a new and better chapter of our lives. But still...

There were other things too. For example, there was a secretary at Robertson's I fell half in love with — this was five years ago. It came to nothing, a few conversations, one lunch. I dreamed about her every night for a month. She had long swaying red hair, but also a rasping voice and a way of dropping her *G*'s that cured me fairly quickly of my infatuation. Nevertheless...

I never told you any of these things because I felt that what I was protecting — your faith in me, my faith in you — was worth a small whittling away of truth. And I have no intention of telling you what happened last night.

But I do, it seems, have a perverse compulsion to write it all down, whether out of a desire for self-flagellation or a wish to obliterate, with ink, what scarcely now seems possible.

You know what Fridays are like. It was the end of a busy week, and I came home with a new contract in my pocket — a restaurant extension at Oak Ridge Shopping Centre, the kind of job I thought we'd have to wait years for. I was euphoric. And Sue had just got her exam results — straight A's — and she was over the moon. It was Mother's night to cook and she did one of her famous pot roasts, which left us all feeling joyful and well provided for. Greg and Jean went off to the Fishnet, Marjorie took the girls — and Mother too — to see *Little Women* (yes, still showing), Tricia had got over her cold and was sleeping soundly, and Norm was in the garage oiling his motorcycle. And then the phone rang.

It was Davina, not quite so frosty as when I'd last talked to her, mellow in fact, telling me that the *Writer's Quarterly* had come out with my poem in it. (Normally it wouldn't have appeared till next fall, but for some reason — Davina's influence, probably — they'd slipped it in the spring issue and sent her an advance copy.) Would I like to see it? Of course I would like to see it. When? As soon as possible. I said I'd be right over.

An hour later I was there. Sue, flushed with academic hubris, came along, and Davina greeted the two of us in one of her South Seas robes, waving a copy of the *Quarterly*. There was my poem, centred on a page of its own, with a little biographical squiggle at the bottom saying *Charles Selby of Vancouver is an architect and poet*. I, too, felt suddenly legitimate. I know now what you meant, Jock. I felt new-born.

We sat on Davina's balcony and drank a large quantity of wine. It was a warm night and unusually clear. Sue talked about her marriage. Davina talked about *her* marriage. I am quite sure — forgive me — that I talked about *our* marriage. We also talked, if I remember, about illusion and truth, betrayal and loyalty, poetry and life. Everything we uttered sounded resonant with meaning.

In time it got cooler, and Sue suggested we move inside. After that there is some confusion in my mind, but I do clearly remember that the three of us were suddenly, some-how, together in Davina's wide bed and that our clothes were in a jumble on the floor. The scene was both awful and glori-ous. Moving between those two other human bodies I felt deeply ashamed and at the same time restored to life.

Today, of course, it is the stink of shame that primarily lingers. It's shapeless, this shame, and sloppy, and has to do with betraying you and betraying me, too, and betraying what has always felt right. I want to weep for that rag-taggle thing that I once thought of as my sense of decency, or was it really a delayed condition of innocence? (I've always suspected a lack of harmony with today's porn-soaked world). I long to blame the booze and the headiness of publication, but it's not enough. I would like to blame Davina and Sue and speculate on their cunning — but can't quite. I want to blame you, too, for going off to Ottawa and leaving me in the hands of…myself, mainly. And of course I keep telling myself that I must erase this whole dishonourable slice of an evening — but here is the worst part: there's a corner of my mind, quite rational, that wants to hang on to what happened, that can't quite bear to let it go. Not yet.

None of this has anything to do with you, dear Jock, or

with our life together, at least I don't think so. What happened was an aberration, something that will never happen again. If I weren't so absolutely sure of this I wouldn't be doing what I am about to do, namely touching this letter with a match and dropping it in the fireplace. A Byronic gesture, maybe, but it will be gone. After that it's a case of forgetting what happened — and remembering too.

Your loving and sadly confused,
Chas

29 Sweet Cedar Drive
North Vancouver, B.C.
4 June

Dear Jock,

Just a short note. (Sorry about the last one.) Not too much news. It was a quiet weekend and I was able to tackle the garden at last, hacking down weeds mainly and putting in a few bedding plants — those white petunias you like along the drive. Magnificent weather. I even took a spin Saturday afternoon on Greg's old bike.

On Sunday we helped Sue move. She finally located a reasonably priced two-bedroom spot in Richmond. It was advertised in Saturday's paper and she jumped at it. A little out of the way, but good value, and there's a playground for Molly across the street.

Hope you got the copy of *Writer's Quarterly*. I asked them to send you one. Doubt if I'll be doing much in that line in the future — too busy, etc. Davina Flowering got a travel grant from the Canada Council — somehow she made peace with them — and is off to England tomorrow.

God, we're rushed at the office, but I'm not complaining. Hope you survive your mother's visit.

Love,

Chas

P.S. Phone! Bills are all up to date.

4 Old Town Lane

Ottawa, Ont.

June 11

Dear Chas,

It's late, but I want to get a letter off to you. The last one, I suppose, since I'll be home in just a few days.

Tonight Mother and I attended the little farewell bash Vance threw for me at the office. It was sweet but rather anti-climactic. Austin wasn't there — seems he had to go to Charlottetown again, his sister is ill — so I won't see him before I go. George and Esther were there, arm-in-arm, and Yvette, whom I've grown fond of. Jessica was damp-eyed, also a little drunk, and gave me a crushing embrace and kissed me on the lips. The lips! I was taken aback — no, I was shocked! Why did that shock me so much? I don't know, but it did. After the lip kiss I stood quietly in the corner for a bit, playing the role of observer and thinking about how much these people have meant to me this year, how well I know them, and how I don't really know them at all.

Vance's Catherine was there, down from Montreal for a bit of slumming. Van's office seemed to belong more to her than to him. She enlightened us all on her views of poverty (it's extent is vastly overrated; nobody can call themselves poor if they own a colour TV; unemployment insurance lets people live like kings) in the middle of which Jessica bellowed, "So long, Jock." (This time I ducked.) She shook Mother's hand and said, "Goodbye, Jock's mother, you raised one hell of a daughter." Then she toasted me (in not-rare burgundy), resisted throwing her glass at the wall, and pressed a farewell card into my hand. Van presented me with a beautiful watercolour of birch trees in an Ottawa park. (I told him I hadn't found enlightenment, but he seemed to have forgotten about that. He didn't try to kiss me; contented himself with a handshake.) We were home by eleven.

Pushed under the door was a farewell gift from Austin. It is a small manuscript of poems entitled "Interlude" that he's just completed. He'll be off to Europe as soon as the report is finished; he has some sort of poet-in-residence and lecture series at a university in Wales. So here I am, feeling honoured, happy, sentimental, sad, confused, and tired. (I've given Mother my bed, and getting to sleep on this old couch of mine is a challenge that demands more than just counting a bunch of sheep.) I'm also feeling somewhat tingly and amazed about a conversation I've just had with Mother.

True to form she suggested a nightcap the minute we walked in the door. Then a wee top-up. She was in a talkative mood and full of nostalgia about the war years in Ottawa. "It must have been lonely for you," I said, "with Dad overseas."

She sipped a bit, looked up cagily, and said, "Well, not too lonely, actually."

There was a long pause, then she said, "I met lots of people. One in particular."

"A man?" I asked brainlessly.

She nodded. She may even have blushed, though it was difficult to tell with the lights so low. "He was very handsome in his uniform," she said. "A flight louie, as we used to call them. We talked a lot. We both loved to read and we had so many thing to talk about." She looked down into the rapidly emptying glass and repeated, "So many things."

"You don't mean to say you had a fling?" I asked, and then wished I hadn't. I wasn't sure what I wanted her to answer.

To my surprise she didn't flare up, she just held out her glass for more sherry. "A pretty pale one by today's standards, if we did," she said.

She said they'd done a lot of deep talking and read T.S. Eliot and Christopher Fry together, but it was wartime and she knew where her loyalties had to lie. "I had Tim, he was only two years old, I couldn't kick up my heels much even if I'd wanted, the way some of them did."

I asked her what happened.

"He was posted overseas and we wrote for a while, but you know how it is." I could tell by the way her eyes shifted that she was dissembling. "When you've got a family, Jocelyn, you have responsibilities beyond your own wants and bit of excitement. You make a decision the day you bring a child into the world, and if you've got the right stuff you'll stick to that decision."

"For life?"

"Oh no, I'm not as old-fashioned as that, but I think a person should give it their best shot for twenty years — per child, that is. I don't think a young person is mature enough to handle a parental split before twenty."

"But what if you were in the grip of — say — your legendary grand passion?"

She shrugged. "Nothing's easy. That's the human condition, isn't it?"

She seemed almost angry as she said this. She got up rather abruptly and went into the bedroom and I sat for a bit, thinking about the mysterious friend that Mother must have loved once, thinking of duty as she had defined it, and the seemingly compatible marriage as I remember it between her and my father. I even felt threatened — Dad was a good person, I truly loved him — to think that once she had wavered, and grateful that she'd found "the right stuff" in herself. I wondered if she'd be so stalwart in today's moral climate.

I thought when she sailed so huffily into the bedroom that that was the end of that, so I pulled out the sofa-bed and prepared for another nocturnal wrestle with its wandering springs.

"Sacrifice and duty are old-fashioned concepts," she called out suddenly from the darkness, "but the Me Generation isn't going to find happiness dangling from the trees of self-indulgence either." With which eloquence she rolled over and started to snore within two minutes.

Our few months of separation, yours and mine, are pretty small potatoes compared to those wartime separations, yet it has been hard on us, Chas. So many things get separated in a separation, not just bodies but all the little threads of concern and necessity that hold people together. And maybe Mother has a point — the kids do need us at this age, and I don't want to let them down any more than I already have.

But can we edge back into togetherness gradually? Give ourselves some breathing space, a chance at transition. (Would you be terribly hurt if I took over the spare room for the first few nights? — if your mother has left, that is, and if you can think of a way to explain it to the kids.) I need time to feel my home fold about me again and let the familiarity ooze back into my bones while Ottawa recedes. Because it will, it will.

I feel as though I've been on a leave of absence. In fact, I'd like to stay home for six months, if we can afford it, and catch up with my life, and with my stretch marks. Yours too.

But I don't want to put pressure on you. You need time too, Chas. You're a published poet! You can't quit now!

Until Sunday —

Love,

Jock

P.S. After all these months of thinking about wealth and poverty, I'm still bewildered — more so than when I ventured forth to set the world straight, back in September. Tell me, Chas, what do those words *mean*?

P.P.S. Jessica's farewell card was a single sheet of paper with the words "I LOVE YOU" printed boldly across it. This has shaken me more than I like to admit.

29 Sweet Cedar Drive
North Vancouver, B.C.
11 June

Dear Jock,

It's hard to believe that in less than one week you'll be home and this *très bizarre* year, as you termed it on the telephone last night, will be over. And of course we'll meet your plane. Why on earth would you even mention taking a taxi all the way to North Van? Never mind that the government would "cheerfully" pay. *We'll be there.*

I can't, it seems, resist sitting down and writing you one last letter, especially since I have the curious notion that it's going to take us a few weeks, and maybe longer, to ease our way back to familiarity, to being able to talk openly again. Christ, to think that we should feel awkward together after all these years. More than awkward — *shy*. And fearful. (Will she approve? Will I measure up? Will I be as good company as the silver-tongued Vance?) Which is why I'm writing to suggest that we take it one day at a time instead of lunging at each other as we did so desperately and foolishly at Christmas — and again in Winnipeg. If necessary, let's be shy and awkward (and polite too) for a few days, like a courting couple or like two people who have to relearn each other's private habits and idiosyncrasies.

You know something? Writing these letters to you all year has had a curious effect on me, letting me know, in fact, what I'm thinking. I'll miss that. Would it be idiotic to suggest that in the future we slip each other a letter now and then? I can imagine myself leaving you notes under your pillow or in the sleeve of your raincoat or under your coffee cup. I can also imagine finding letters from you pinned to the shower curtain or folded in my pants pocket, notes full of your old corny jokes, but also those surprising disclosures that you make from time to time and that I've been too preoccupied in the past to notice.

Dear Jock, you'll be happy and relieved to know that you will be returning to a rapidly emptying household. Marjorie and Laurie moved back across the road a week ago and are now in the midst of what Marjorie calls a trial reconciliation. "You won't be seeing much of me for a while," she said, "because Gus and I are going to be very busy trying to put the scrambled eggs back into the egg shells." I told her I understood perfectly, and oddly enough I do, despite the fact that I never found out what happened between them. All I know now is that Gus is "getting help" and Marjorie is "getting support," and that for some reason Laurie has come through relatively unscathed.

Norm and Jean blasted off yesterday for Kamloops where

Norm has been accepted (conditionally) as an apprentice at the mill and Jean has something sure (almost) lined up at the Silver Rail Bar. (I suggested she give teeth one more try, but she says she's found her calling and it's hoisting trays.) All of us, Tricia included, celebrated their good fortune with a farewell lunch at the Fishnet, codfish cakes and beer served by none other than your son, Greg, who whispered into my ear that it was okay if we didn't want to tip. And so, suddenly, the house is quiet. We all miss Tricia, but it's nice to go into the bathroom and not fall over a carton of Pampers.

And Mother left this morning. When I came in to breakfast she was sitting at the table next to a packed suitcase. "I've missed my own place," she said, "and Jock will be back from Halifax soon." She then launched into a disjointed and halting lecture — many nervous sips of coffee — about responsibility to one's children and the terrible perils of separation. "And I speak from experience," she said with a certain sly emphasis. As propaganda it was feeble, but I found myself nodding in agreement. Because I do believe, Jock, that we took an enormous chance, far riskier than we realized, when we set this year into motion. In fact, it scares the hell out of me to think how much damage we might have done to each other and to the kids.

Of course there have been some good things. I've learned to iron reasonably well and I've written two pomes. (Please overlook flippancy.) The kids' more vulnerable sides have been revealed to me, as well as their occasional good humour and resilience. I've made and lost a good friend (Gil) and tried out a few other friendships for size, some more successful than others, but all interesting. And I'm on better terms with The Mothers, though I'm not sure how this happened or if it will last. In short, everything is different and yet the same.

Except us, that is. I think it's entirely possible that we

(you and I, lovey) are not quite the same people we were a year ago. Things have happened to us both, and I suppose that some day we'll want to talk about it all. But let's not, for God's sake, feel obligated to sit down the minute you get home and "discuss our relationship." I'm not ready for it, and I suspect you aren't either. As a matter of fact I'm feeling fairly fragile and thought I detected a little fragile rustling in your last letter — am I right? Never mind, don't tell me.

By the way, if you don't feel like rushing back to work for a few months, I think we can manage financially. The Sun Spot is averaging at least two new orders per month, and some of the work is even moderately exciting. We won't get rich, no yachts on the horizon, but there's enough give in the cash-flow these days for you to take some time off if you want. Anyway, it's something to think about. You might also want to think about the possibility of adding a balcony to our bedroom. We could do it fairly inexpensively, and it might be nice to sit out there in the summer and count the stars. Or reminisce about our celibate season.

That is, if summer ever comes. The weather has been cold and rainy and blowing like hell. I'm having second thoughts, in fact, about your suggestion of Christmas in Hawaii. The kids would love it, and so might we. Maybe you could pick up some brochures. Never mind — I will. Onward!

Your loving,
Chas

Afterword

Carol Shields and Blanche Howard are both award-winning writers, each well established in Canadian letters. And in this work letters are the thing. *A Celibate Season* is an epistolary fiction text with a twist — two characters take up the pen: the wife and husband team of Jocelyn (Jock, a lawyer) and Charles (Chas, an architect). The season of their celibacy is brought on when they decide that Jock should accept a nine-month appointment as legal counsel for a national commission on poverty and women. She flies off to Ottawa, while Chas (unemployed anyway) moves into the kitchen and into the role of single-parenting their teenaged children Mia and Greg. The text comprises the letters they fire (at times like ammunition or live volleys) back and forth across the nation, as they adjust to their new roles/lives, as they grow and stretch — from Burrard inlet to the Rideau Canal.

Every thread of this text's fabric (to use a domestic metaphor) in some way contributes to a highly wrought pattern of the ways that labour and identities are/can be divided up in the average heterosexual partnership. This art is an act of symmetry. Its pattern stresses balance — what it is, how to get it, why we need it. Proportion is suggested first by the title, which may recall the comforting cliché of Ecclesiastes, "to everything there is a season." More pointedly it recalls a letter to the Corinthians in which St. Paul asserts that celibacy is desirable within marriage, but only for a "season," after which time, he urges, husband and wife should "come together again; otherwise, for lack of self-control, [they] may be tempted by Satan" (1 Cor. 7:5). During the celibate season both partners are to care for "the Lord's business" rather than the "worldly things" that occupy the married mind (1 Cor. 7:32-34). Paul's is a plea for balance.

The application of Paul's words to Jock and Chas is clear: they are indeed freed of their *usual* cares by this hiatus from co-habitation. Each partner stumbles onto "what really matters" — not the Lord's business, exactly, but new challenges, "Bigger Issues," moral/philosophical concerns that those of us who remain trapped by phone bills and eggplant casseroles just can't see. Growth occurs outside of habitual living and, ironically, in the absence of either procreative or recreational sex.

But Chas and Jock do not heed Paul's advice; they remain apart too long. In fact, their main point of contention comes to be whether (and how) they will end this "season," which threatens to be extended if Jock's appointment is renewed. They don't "come together again." They don't have sex. What's more, they don't see things — values, friends, their home — with the same eye(s) any more. They become attracted / attractive to members of the opposite (and occasionally the same) sex. They fall out of step with their marriage.

While Chas and Jock try to re-balance their single and married lives, Shields and Howard explore the balancing of space, or rather spaces — public and private, east and west. The text's symmetry comes from its construction by alternatives, beginning with the alternating voices thrusting us between Vancouver and Ottawa, kitchen and meeting room, Poetry and Poverty. In Ottawa, the (stereo)typically masculine, public realm of offices, politics, meetings and rivalries, Jock learns to move beyond her own immediate world of the family to consider "what really matters"; on the rainy west coast, Chas takes up the domestic challenge and becomes ensconced in the kitchen, the seat of family and food, gossip and love.

Shields and Howard manoeuvre skillfully between these worlds, which remain in dialogue, not opposition. And neither world is identified with only one gender: although the kitchen and kids seem primarily to have been Jock's domain, Chas adjusts and copes. He becomes embroiled in the lives of neighbours, kids and family to a degree shared only by the most devout of stay-at-home parents. He is the one home when his daughter Mia weeps when her first period begins; he is the one home when a neighbour, leaving an abusive husband, crosses the street seeking shelter. For her part, Jock grows into the role of the distant professional parent with only minimal resistance. Early letters are filled with mother-at-a-distance contributions to family needs such as food ("My God, the lentils! I bought two jars; . . . seems a shame to waste them") and ballet costumes ("Sequins! . . . Don't worry, I'll think of something."). But as the months pass and her consciousness is raised (and the pay begins to roll in), Jock meddles less with her family's affairs and grows more self-involved. Ironically, her self-involvement is spurred on by her work on the Commission, through which she learns about women and poverty and begins to feel she has stumbled onto "what really matters": national questions of economic and social inequities, the ghettoization of women in demeaning, poorly paid occupations, and the scandalous abuses of privilege by (white/male) politicians — and commissioners, like her.

As Jock becomes politicized, Chas is increasingly poeticized. He takes creative writing classes while she practices her French. Each crosses into a new realm — public or private, national or familial — as if gliding across a continuum: if Chas and Jock were moving on escalators in a department store, we might imagine them shaking hands at precisely mid-point, as one slides up, the other slides down. But as such a metaphor implies, this movement is not without value. These characters' changes are balanced, but not equal: despite the attention and sympathy given each space, each experience, certain cues in the text direct our allegiance toward house and home. Particularly, a lushness of symbol and metaphor conspires to sketch Chas' world as verdant and warm, inclusive and loving; it is allied with all that screams out "life." Early on in their separation, the characters speak frankly to one another about stagnation, and even apply to themselves the metaphor of pot-bound plants desperately needing more room but feeling an initial shock over the unaccustomed freedom. The impulse to describe Jock in these terms, as being uprooted — or transplanted — is understandably overwhelming, and belies the text's attitude toward home as source and life itself. While away, being nourished on politics and feminism, Jock loses her appetite. She is liberated, she has her consciousness raised, she is independent, but she is also starving.

If we had any doubts that home is where the kitchen is, where our nourishment should be found, Shields and Howard remove them by inscribing in Chas' kitchen the traces of the conception of life itself. Moving his desk from the basement to the kitchen as soon as Jock leaves for Ottawa, Chas quickly casts his creative architect's eye about him and begins scheming about how best to let the sun in. He builds a solarium — a big, sunny nest in the middle of the kitchen. He fills it with plants. He makes it green and bursting with life. He makes it inviting and safe.

Unfortunately, he also makes it his, overlooking Jock's prior territorial rights to that space, and his renovations become the focal point of their increasing alienation and separate lives. What results is breakdown — in communication, in correspondence, perhaps in marriage. But as Jock comes slowly to terms with no longer "knowing" her home, we can't help but admire this locus of growth and light, and feel the plants thriving and the rain pounding around us as we're snuggled warmly in this womb on the we(s)t coast. All the while, though, Shields and Howard seem to affirm their relationship rather than mourn it, a reading encouraged by the other metaphor used by Jock and Chas to make sense of their estrangement: they come to view their relationship as developing "stretch marks," and come to understand that the body that is their marriage has scarred and torn, but is still intact. Implicit in this generative metaphor are both the permanently altered self-image of the maternal body and the fact of creation: what Chas and Jock give birth to is change — their new and newly evolving bond, one that includes tears and imperfections.

Where Jock and Chas falter, the text remains true to the gospel of symmetry and balance, as if on their behalf. This work's got rhythm: through the dialogue of the letter, through the parallel four-letter nicknames the partners have for one another, even through the alternating placement of the inside address — to the left in Chas' letters, to the right in Jock's — we see two sides to everything. But we also see preference. Without ever identifying what they privilege with the construct "mother," that is, without limiting this role to the female, Shields and Howard let it be known that the homebody-who-also-works is, to them, closer to some vital centre of value than is the working-spouse-who-shares-in-house-duties. Hearth and home prevail; we should all be so lucky to earn our daily bread in such a space.

— Meg Stainsby